What Reviewers S  Work

It Should be a Crime

"Law professor Morgan Bradley and her student Parker Casey are potential love interests, but throw in a high-profile murder trial, and you've got an entertaining book that can be read in one sitting. Taite also practices criminal law and she weaves her insider knowledge of the criminal justice system into the love story seamlessly and with excellent timing. I find romances lacking when the characters change completely upon falling in love, but this was not the case here. I look forward to reading more from Taite."—*Curve Magazine*

"This [*It Should be a Crime*] is just Taite's second novel…but it's as if she has bookshelves full of bestsellers under her belt."—*Gay List Daily*

"Taite, a criminal defense attorney herself, has given her readers a behind the scenes look at what goes on during the days before a trial. Her descriptions of lawyer/client talks, investigations, police procedures, etc. are fascinating. Taite keeps the action moving, her characters clear, and never allows her story to get bogged down in paperwork. *It Should be a Crime* has a fast-moving plot and some extraordinarily hot sex."—*Just About Write*

Do Not Disturb

"Taite's tale of sexual tension is entertaining in itself, but a number of secondary characters…add substantial color to romantic inevitability."—Richard Labonte, *Book Marks*

Nothing but the Truth

"Author Taite is really a Dallas defense attorney herself, and it's obvious her viewpoint adds considerable realism to her story, making it especially riveting as a mystery. I give it four stars out of five."—Bob Lind, *Echo Magazine*

"As a criminal defense attorney in Dallas, Texas, Carsen Taite knows her way around the court house. This ability shows in her writing, as her legal dramas take the reader into backroom negotiations between the opposing lawyers, as well as into meetings with judges. Watching how Carsen Taite brings together all of the loose ends is enjoyable, as is her skillful building of the characters of Ryan and Brett. *Nothing But the Truth* is an enjoyable mystery with some hot romance thrown in."—*Just About Write*

"Taite has written an excellent courtroom drama with two interesting women leading the cast of characters. Taite herself is a practicing defense attorney, and her courtroom scenes are clearly based on real knowledge. This should be another winner for Taite."—*Lambda Literary*

The Best Defense

"Real life defense attorney Carsen Taite polishes her fifth work of lesbian fiction, *The Best Defense*, with the realism she daily encounters in the office and in the courts. And that polish is something that makes *The Best Defense* shine as an excellent read."—*Out & About Newspaper*

Slingshot

"The mean streets of lesbian literature finally have the hard boiled bounty hunter they deserve. It's a slingshot of a ride, bad guys and hot

LETTER OF THE LAW

women rolled into one page turning package. I'm looking forward to Luca Bennett's next adventure."—J. M. Redmann, author of the Micky Knight mystery series

Beyond Innocence

"Taite keeps you guessing with delicious delay until the very last minute…Taite's time in the courtroom lends *Beyond Innocence* a terrific verisimilitude someone not in the profession couldn't impart. And damned if she doesn't make practicing law interesting."—*Out in Print*

"As you would expect, sparks and legal writs fly. What I liked about this book were the shades of grey (no, not the smutty Shades of Grey)—both in the relationship as well as the cases."—*C-spot Reviews*

Battle Axe

"This second book is satisfying, substantial, and slick. Plus, it has heart and love coupled with Luca's array of weapons and a badass verbal repertoire… I cannot imagine anyone not having a great time riding shotgun through all of Luca's escapades. I recommend hopping on Luca's band wagon and having a blast."—*Rainbow Book Reviews*

"Taite breathes life into her characters with elemental finesse… A great read, told in the vein of a good old detective-type novel filled with criminal elements, thugs, and mobsters that will entertain and amuse."—*Lambda Literary*

Rush

"A simply beautiful interplay of police procedural magic, murder, FBI presence, misguided protective cover-ups, and a superheated love affair…a Gold Star from me and major encouragement for all readers to dive right in and consume this story with gusto!" —*Rainbow Book Reviews*

Switchblade

"I enjoyed the book and it was a fun read—mystery, action, humor, and a bit of romance. Who could ask for more? If you've read and enjoyed Taite's legal novels, you'll like this. If you've read and enjoyed the two other books in this series, this one will definitely satisfy your Luca fix and I highly recommend picking it up. Highly recommended."—*C-spot Reviews*

"Dallas's intrepid female bounty hunter, Luca Bennett, is back in another adventure. Fantastic! Between her many friends and lovers, her interesting family, her fly by the seat of her pants lifestyle, and a whole host of detractors there is rarely a dull moment."—*Rainbow Book Reviews*

Courtship

"The political drama is just top-notch. The emotional and sexual tensions are intertwined with great timing and flair. I truly adored this book from beginning to end. Fantabulous!"—*Rainbow Book Reviews*

"Taite keeps the stakes high as two beautiful and brilliant women fueled by professional ambitions face daunting emotional choices… As backroom politics, secrets, betrayals, and threats race to be resolved without political damage to the president, the cat-and-mouse relationship game between Addison and Julia has the reader rooting for them. Taite prolongs the fever-pitch tension to the final pages. This pleasant read with intelligent heroines, snappy dialogue, and political suspense will satisfy Taite's devoted fans and new readers alike."—*Publisher's Weekly*

Lay Down the Law

"Recognized for the pithy realism of her characters and settings drawn from a Texas legal milieu, Taite pays homage to the prime-time soap opera Dallas in pairing a cartel-busting U.S. attorney, Peyton Davis, with a charity-minded oil heiress, Lily Gantry."
—*Publishers Weekly*

"Suspenseful, intriguingly tense, and with a great developing love story, this book is delightfully solid on all fronts. This gets my A-1 recommendation!"—*Rainbow Book Reviews*

Reasonable Doubt

"I was drawn into the mystery plot line and quickly became enthralled with the book. It was suspenseful without being too intense but there were some great twists to keep me guessing. It's a very good book. I cannot wait to read the next in line that Ms. Taite has to offer."
—*Prism Book Alliance*

Above the Law

"…readers who enjoyed the first installment will find this a worthy second act."—*Publishers Weekly*

"Ms Taite delivered and then some, all the while adding more questions, Tease! I like the mystery and intrigue in this story. It has many 'sit on the edge of your seat' scenes of excitement and dread (like watch out kind of thing) and drama…well done indeed!"
—*Prism Book Alliance*

Without Justice

"Carsen Taite tells a great story. She is consistent in giving her readers a good if not great legal drama with characters who are insightful, well thought out and have good chemistry. You know when you pick up one of her books you are getting your money's worth time and time again. Consistency with a great legal drama is all but guaranteed."—*The Romantic Reader Blog*

"This is a great read, fast-paced, interesting and takes a slightly different tack from the normal crime/courtroom drama having a lawyer in the witness protection system whose case becomes the hidden centre of another crime."—*Lesbian Reading Room*

By the Author

Truelesbianlove.com

It Should be a Crime

Do Not Disturb

Nothing but the Truth

The Best Defense

Beyond Innocence

Rush

Courtship

Reasonable Doubt

Without Justice

The Luca Bennett Mystery Series:

Slingshot

Battle Axe

Switchblade

Bow and Arrow (novella in Girls with Guns)

Lone Star Law Series:

Lay Down the Law

Above the Law

Letter of the Law

LETTER OF THE LAW

by

Carsen Taite

2017

LETTER OF THE LAW

ISBN 13: 978-1-62639-750-7

This Trade Paperback Original Is Published By
Bold Strokes Books, Inc.
P.O. Box 249
Valley Falls, NY 12185

First Edition: May 2017

CREDITS
Editor: Cindy Cresap
Production Design: Susan Ramundo
Cover Design By Sheri (graphicartist2020@hotmail.com)

Acknowledgments

Big thanks to the usual suspects. VK Powell and Ashley Bartlett, the best first readers and butt-kickers a girl could have. Rad and Sandy Lowe for running a top-notch publishing house that provides me with all the support I need and lots of room to grow. Cindy Cresap, my smart, witty editor who whips all my manuscripts into shape. Ruth Sternglantz for your magic marketing skills. All the associates at BSB who lend their time and talent to make our books shine.

A special shout out to all my BSB sister and brother authors who never fail to amaze me with their generous support and encouragement. Thanks especially to Barbara Ann Wright, Melissa Brayden, Nell Stark, Trinity Tam, and Ali Vali who joined me on a tour of McMahon of Saratoga Thoroughbreds during the last BSB retreat so I could get a close up look at a horse breeding operation as research for this book.

Thanks to Sandy Thornton and Sheri Campbell for all the work they do to organize the Women with Pride book club each month and big hugs to all the members who make the club a bright light for lesfic authors and readers alike.

To Lainey, my amazing wife, cheerleader, and confidant. Thanks for making this wonderful life possible. Couldn't do it without you. Wouldn't want to.

And to my readers. Your kind words of encouragement and loyal support are appreciated more than you can ever know. I write stories because you read them. Thank you, thank you, thank you.

Dedication

For L Always

CHAPTER ONE

Bianca Cruz clenched her jaw and glanced at the clock on the wall as she waited for the judge to make his ruling. She'd worked her whole life to become a litigator, but now that she'd achieved success in the courtroom, her most important work was taking place outside of it, and she wanted nothing more than to get back to the task force's clandestine operation.

Finally, the judge sustained defense counsel's objection and motioned for Bianca to continue. Breathing a sigh of relief, Bianca announced, "I have no further questions."

"May the witness be excused?" Judge Casey directed the question to defense counsel, and Bianca shot a glare at her adversary, daring him to ask more questions. What was supposed to have been a straightforward hearing on a motion to suppress, lasting a couple of hours at most, had turned all O.J. Simpson right out of the gate. They'd started at eight this morning. Now it was almost seven p.m., and they'd only had a quick thirty-minute lunch break which Judge Casey had grudgingly granted. Casey hated taking breaks almost as much as he loved his reputation as the hardest working jurist on the federal bench. Bianca would never understand why he cared so much, considering his bench was a lifetime appointment. It wasn't like he was going to get impeached because he went home at five o'clock.

"No, Your Honor, that was my last witness," the defense attorney said. "Would you like to hear argument now?"

Bianca tapped her fingers on the table, no longer bothered with trying to hide her annoyance. The law was clear, and the facts supported her position about the admissibility of the evidence in what amounted to a standard case of drug trafficking. The defendant had been stopped by a Texas State Trooper for speeding on Interstate 45, a known route favored by drug mules looking to get product in country. The defendant had failed to produce his ID, stating he must have lost it somewhere on his trip, and he was evasive when the trooper asked him simple questions about his destination. Suspecting there was more to the story, the trooper had called for a K-9 unit, and the troopers recovered eighty pounds of weed along with a few fat stacks of hundred-dollar bills.

Defense counsel had mounted an all-out assault on Bianca's short presentation of the evidence with a show-all-your-cards, trial-style display, including an expert witness on drug-sniffing dogs and three witnesses to lie about the defendant's real plans that of course had nothing to do with drug smuggling. When Bianca had received the defendant's list of witnesses earlier that week, her first reaction had been to respond with a list of her own, including an expert, but her mentor, Peyton Davis, had talked her down, and she'd chosen instead to rely on the experienced testimony of the state trooper along with the clear view of the entire incident as it had been recorded on his body cam. She'd presented her best case, and now that it was time to argue, she had little more to say and a strong desire to break for the night. When defense counsel finally finished his over-the-top diatribe, she spent less than five minutes making her key points.

"Well, counsel," Judge Casey said, "you've given me a lot to think about. I think considering the time, we'll adjourn for now and I'll issue my opinion in the morning."

He'd probably stay up all night writing it, but Bianca was so happy to hear the words, she nearly shot out of her seat, already reaching for the powered-off phone in her bag, certain when she turned it on, it would be on fire with messages.

She wasn't wrong. When she reached her car, she took a moment to scroll through her messages while she let the Miata's engine warm up.

Mom, can't wait to tell you what happened today! You're going to go crazy!!

Bianca smiled at her daughter's hyperbole and scrolled to the next message, this one from her own mother.

Those people know you have to eat sometime, don't they? Or do they ignore their mothers too?

A few more clicks revealed more of the same. Bianca tossed her phone back in her bag and drove out of the lot behind the federal building, finally on her way home. She spent the drive reflecting on how much her life had changed over the past few years. She'd gone from being a lackey of sorts, drafting motions and doing research for other AUSAs, to handling her own docket while working on a covert task force investigating both the Zeta Cartel and the potential of a leak inside the US Attorney's office threatening their investigation. She had a lot to lose, but she was doing what was right and that was all that mattered.

When she finally reached home, Bianca had switched gears, replacing legal analysis with thoughts of family, but as she stepped up to the front door of her house, work rushed back in. She paused with her hand on the handle to her front door, torn between answering the buzzing cell phone in her purse and ignoring it in favor of a family dinner. The smell of her mother's posolé voted for the latter, but the buzzing phone was a significant distraction. She pulled the offending device from her purse, glanced at the screen, and knew it would keep ringing until she answered.

I'll make it quick. She almost believed the lie before she punched the answer button and let reality flood in. "This better be important," she said curtly.

"Are you at the office?" Dale asked.

Dale Nelson was a DEA agent who worked with her on the task force. Bianca had spent most of the weekend with Dale and other members of the task force after a nationally-known investigative reporter, Lindsey Davis, had been kidnapped by members of a drug cartel. Lindsey was safe and sound, but her rescue raised more questions than answers, and now the task force was spinning in several different directions, not entirely sure which one would lead to the capture of the criminals they were trying to take down.

Bianca liked Dale, even enjoyed her company. Most of the time. But after a bruising day in court, she needed to erect a wall between the part of her dedicated to taking down heinous criminals and the part determined to spend a normal dinner with her daughter and her mother. "I'm at home. If you're going to mess with family time, prepare for the fallout."

Dale laughed. "No need to threaten me. It can wait until tomorrow. I just wanted to know if you'd seen the article in the *Morning News*, and let you know we were able to run down some additional information about the other owner of Valencia Acres. You're not going to believe what—"

A sharp scream from the other side of the door interrupted Dale's announcement and almost caused Bianca to drop the phone.

"What was that?" Dale asked.

Bianca jerked on the handle with one hand and pounded on the door with the other. Her phone was jammed up under her chin and she ignored Dale's increasingly loud "are you okays" while she focused all her energy into getting into her house, but the door resisted her attempts to break through.

Of course it was locked. She jammed the key into the lock and turned again, barreling through the entryway faster than the heavy door could move, slamming into the wall at the end of the foyer. Her phone clattered to the ground, cracking against the hard tile and skittering to a stop at the feet of her mother who stood to the side with her hands on her hips.

"*Mija*, where is the fire?"

Semi-conscious of the fact Dale's pleas for information were still wafting up from the downed cell phone, Bianca ignored her mother's question and asked one of her own. "I heard screaming. What's going on?"

"*No se.* Emma is talking to one of her friends on the phone. I told her three times you were going to be home soon and she needed to get off the phone, but…" Her mother placed her hands over her ears to demonstrate her granddaughter's behavior. Before she could say anything else, another sharp scream filled the air, but this time the screamer bounded into sight.

"Mom!"

Bianca shook her head. "Emma, are you trying to give me a heart attack?"

Emma cocked her head. "Mom, don't be silly. The likelihood of someone your age having a heart attack is pretty slim. Besides, I'm so excited to see you. I have amazing news!"

"What's going on?"

As one, Bianca, her mother, and Emma looked down at the floor where the question blared from Bianca's forgotten phone. "Oh crap," Bianca said as she reached down and scooped up the phone.

"Language!" Emma and her mother said at the same time.

"You two are spending way too much time together. Hold that thought." She held the phone to her ear. "Dale, are you still there?"

"Is everything okay? I'm in my truck. Should I head that way?"

"Everything is fine, except for the derelicts living at my house. Seriously. Can I call you back in the morning?"

"Absolutely. Go be with your family. I'll fill you in tomorrow."

Bianca set the phone on the counter and turned her attention to her daughter. It never failed to surprise her that Emma looked exactly like the father she'd probably never know, and almost nothing like her. Where she was petite, Emma was tall, with long legs and willowy arms. And Emma possessed a natural athletic grace that made Bianca look even more clumsy than she actually was. Bianca embraced their differences, never letting them interfere with the close relationship she and Emma shared. "Tell me, what's all the screaming about?"

"I'm going to be the lead in the school play. It's a remake of *Romeo and Juliet* and I'm, you know, Juliet. Jake Swan is Romeo. He's a hunk."

Bianca's stomach turned at the boy-crazy look on Emma's face, and she had to resist the urge to shut it down, instead opting for a more subtle approach to gather information about the boy who'd captured her daughter's attention. "That's exciting, bug. Tell me about your costar. What's Jake like?"

Emma settled into a chair at the table. "I don't know him very well, but he seems super nice. He plays basketball and he's the eighth grade class president."

Bianca bit down hard on her tongue to keep from shouting *eighth grade*! She glanced over at her mother, standing behind Emma, shaking her head. She had no doubt there would be a full round of "see what I went through when you were young" after Emma went to bed. Resisting every protective urge she felt, Bianca pared her response down to a simple. "He sounds nice. Maybe I will get a chance to meet him soon."

"Sure, Mom. How was your day?"

The sudden switch in subjects restored her faith that Emma wasn't entirely boy-crazy, and Bianca sighed with relief. "Long, but I'm glad to be home. Did your abuela make us *posolé* or is my nose just wishing it was so?"

Her mom cleared her throat. "It's not polite to talk about me like I'm not here."

Bianca laughed at her mother's stern tone and faux frown. She knew her mother would cook for her every night if she allowed it, but she tried to keep some form of normalcy with her erratic schedule. Lately, it had been even more unpredictable, and she didn't know what she would've done if her mother didn't live down the street, ready to fill in at a moment's notice. "Sorry, Mama. I just didn't want you to get a big head."

"Enough already." She pointed at the table. "Sit down, both of you. Your dinner is getting cold."

Bianca took two steps toward the kitchen table when her cell phone rang again. She recognized the ring tone right away. She'd programmed it into her phone on her first day at the US Attorney's office, when her boss, Herschel Gellar, informed her she might be called upon at all hours and he expected her to be available. He'd rarely called her himself and, considering the events of the last week, she was reluctant to hear whatever he had to say.

"Don't answer it," her mother said.

But Bianca was already reaching for the phone. "I have to." She punched the line to answer. "Cruz here."

"I heard your hearing went well today."

"I think so, sir. Judge Casey said he'd take it under advisement."

"His clerk thinks it's a slam dunk. I bet you get your opinion in the morning. Speaking of which," he said in the poorest of segues, "Did you see the article in the paper this morning?"

The article again. "Actually, no. I was busy preparing for the hearing, but I plan to read it tonight."

"Good. Do that. And I need you to come in early tomorrow." He lowered his voice to a conspiratorial whisper. "It's important that I talk to you before anyone else is here. Privately."

Uh-oh. Something was up and it wasn't good. She and the rest of the disbanded task force had been working off the books for the last two weeks, running around behind Gellar's back to shore up the case against the Vargas brothers that he seemed to have shuttled to the back burner while he focused on what appeared to be a personal vendetta against a prominent Dallas oilman. Had he figured out his team wasn't playing by his rules anymore?

All she could think about was that she needed to get off the phone and call her friend and mentor, AUSA Peyton Davis. Peyton was the de facto head of their task force and she also happened to be in a relationship with the daughter of Cyrus Gantry, the focus of Gellar's prosecution. Gellar's voice faded in the background as she parsed through the complications of her professional life.

"Are you there, Cruz?"

"Yes, sir. I'll be there. First thing in the morning." She waited until he clicked off the line before she did the same. When she looked up from the phone, she saw both her mother and daughter staring at her. "What?"

"You don't have to go now, right?" Emma asked, her voice quiet with disappointment.

"No, bug. I do not." She held up the phone and made a show of turning down the volume. "And no more interruptions. It's time for dinner." She tossed the phone on the counter next to the current edition of the *Dallas Morning News*. She was dying to read the article now that both Dale and Gellar had mentioned it, but for the next couple of hours, her primary focus was her family because no matter how complicated her career had become, the simple pleasure of a home-cooked meal shared with the people she loved was the most important part of her life. She would let nothing steal these simple pleasures from her.

❖

Jade Vargas climbed the steps to the front porch, her boots clomping against the wide planks of wood and echoing in the cool night air. She wasn't expected until the weekend, and she hoped the key was hidden in the same place it always was since the quiet signaled no one was home to greet her.

She rested her suitcase against the door and pried away the already loose board in the railing. Within seconds, she freed the key and let herself into the ranch house.

"Hello?" she called out as she parked her suitcase in the front entry and made her way back to the kitchen. "Is anyone home?" The hum of the refrigerator cut through the silence, and she let out a huge breath in relief. The delayed flight home after a month of living out of her suitcase had taken its toll, and all she wanted was a stiff drink and her own bed.

She rummaged through the cabinets. Sophia didn't favor strong spirits, and she had a tendency to push Jade's prized finds to the rear of the cupboard when she was traveling, but it only took a few moments to locate one of the bottles. Jade pulled down the beautiful bottle of Amor Mio along with one of the handblown shot glasses she'd purchased on one of her trips to Mexico last summer. She'd purchased the bottle for its beauty, thinking even if the tequila inside was shit, at least she'd have a lovely vase, but to her surprise, the extra añejo liquor was delicious. She poured two fingers of the amber liquid into the glass and took a generous sip, enjoying the complex layers of hazelnut, chocolate, and cinnamon. She took another drink, sank into a chair at the kitchen table, and twisted her neck back and forth to shake loose some of the tension brought on by a day of travel.

Her hand rested on a stack of mail and the current edition of the *Dallas Morning News*. She sorted through the envelopes, mostly bills, before brushing the mail aside to check out the day's headlines. She'd expected a little light reading before bed, but the glaring headline over the fold grabbed her attention. *Local Oilman Facing Life Sentence.*

Could it be? She unfolded the paper and spread it out on the table, quickly scanning the lead. *Cyrus Gantry, President and CEO of family-held Gantry Oil, is the target of a multi-jurisdictional investigation led by a task force of federal agents seeking to root out the drug trade in North Texas.* Jade gasped at the sight of the familiar name and she took another drink, more than a sip this time, before diving back into the article.

A federal grand jury issued subpoenas over the last few weeks, allowing the FBI to search all of Gantry Oil's offices in the district. Sources close to the investigation say the search yielded evidence that implicates Gantry in a complex money laundering scheme with known drug lords, Sergio and Arturo Vargas, captains of the local faction of the Zeta Cartel.

At the sight of the familiar names, Jade set the paper down, not entirely sure she wanted to know more. These stories never ended well, but curiosity won out and she kept reading.

The subpoenas were the culmination of the work of a task force organized by US Attorney Herschel Gellar. Gellar put together law enforcement personnel from the FBI, DEA, ATF, and Texas Rangers to work with prosecutors in his office to investigate the activities of the Vargas brothers. One of the AUSAs originally assigned to work on the task force was Maria Escobar, a decorated JAG attorney who came to work for the Northern District of Texas US Attorney's office following two tours in Afghanistan. Last year, AUSA Escobar was gunned down in front of her house, and the murder, while as yet unsolved, is widely believed to have been committed by members of the Zeta Cartel sending a message to law enforcement about the investigation.

Jade shook her head as her suspicions were confirmed, but she was too far into the article to stop reading now.

Escobar was survived by her wife, DEA Special Agent Dale Nelson, also a member of the task force. Agent Nelson, along with the other members of her team regrouped, and AUSA Peyton Davis, a native Dallasite, transferred home from the Department of Justice to take over Ms. Escobar's role as the attorney liaison to the law enforcement team. In early October of this year, Nelson and Davis, following up on a lead that one of the Gantry Oil's trucks had been used to transport undocumented immigrants over the border, were involved in a shootout at a local warehouse owned by Gantry. Agent Nelson was injured, but not deterred. Within a week, subpoenas were issued for all of Gantry's offices, and forensic accountants began combing through evidence regarding his business transactions.

Sources surmise the pressure on Gantry caused the usually elusive Vargases to surface. Just days following the search of Gantry's offices, Arturo Vargas was arrested outside of Dallas at the ranch of his estranged sister, Sophia Valencia, where he was holding Sophia and Cyrus Gantry's daughter Lily at gunpoint while trying to steal Valencia's prize stallion, Queen's Ransom, last year's winner of the All American Futurity. Arturo was shot during his apprehension, and after his condition stabilized, he was transferred to the Federal Detention Center in Seagoville where he is being held pending additional charges. Neither of the women would meet on the record to discuss why Arturo was targeting them.

Jade gulped the tequila this time, no longer caring about layers of complexity in the drink. She'd already known some of what she just read, but seeing the story stripped down to the bare facts brought home how close she'd come to losing Ransom.

Last week, the investigation took a twist when internationally known investigative reporter Lindsey Ryan was kidnapped outside of city hall while she was in town to cover a DEA Drug Take Back event. Ryan was held hostage pending the release of Arturo Vargas. The kidnappers were arrested at a farm near Denton where they were holding Ms. Ryan. They had forced her to make a tape calling on US Attorney Gellar to set Arturo free and drop all charges against both Vargas brothers in exchange for Ryan's safe release. No one was injured during the raid that freed Ms. Ryan, but sources close to the investigation intimate the kidnappers' motives were more complex than securing Arturo Vargas's freedom.

Sergio Vargas remains at large, and he is now listed among the FBI's Ten Most Wanted. Authorities continue to pursue all leads and have opened a hotline and offered a reward for anyone who has information that might lead to his arrest. In the meantime, the clock is ticking on Cyrus Gantry who remains free pending formal charges, but whom Gellar has told his staff will not survive this year without an indictment implicating him not only on charges of money laundering for the Vargases' operation, but for other crimes as well. No one would speak on the record about what these other crimes might be, but sources close to the investigation tell us Gantry is likely to be charged as part of a conspiracy that may extend far beyond money laundering and could also be connected with the murders committed by the Vargases as part of their criminal enterprise.

Jade let the paper fall back to the table and took a long drink of her tequila. Before she could process the bombshells contained in the article, she heard a door slam and the sharp staccato of heels on the wood floor.

"I was gone no more than an hour and I come home to find you raiding the liquor. You know I don't like it when you drink spirits."

Jade raised the glass in a mock toast and smiled at her mother. "If you really objected, you could pour it out when I'm away."

It was Sophia's turn to smile. "What? And have you go running off to the nearest bar instead of staying here with me?"

"You know me so well."

Sophia held out her arms. "Put down that glass and say hello to me."

Jade pitched the remaining drops of tequila down her throat and slid the glass onto the counter. She stepped into her mother's arms. The embrace was as awkward as always, but as Sophia pressed her closer and stroked her hair, Jade sensed an undercurrent of nostalgia. Had Sophia truly missed her for more than her help running the ranch? She had been gone for a while, but she'd taken extended trips before without this kind of welcome when she returned. Something had prompted Sophia to offer a rare display of motherly affection.

When Sophia released her, Jade backed away, wondering if her observation was fact-based or tequila-inspired. Didn't matter either way. She would be here at the ranch for a while and then she'd leave. She never stayed long enough for the discomfort of their differences to get in the way of business. Sophia might be her mother, but their relationship as business partners was their strongest bond. "Is everything well?"

"The horses are fine. How was your trip?" Sophia asked, as if reading Jade's mind.

"Good. I made a few purchases, and they'll be delivered in the next couple of weeks."

Sophia pointed at the small suitcase. "I'm certain you left here with more than one tiny bag. Did you trade your belongings for the new horses?"

Jade laughed, relieved at the mundane topic of conversation. "The airline lost my checked bags. Supposedly, they are somewhere in the Midwest and they swore they would have them to me by tomorrow." The reminder of the rotten travel day she'd suffered through brought on another wave of exhaustion and Jade yawned. "If you don't mind, maybe we can talk details tomorrow. It's been a long day and I'm beat." She didn't wait for a response, instead reaching for her suitcase, but Sophia's hand on her arm stopped her getaway.

"Actually, I need to talk to you about something and I'm afraid it cannot wait." Sophia pointed at the paper on the table. "Did you read the article?"

Jade braced at the ominous tone in her mother's voice. She hadn't had enough tequila to stomach more unpleasantness, but if she didn't hear her out now, her sleep would be ruined while she wondered what was so important that it couldn't wait until dawn. "I did. What is it?"

Sophia strode over to the refrigerator and opened the door. "Would you like something to eat? How long has it been since you've had a home-cooked meal? I could make you an omelet."

Jade gritted her teeth to stave off her building frustration and resisted the urge to point out she rarely had home-cooked meals even when she was home. "I'm not hungry, but I am very tired. Perhaps you can tell me what's on your mind and then I can get some sleep."

Sophia shut the refrigerator door and slowly turned to face her. Her expression was an odd mixture of expectation and dread, and she flinched as the words tumbled from her lips. "Lily Gantry was here. She's been here several times. She knows."

Jade's gut clenched and she sagged back against the counter, all thoughts of sleep vanished with the vague, yet ominous revelation. "What does she know?"

Sophia's gaze darted around the room, but Jade wasn't about to let her off so easily. Some small part of her knew this day might come, but as time passed, she'd grown to think maybe it never would. Now that it had, she needed to be prepared. "What does she know?"

"She knows everything. Except…"

"Except what?" Jade was certain she knew the detail her mother had left out, but she had to hear her say it to make it real.

"Except she doesn't know about you. She doesn't know she has a sister."

CHAPTER TWO

It was almost dawn when Jade strode through the tall double doors of the climate-controlled stallion barn that supported her standard of living. After her mother's bombshell the night before, she craved the sweet smell of hay and the soft whinnies from the horses as she walked by their stables. The peace of this place never failed to soothe her, especially when she returned from a long trip away. She loved every one of these proud, beautiful animals, not for the trappings they'd afforded her, but for their gentle, unconditional affection. Jade walked through the wide hall, stopping at every stall to greet each one. These horses were her family, more so than the woman who'd given birth to her, the father she'd never know, or the half sister she didn't want or need.

Family. The concept was bittersweet. She'd known Lily Gantry was her half sister since before they'd moved to Valencia Acres. She'd started figuring it out when she'd seen Lily's father, Cyrus, at the much smaller ranch they used to own down in the valley. She'd been a teenager then. Her mother had introduced Cyrus as a family friend, but by his fourth visit, she knew differently. The casual way he interacted with her mother, who had a tendency to hold most people at arm's length, the lavish gifts he gave her were signs there was more to their relationship. When she spotted his car in the driveway before dawn, and then saw him sneaking out wearing the same clothes he'd had on the night before, her suspicions were confirmed.

One day she'd gone through his wallet while he was doing God knows what in her mother's room, and she'd seen a picture of his daughter, Lily, sitting astride a gorgeous mount. Something about the picture was deeply familiar, and she spent days trying to figure it out. When she came across the same picture in her mother's bureau, the mystery was solved. Lily and Sophia looked so much alike except for the one or two features Lily shared with Cyrus. She hadn't known if she should be more shocked by the fact her mother was sleeping with a married man or that Sophia had chosen to keep her daughters apart, allowing them to grow up as strangers occupying separate worlds.

Jade shook away the thoughts and returned her attention to her horse family. She took her time, greeting each horse in turn, but seeking out one in particular. When she finally reached the largest stall, she waited by the gate, quietly watching her favorite stallion, Queen's Ransom. She didn't wait long before he lifted his nose, sniffed the air, and stepped to her, nickering his pleasure at her return. Ransom had won the All American Futurity the year before, and now he was the most valuable asset of Valencia Acres, commanding substantial stud fees.

"Did you miss me?" Jade asked, nuzzling her face against his. "I bet Sophia's spoiling you rotten. When's the last time you went on a hard ride?"

Ransom answered by thumping a hoof against the ground and rubbing his massive midsection against the gate. His eager response sparked an idea, and Jade acted quickly before she could change her mind or consider the consequences. She told Ransom she'd be right back and strode to the tack room where she selected a bridle, blanket, and saddle before making her way back to the stall. When she returned, Ransom danced at the sight of her, confirming her hasty decision. She gave him a thorough brushing and then led him past the other stalls and out of the barn. Outside, in the cool, dark air of morning, she tacked him up and climbed into the saddle. Once astride Ransom, she finally felt like she was home. With only a passing thought to what her mother would think of her taking their most valuable possession for a trail ride, she pressed the heels of her boots into Ransom's side and they rode toward the rising sun.

❖

Bianca swiped her card to open the private entrance to the US Attorney's suite of offices and eased down the hall, hoping she'd beaten her boss into the office. She'd need a full cup of coffee and a few moments to gather her thoughts before she faced whatever surprise he had in store. She fired up her computer. While it came to life, she gulped the lukewarm coffee she'd brought from home and mentally retraced the newspaper article she'd read that morning as well as her own recollection about the events of the last month, looking for any clues as to what Gellar might be on to.

Since the time Peyton Davis had returned to town to take the reins of the Zeta Cartel task force, events had occurred at a breathtaking pace. At first, Bianca had been reluctant to accept Peyton's leadership. Bianca had had a close professional relationship with Peyton's predecessor, Maria, and considered her a mentor, which had made it difficult to accept anyone taking her place. But it didn't take long for Bianca to realize Peyton was a tough, no-nonsense lawyer who was more interested in justice than politics, which had quickly earned Bianca's respect. Even when it turned out Peyton had fallen in love with the daughter of Cyrus Gantry, a well known local oilman accused of conspiring with the Vargas brothers, Bianca still trusted Peyton's judgment over that of her boss who seemed singularly focused on Gantry as if to settle some unspoken vendetta.

Gellar's obsession had recently turned into questionable behavior, and two weeks ago, he'd disbanded the task force and made several dubious decisions that placed all of their hard work in jeopardy. Unwilling to accept Gellar's decisions, Peyton and Dale had taken the reins and urged the group to operate underground. Now she and the others were leading double lives, working regular dockets and caseloads while using every spare moment to find Arturo's fugitive brother, Sergio, and shut down the illegal activities of the Cartel. Just last week, investigative reporter Lindsey Ryan had agreed to join their team, and they were ready to take their underground investigation to the next level.

Had Gellar caught on? Was that the reason for this secret, early morning meeting? Bianca pulled out her phone and sent a quick text to Peyton. *Early meeting with the boss at his request. Any ideas?*

She tapped her fingers on her desk while she waited for a reply. She didn't wait long.

No idea, but you got this. Call me after.

Bianca took a deep breath and replayed the events of the last week, certain they carried a clue as to what Gellar wanted. Lindsey had been in town to do a piece on the DEA for *Spotlight America*, a prime-time TV news show. Lindsey had been paired with Dale, who'd spent the entire week showing Lindsey around during the day and working on the task force in whatever free moments she could grab. Despite Dale's best efforts, Lindsey had figured out something else was up and discovered that Dale, Peyton, Bianca, and a few others were holding meetings at Peyton's ranch. Before she could confront them about it, Lindsey had been taken hostage and held until the kidnappers' demand to drop the investigation into the Vargases was met. After Lindsey was rescued, they'd figured out she'd actually been taken by the Barrio Aztecas, sworn enemies of the Zetas and Sergio and Arturo Vargas. Unable to figure out the kidnappers' true motive, the task force made a pledge to double their efforts and scrutinize everyone outside of their tight-knit circle, including Gellar. They planned to ask Lindsey to use her investigative skills to help them root out the truth.

A sharp knock on her door rousted Bianca from her reflections. Herschel Gellar stood in her doorway, and she rose to greet him. "Good morning, Mr. Gellar. I didn't realize you were here."

His eyes swept the room. "I just arrived. Thanks for coming in early. Come to my office?" He turned and walked away before she could answer, but it had been more of a command than a question. Bianca grabbed a notebook and followed him down the hall.

His office was opulent, furnished with an expensive, expansive desk, a comfortable sofa, and large leather club chairs. The walls were lined with photos of him glad-handing many notables from politicians to celebrities and gilded certificates lauding him for his service to his country. She wasn't impressed. In the three years she'd worked for the office, she'd found him to be a fickle, sometimes oppressive personality, prone to temper and personal bias. If the work were less challenging or rewarding, she would've sought a position elsewhere long before. Shortly after she joined the office, Maria had convinced her to stay after one particularly challenging exchange with Gellar, and then Maria had become her mentor. When Maria died, Bianca had stayed out of allegiance, dedicated to finishing the work they'd started, which included avenging Maria's death. Dedication was the reason she was still working with the task force, despite the risk it posed to all of their careers if they were caught conducting an unauthorized investigation.

"Have a seat, Bianca." He waved her toward one of the chairs directly across from his desk. "We've got some things to discuss." He crossed his hands and stared intently into her eyes. "Things best dealt with face-to-face."

She sat down but stayed on the edge of the seat, unwilling and unable to relax until she knew the impetus for this secret meeting. She rubbed her hands and braced for questions about whether she was the source referenced in the article. "What can I do for you?"

"Well, that's a good question. The truth is, it depends." He leaned back in his chair, feigning relaxation, but Bianca wasn't fooled. She would stay on alert until she was certain he wasn't toying with her. "I seem to recall that you and Maria Escobar were pretty tight."

It wasn't a question, but she knew he expected some kind of response. Thrown because she hadn't expected him to mention Maria, she took a beat to gather her thoughts. Tight wasn't the word she'd use to describe her relationship with the now deceased AUSA who'd been married to Dale Nelson, but she needed to say something. "Maria was very helpful when I was starting out. Federal criminal practice is different from what I was used to at the DA's office."

She came to this meeting expecting to have to dissemble, but everything she'd said so far was the truth. After graduating from Georgetown Law School and a judicial clerkship, Bianca had worked as a civil litigator. Her only criminal law experience consisted of a six-month stint in Fort Worth at the DA's office as a lawyer on loan. The call of the criminal courts had been exciting enough to lure her from the otherwise lucrative practice of big law to pursue a position with the US Attorney's Office, but nothing she'd learned had prepared her for the unending stream of cases exposing the vast criminal network in the Dallas Fort Worth area. Being part of the task force had given her the support she needed to navigate through her new career, and she'd come to rely on the strength in numbers that came with being part of the team. But here she was, facing Gellar on her own, wondering why he was asking about a dead prosecutor. She elected to get right to the point. "Do you mind if I ask why you brought up Maria?"

He grunted and leaned back in his chair. "Do I mind? No, I don't mind. I guess I want to know why one of my prosecutors was killed and no one seems interested in putting away the man who was responsible for her death."

His face grew increasingly red as he spoke, and his tone was harsh. Bianca could do little more than stare. Of all the things he could've hauled her in to discuss at the crack of dawn, she'd never expected Maria's death to be one of them. The general consensus of everyone in the office and the DEA was that Maria had been gunned down by several of the Vargases' lieutenants, but they'd never caught the gunmen. Gellar's reference to a single man didn't jibe with the facts. "I'm sorry, I don't think I know who you mean."

"Cyrus Gantry, of course." Gellar punctuated his declaration with a slap of his open palm on the desk. "It's clear to me he arranged for Maria's death to divert attention from his illegal dealings with the Vargases. She was getting too close to the truth and he took her out."

A surge of anxiety-producing heat coursed through Bianca's body, and she scrambled for air. Gellar's obsession with taking down Gantry was already bordering on self-serving, but nothing the task force had uncovered implicated Gantry in Maria's death. Of course, they'd never had any reason to consider he might be involved, but her gut told her Gellar's focus on Gantry was suspect. She cast about for something to say, acutely conscious she needed to tread carefully. "You're absolutely right. I don't think anyone has directly pursued that angle. What would you like me to do?"

She'd apparently said the right thing because his eyes gleamed with satisfaction. He reached into his desk drawer and pulled out a slim folder that he pushed toward her. "That is a draft of an amended indictment which I plan to share with the grand jury in two weeks. I would like you to meet with the case agent, Tanner Cohen, and go over every detail in there and prepare a summary of the evidence for the grand jurors. Line up the witnesses—I have a list in there. Make sure everyone is on board. Whatever else you're working on can wait. Do you understand?"

She nodded in agreement, but it was a lie. How could she be expected to understand when she didn't know what he had in mind? She desperately wanted to open the folder and glance at the indictment, but his stern expression made it clear he wanted unconditional acceptance. The sooner she could get out of here, the better off she'd be. She took a risk and stood. "I'd better get started."

He waved a hand in her direction. "Yes. Keep me updated. I expect a report by the end of the week." He looked back down at his desk and thumbed through some papers. She took the abrupt switch of his attention as a signal to leave, but before she reached the door, he called out. "Oh, and, Bianca?"

"Yes?"

"I picked you for this assignment because I have high hopes for you. I trust you're not going to disappoint me."

She turned to face him, but his focus was back on the papers in front of him. Good thing because she wasn't sure she could lie with both her eyes and her mouth. "I don't plan on it."

Back in her office, she opened the file, quickly skimmed over the contents, and gasped as she read the text of the draft indictment. Instinctively, she picked up her phone to text Peyton, but hesitated with her thumbs hovering over the screen. Gellar was paranoid, and she had no idea where his paranoia might lead. Better she have an in-person conversation with Peyton than one that could be traced and misinterpreted. Dale needed to be in on this as well since she'd made catching Maria's killers part of her life's work. Bianca reached for her desk phone and risked making a call since that would be easier to explain away than a text. Peyton answered on the second ring.

"We need to meet," Bianca said.

"Tonight, my place?"

"Sooner, and Dale should be there."

"Actually, she and I are both headed out to Sophia's. Should I swing by and pick you up?"

She didn't have any settings on the docket and could easily duck out. Meeting at Sophia's ranch was the perfect solution, but she couldn't risk someone seeing her leave with Dale and Peyton since they were all supposed to be working on different cases. She had a different idea. "I'll meet you there."

Chapter Three

Jade took her time on the ride back to the ranch house. She wasn't anxious to hash over her business plans with her mother, but she knew they would need to discuss the recent purchases she'd made and plan for the arrival of the new horses. In a few weeks, it would be time to renew marketing efforts to ramp up for the next breeding season, and based on the observations from her ride, there was a lot of work to do before spring. The outer edges of the property were leased out to local farmers who rotated various crops throughout the year, but the parcels she and Sophia retained needed attention: fences in disrepair, trees in need of thinning, bridle paths cleared. Sophia wasn't minding the property in the manner she'd come to expect, and Jade wondered what had distracted her.

She heard hoofbeats and saw Sophia galloping toward her on Descaro, a chestnut mare. There was no denying her mother was a striking woman, and age had only increased her beauty. What mystified Jade was why her mother would settle for a lifetime affair with a married man, especially when the rest of her family loathed that man, and she was accomplished and attractive enough to have anyone she desired.

She'd asked outright in the past, but Sophia's answers had always been thin and veiled. She never mentioned love, but what other ties could she and Cyrus have? They hailed from completely different worlds—Cyrus from privilege and Sophia from finger-clawing labor and desperation. Lily, the daughter that had been born from their affair, hadn't known either of them were her birth parents, so staying together for the sake of the child hadn't been the motivation.

Until now. Lily Gantry had discovered Cyrus and Sophia were her birth parents just a few weeks ago. Jade wondered if Lily's discovery would change things for either of their families. Did her uncles know about Lily? She'd be willing to bet they would not be happy to learn a Gantry had Vargas blood running through her veins. Before she could contemplate the issue further, Sophia's mount thundered to a stop beside her. Ransom and Descaro nickered at each other, and Jade pulled Ransom back, squaring her shoulders for the scolding she was about to receive.

"I wish I'd known you were going for a ride."

Jade leaned down and ran a hand along Ransom's jaw. "So you could tell me not to ride him?"

"He's your horse. You can do what you want."

Jade shook her head at Sophia's disapproving tone. Ransom was hers, purchased with her own money, but he belonged to the ranch, and right now, he was their primary breadwinner. If she had a proper sense of family, maybe Jade would defer to her mother's wishes more, but years of forced independence couldn't be overcome with a few touching moments of familial solidarity. Still, she reacted defensively. "He is my horse, but I'm happy to have him here where he is happy and can make us both a good living. Perhaps you could trust me to take care of him in the same way you trust me to run this business."

"Fair enough."

Jade nodded. "Speaking of which, I noticed a few areas that need some attention."

Sophia winced. "I've had a lot on my mind since you've been gone. I haven't had a chance to tell you everything."

"You have more surprises?" Jade tensed. "First, I come home to find you've decided to be a mother to a stranger and now what? Are you going to tell me I'm not really your daughter?"

Jade watched Sophia's face for clues, but all she saw was a sharp wince of pain for which she had no sympathy. "You expected me to take last night's news in stride and not be affected at all? I need some time to get used to the idea that you have cozied up to Cyrus's daughter. She might be your family, but she's not mine."

"But she is," Sophia insisted, her tone pleading. "She's your half sister. I think if you would get to know her—"

"I know her. She's a debutante, adoring daughter to a rich gringo family who never had to work a day in her life. Don't even bother with the poor little adopted girl, didn't know who her real parents were sob story. I doubt she had time to notice between social events."

"Jade, you don't know her at all."

"And I don't plan to. Now, do you want to tell me what's on your mind or should we talk about the ranch repairs that haven't been done?"

Sophia looked around. "Let's ride back and talk at the house. I have a lot to tell you. No sense in the horses just standing here waiting on us."

Jade answered by nudging Ransom forward into a fast-building run. Seconds later, she could hear Descaro trying to keep pace behind her, but Ransom picked up speed without any urging from her. For the few minutes it took to close the distance to the stables, she forgot all the complications of her dysfunctional family and surrendered to the autumn wind in her hair, the cool breeze across her face, and the majestic beauty of her galloping stallion. So lost was she in the feel of the ride, it took a moment after they'd stopped for her to notice the two unfamiliar vehicles in the drive.

A large Ford pickup and a tiny Miata. Potential clients? Most made appointments, but occasionally interested breeders dropped by to check out an operation before they made a decision about breeding. The ranch's website encouraged visitors, a fact Jade was instantly grateful for since she'd love a distraction from whatever weighty topic Sophia wanted to discuss.

She remained in the saddle and walked Ransom to the edge of the drive. If these visitors were looking for references, they could find none better than her mount. Might as well give them an up-close look.

A tall, rangy woman stepped out of the driver's side of the truck and looked around. She was dressed in well-worn jeans and dusty boots. Jade couldn't tell much else about her since her shades blocked her expression. The passenger door opened and another tall woman, similarly dressed, walked around the side of the truck. They could be potential buyers who'd dropped by to visit or perhaps they had an appointment with Sophia and she hadn't bothered to mention it. One look at her mother dispelled that notion. Sophia's jaw was set. Her gaze cast about wildly as if these visitors would disappear if she avoided eye contact.

Jade walked Ransom closer, enjoying the height advantage. She started to call out a greeting to the women, but before she could say anything, the door to the Miata opened and a voice called out. "I told you I could make it down the drive, but thanks for waiting. Next time—"

The woman stopped mid sentence and looked up at Jade. "Wow, who's this super tall stranger?"

Jade couldn't help but grin as the woman's hand flew up to her mouth. While the woman cast an embarrassed look at her acquaintances, Jade took advantage of her diverted attention to assess this stranger.

Unlike the other two who'd arrived in the pickup, this woman was dressed more suitably for an office than a ranch in a metallic blue sheath dress and matching jacket, but it was the high-heeled, black patent, T-strap sandals with the perfectly pedicured toes that captured Jade's attention and caused her to suck in a breath. She probably spent too many seconds staring at the pop of purple color on the woman's toenails before she collected her thoughts. The first thought was that the tall heels were a sure sign this chick was completely out of her element at the ranch. What was she doing with these other two who looked like they worked with horses? Maybe she was one of those women who fancied having a few horses without a clue what to do with them and she'd brought along her pals to give her advice.

Jade started to shrug off the encounter as more likely a pain than a real prospect, but when she looked into the woman's face she was struck by her beautiful light brown skin and very expressive, deep brown eyes, and her usual reticence faded. "I'm Jade. I am tall, but the horse is doing most of the work in that department." She dismounted and gathered Ransom's reins in one hand, holding the other out. "And you are?"

"Bianca Cruz."

Jade was pleased when Bianca's grasp was firm and strong. "May I show you around the stables? Maybe even a ride so you can see the ranch?"

"Uh…" The wattage of Bianca's smile dimmed a bit as she glanced at the two women who'd arrived just before her.

Jade followed her gaze, reluctantly remembering they weren't alone. In the few minutes since she'd locked eyes with Bianca, she'd forgotten about the other strangers, her mother, and her work. She had plans for Ms. Cruz. She'd show her the horses, the ranch, and then whatever else she wanted to see. Normally, she reserved her conquests to her trips on the road. It was less complicated to engage when she knew she'd be leaving soon, but she was captivated by Bianca. Enough to break a few rules. She crooked her arm. "Come on. My mother will talk to your friends, while you and I get to know each other better."

Bianca's eyes were locked on her now, and Jade was certain she'd won her over. She took a step closer to seal the deal, when one of the other women, the one with the dark shades, called out, breaking the spell. "Bianca, can I talk to you for a second?" A beat passed. "Now."

Bianca's brow furrowed and she squinted like she'd just shaken out of a dream and wasn't sure where she was. Bianca shot her an apologetic glance, extracted her arm, and started picking her way down the gravel drive in her too-tall heels. One step, two steps before her heels lost their battle with loose rock. Jade sprang forward, catching Bianca as her feet skated out from under her.

❖

Bianca barely felt the ground slip away before strong arms cradled her and she was looking skyward. But the big blue sky was no match for the full lips and dark, steamy eyes of her savior. Jade. She had no idea who Jade was, but she made an instant pledge to find out everything about her, starting with where Jade had been all her life.

"I'm sorry about that. Clumsy, I guess."

Jade eased her upright. "Anyone would be clumsy in those heels. You're not exactly dressed for a ranch."

"True." Bianca looked over at Dale and Peyton who were shaking their heads, and she snapped back to reality. She wasn't dressed for a ranch because she'd just come from the office. The office where she'd received important information about the investigation that she needed to share with Peyton and Dale as soon as possible. She'd thought she'd have time for a quick conversation with them before they talked to Sophia, but she hadn't planned to meet this female Don Juan astride a beautiful horse, let alone fall into her arms.

She stood up straight, brushed the wrinkles from her suit, and assumed her most professional tone. "My friends," she pointed at Peyton and Dale, "and I are here to meet with the owner of the ranch. Maybe we could talk again after our meeting?" She couldn't resist leaving the possibility open. She didn't know who this woman was, but she knew for darn sure she wanted to find out.

Jade's eyes went from warm to distant in the span of a few seconds. "The owner? But…" She followed Bianca's gaze to her mother. "Ah, you must mean Sophia Valencia? Yes, she is the grand dame of this ranch." She swept an arm in mock grandeur toward Sophia. "By all means, discuss your business with her." She didn't wait for a reply as she grabbed the reins of her horse, and walked toward the stables with her gorgeous mount.

Bianca knew she'd said something wrong, but she didn't have time to figure it out before Dale called out to her again. She walked over to where Dale and Peyton were standing, but chanced one look over her shoulder at the stunning beauty who had rescued her from falling.

Dale grabbed her arm and whispered, "I see that look in your eyes. Save it until we can talk." She and Dale joined Peyton who was standing next to Sophia. Sophia didn't look happy to see them, and she didn't hesitate to let them know in an angry whisper.

"You cannot just show up like this. What if I have company or business dealings? How do I explain who you are?"

"You tell them you have business with us too," Peyton said in the calm and cool tone that was her trademark. "We do have some unfinished business, after all. Now, why don't you invite us inside unless you need to talk to that woman?"

Bianca risked a glance back at the woman who'd captured her attention to the point of distraction, but she was gone. Bianca shook away the disappointment and followed the group into the house.

A few minutes later, they were seated around Sophia's kitchen table. Sophia sat at the head of the table, her hands clasped in front of her, and the air was thick with apprehension. Bianca glanced at Peyton and Dale. Under normal circumstances, Peyton would be the one to lead this interview, exchanging good cop/bad cop roles with Dale, but normal wasn't at play since Peyton was in love with Sophia's daughter. Truth was, Peyton probably shouldn't even be here, but it wasn't Bianca's place to toss her out. If Dale, a stickler for making sure this investigation stayed on track, had no problem with Peyton's presence, then she was on board as well, but she'd do everything in her power to make sure they got what they came for.

Bianca turned in her chair and faced Sophia. "We need to talk. You get that right?"

Sophia's eyes closed and she nodded her head like she was whipped. "I know."

Bianca shot a look at Dale who motioned for her to continue. She did a mental inventory of the things they wanted to know and settled on the one that had been bothering her most. The week before they had set up a prison visit so Sophia could see her brother Arturo. The purpose of the visit had been for her to get him to disclose the whereabouts of their other sibling, Sergio, who'd been on the run ever since Arturo had been arrested. Dale had been at the prison listening in on the conversation which had been completely without substance until the very end when Arturo pulled Sophia out of range of the prison microphone and delivered an ominous warning. Bianca decided to start there. "Let's start with what really happened when you went to see Arturo in prison. Tell us again what he said to you."

"He spoke about the threat on Lily's life. He said Sergio wasn't the one threatening Lily. He said she may be a…" she winced, "a gringo, but she is part of our blood and it would take an act of complete betrayal for them to go against blood."

"Did he tell you who did make the threat?" Bianca held back a shudder as she recalled the image of the threat against Lily, painted with what was determined later to be animal blood.

"No."

"That's not what you told Peyton before." Bianca looked between Peyton and Sophia.

"I'm telling the truth. He didn't give a name. He said only that it was someone who works with you. It could be anyone, I suppose." She gave them each a pointed look. "It could be one of you for all I know."

Dale started to move out of her chair, but Bianca waved her back. "Really, Sophia? You honestly think one of us would threaten your daughter? Peyton is in love with her and Dale has taken a bullet during this investigation. And me? What would be my motive?"

"Your motive for what?"

They turned as a group. Jade stood in the doorframe of the kitchen. Jade. She wasn't quite as tall now, having switched her boots for loafers, but she was every bit as striking as she had been sitting astride her horse, looking like a model for *Cosmo*. Before Bianca could form words, Dale jumped in.

"Excuse me, ma'am, but we have private business with Ms. Valencia."

Jade's full, luscious-looking lips curled into a sly smile. "Is that so?" She didn't wait for an answer before directing her next question directly to Sophia, in Spanish.

Bianca listened and then replayed the words in her head. Jade had just asked Sophia why she had brought these people around their family. Bianca looked back and forth between them as clarity dawned. She'd been too distracted to notice the similarities before, but with the two women standing so close, it was impossible to miss. She blurted out her observation to Sophia. "Is this woman your daughter?"

Sophia flinched, but Jade merely laughed, a hard, brittle sound. She held a hand out to Bianca. "I guess dear Mother didn't tell you her other daughter had come home. Jade Vargas."

Bianca stared at the hand extended her way, surprise robbing her of the ability to engage in normal social graces. Vargas. She knew Sophia had changed her name long ago, when she had fallen in love with Lily's father and defied her brothers' insistence she remain engaged in the family enterprise. But Jade, her daughter, said the name Vargas with a cocky attitude, like she was proud of it.

Thankfully, she was spared having to come up with a suitable response because Dale asked, "You're Jade Vargas?"

"I believe I already said that, but you people have yet to answer my question. Who are you and what are you doing here at our ranch?"

"Your ranch?" Bianca managed the feeble question, but it was Dale who answered.

"Yes, she's the other owner of Valencia Acres. That's what I called to tell you last night, although I didn't know Jade was Sophia's daughter at the time." Dale turned to Peyton. "I'm guessing by the look on your face you didn't know either."

"I didn't. And I seriously doubt Lily has any idea she has a sister."

"Half sister," Jade corrected her.

"I was going to tell her," Sophia said. "When the time was right."

A loud slap echoed through the room, and they all turned toward the sound as Jade's hand was raised to strike the counter again. "It's time for one of you to answer my question. Who are you and what are you doing here?"

Bianca looked at Peyton who shook her head. Peyton couldn't handle this, and no one should expect her to. Dale could, but this situation required a more delicate approach than Dale's rough and tumble style. It was up to her. Damn. She looked up into the deep, rich brown eyes of the most gorgeous woman she'd ever met and sighed. Jade Vargas—secret sister of Peyton's girlfriend, niece of drug dealers, crazy good-looking horsewoman. Yeah, she could handle her. No problem.

CHAPTER FOUR

Jade tapped the floor with her foot, but her hold on her patience was tenuous at best. She'd heard exactly enough of the conversation these women were having with her mother to know they were up to no good. Her uncle's name, the reference to prison, and threats of violence. She was no stranger to the darker side of her heritage, but these people were outsiders and she couldn't understand why Sophia was discussing her uncles with them. She was most surprised when the petite woman who'd caught her eye out by the stables rose to greet her challenge.

"I think we got off on the wrong foot," she said, sticking out her hand. "I'm Bianca Cruz and these are my associates, Peyton Davis and Dale Nelson."

Jade tore her thoughts from the distracted notion that Bianca was a lovely name and glared at the other women, whose names she recognized from the news article she'd read the day before. "You're police?"

"Not quite," Bianca said. "Peyton and I are with the US Attorney's office. Dale is with the DEA."

"So only one of you," Jade pointed at Dale, "is with the police and," she turned back to Bianca, "you and the other one put people in prison for a living." She surveyed their faces, but couldn't quite glean who was really in charge, so she turned back to Bianca and fixed her with a piercing stare. "I suppose you are responsible for my uncle Arturo's incarceration?" She delivered the words calmly and easily. Years of practice had equipped her with the tools to take apart any sort of adversity.

The woman named Peyton stood up. "Actually, I'm the one who put your uncle in prison, and with good reason. He tried to kill your mother and your sister."

"I do not have a sister," Jade growled, her eyes still focused on Bianca who hadn't flinched during this entire exchange. "Lily Gantry is not my sister. And if Uncle Arturo wanted her dead—if he wanted anyone dead—they would be finished." She drew her finger across her neck as she spoke. Bianca watched her every move, the only reaction a slight wince. "Did you come here to warn me about my own relatives or do you have some other reason for intruding in our home?"

Peyton started to speak, but Bianca put a hand on her arm. "We're here because we need your mother's help with a very important case. Maybe your uncles are involved, maybe they aren't, but we need your mother to talk to Arturo because it's becoming clear he knows something that can help us."

Jade laughed. "And you think he'll help you? Then you have no idea who you're dealing with." She tore her gaze away from Bianca and turned to face her mother. "We need to talk, but first you need to get these people out of here and make it clear they will need a warrant if they wish to come back. Are we in agreement?"

Sophia didn't answer at first, casting a glance in the direction of the law enforcement posse. Peyton's face was red with anger. Dale met her eyes, but Jade couldn't read her expression, and Bianca looked…hopeful. Silly, but there was no other way to describe the eager anticipation in her caramel eyes, and Jade experienced a tinge of regret at dashing her hopes, but she didn't waver. She'd lived her entire life in the shadows of law and order, and she wasn't about to invite the shadows in.

Sophia finally got the point. She rose and ushered the women through the kitchen and out of the house. Resisting the urge to watch as Bianca walked past her, Jade pulled a bottle of water out of the fridge and listened for any signs of resistance from the departing visitors. She heard snippets of conversation, "I'm sorry," "she's not always like this," "too much traveling," and then the front door shoved shut and her mother's footsteps echoed across the wood floors.

Jade downed half the bottle in one drink and looked up to see her mother framed in the doorway. "They're gone?"

"Yes."

"They shouldn't be here."

"It's complicated."

"Everything is, but complicated doesn't mean it's hard to decide between safety and danger."

"Peyton is Lily's girlfriend."

Jade nearly choked on a gulp of water. "Perfect. I suppose while I've been gone you've all been sitting around discussing our private business? Lily Gantry hasn't earned her way into this family. And do you think it's a coincidence that AUSA Peyton Davis is dating your rich half-white daughter who just happens to be Cyrus Gantry's only child?"

"They're in love. Peyton seems like a good match. She is very protective."

"Love is a means to an end. I'm sure they are very much in love. The question is why, after all these years of estrangement, are you letting Lily and her band of law enforcement friends into our lives when you know they mean us harm?"

Sophia grabbed her arm and pulled her into a half hug. "I would never do anything to hurt you, Jade. I promise. I do not think Peyton is a danger to us."

"And what about the others?" Jade didn't name her, but Bianca's hopeful expression had burned its impression in her mind. "This Bianca. Is she a danger?"

Sophia's look was penetrating, but Jade didn't duck the inspection. She doubted her mother could read her mind, and she had confidence Sophia would take her inquiry at face value. Hell, they'd spent most of their lives misunderstanding each other. The very idea Sophia had suddenly developed the power to intuit her thoughts was laughable.

"I doubt it," Sophia said. "She seems like a nice girl. She's always been very courteous to me. She seemed almost reluctant to have me go see Arturo at the prison, like she hated having to ask me to be close to him after he threatened me."

Jade nodded, satisfied her mother's assessment was similar to her own. Bianca Cruz was a nice girl and she had no business sniffing around the Vargas family. In Jade's experience, nice and courteous girls wound up on the losing end of just about everything, which is why she declined to either be one or to be with one.

❖

"I suppose that could've gone worse," Dale said as they walked to their cars.

Bianca punched her arm and motioned to Peyton who looked like she was ready to hit someone. She couldn't recall ever seeing Peyton angry. Fierce and determined, yes, but never angry. She tapped her on the shoulder. "Hey, are you okay?"

Peyton offered her a half smile. "I will be once we get to the bottom of this." She shook her head. "I can't figure her out."

Bianca nodded. "I know. She just shows up out of the blue and thinks she can interfere in our investigation when she has no idea what's really going on." Gall spurred her on. "Do you think she's working with her uncles?" She stared at Peyton who, instead of an answer, gave her a puzzled look. "What?"

"I was talking about Sophia."

"Oh." Bianca tried to will away the blush burning up her neck. Everything about Jade Vargas, her easy athleticism, devastating good looks, and her stormy temper kicked up emotions she hadn't felt in a very long time. She was using anger to mask agitation, but she wasn't ready to admit the agitation was born of arousal, and she hoped it didn't show.

"But you're right," Peyton said. "Jade Vargas looks like trouble. It bothers me that Sophia never mentioned her, especially since it looks like she has quite a bit of influence over Sophia's business. If nothing else, Jade is going to be an impediment to what we have planned."

Bianca nodded. When they'd sent Sophia to meet with Arturo the first time, her job had been to convince Arturo she could help him launder money for his operation now that his go-to source, Cyrus Gantry, was under the microscope of a federal investigation. Bianca had come up with the idea, and she and the rest of the task force had constructed the scheme in an attempt to lure Arturo's fugitive brother Sergio out of hiding. The plan had seemed foolproof at first, but the mystery surrounding last week's kidnapping and subsequent rescue of investigative reporter Lindsey Ryan, and now the sudden appearance of Jade, a Vargas child they hadn't known existed, threatened to throw a wrench in the works. "I guess we need to find out everything we can about Jade." She looked over her shoulder as if by speaking her name, she might have conjured Jade's appearance, but despite the fact they were still standing in front of the house, no one had shown up to run them off. "And I still need to talk to you about my news, but maybe we should go somewhere else."

"I know a good diner off 35," Dale offered. "Let's meet there."

Bianca started her car and motioned to Dale and Peyton to leave first, but they waved her on. Darn. She'd had enough trouble traversing the drive on the way in, she wasn't certain her Miata could make it back up the steep grade, and she wasn't thrilled about making the effort while Dale and Peyton looked on from the comfort of Dale's massive pickup. Even more mortifying would be if Jade walked out onto the front porch and saw her wheels spinning on the loose gravel.

She shook away the thought. Why should she care what a total stranger thought about her ability to maneuver her car over unfamiliar terrain? She shouldn't, but she couldn't deny the deep impact of her brief interaction with the enigmatic woman. She tightened her grip on the steering wheel and dug deep for a Zen moment before she hit the gas, murmuring thanks when the little car took the hill like a champ, but feeling a tinge of regret she hadn't been treated to a last-minute glimpse of the captivating Jade Vargas.

A short drive later, she pulled off the highway at the exit Dale had texted her and located the diner. By the time Dale and Peyton arrived, she was already seated inside. A waitress with a loosely coiffed bun ambled over to her table and asked if she wanted something to drink. Bianca ordered coffee and asked for a couple more menus. The waitress sighed and wandered off. Bianca recognized the signs of preoccupation and wondered what her life was like outside this tiny restaurant. Was she a single mother? Was she working her way through school? Did she care for an elderly relative?

Bianca reflected on the many similarly thankless jobs she'd worked on her journey to her current career. She'd zoomed through college and law school in a blur of child raising, working two jobs, and studying. Thankfully, she'd had parents who, although they hadn't had extra money to pay for the school of her dreams, had contributed their time and willingness to help out with Emma. The hardest time of her life had been when she'd traveled across country to attend Georgetown for three grueling years of law school. When her fellow students drank away their stress during weekly happy hours, she'd gone straight home every afternoon to make sure Emma had a hot meal for dinner and the same kind of one-on-one attention she'd received from her own mother. She was well acquainted with the frustration of too much to do and not enough time or energy to make it happen. But with the help of her family, she *had* made it happen, and she couldn't help but attribute some of it to Emma. Without the responsibility of raising a daughter on her own, she might have spent more time drinking pitchers of beer than studying outlines of con law and wound up chasing ambulances instead of criminals.

"Daydreaming?" Dale and Peyton towered over the table.

"Sit down, both of you. You're making me feel like I'm trapped in a forest of redwoods."

They slid into the booth across from her and Dale spoke first. "What was so important you drove all the way out here in your toy car?"

Bianca refused to rise to the ribbing, but now that the time had come to tell them about her morning meeting with Gellar, she dreaded the reaction. "Order something easy, overtip the waitress, and I'll tell you whatever you want to know."

Dale gave her a funny look, but waved the waitress over and dutifully ordered scrambled eggs, bacon, and coffee for both her and Peyton. When they were alone again, she leaned in. "Now?"

"Gellar is going to charge Cyrus Gantry with Maria's death." Bianca blurted out the words and braced for the fallout. Peyton, who'd looked like she was miles away when they walked in, snapped to attention, but it was Dale she was worried about the most. She was right to worry.

Dale slammed the table with her fist and her eyes burned with anger. "No fucking way."

Dale's angry whisper wasn't quite whisper enough, and Bianca put a hand over her still formed fist. "Yes, but I think we can do something about it. Gellar put me in charge of preparing the grand jury presentation."

"All right then," Dale said, waving her arms. "All you have to do is throw the game. Grand jurors are smart enough to know when a prosecutor's heart isn't really in it."

Bianca's heart hurt at the hopeful expression in Dale's eyes, but she had to be honest. "There's no way Gellar is going to let me handle the presentation. My assignment was clear. Work with Tanner to line up all the witnesses and make sure there are no holes in the case. He's confident the grand jury will indict. Even if he somehow agreed to let me handle the presentation and they don't indict, Gellar will start over with a new panel. He's obsessed."

Dale put her head in her hands, and everyone at the table was silent until she looked back up to face them. "Peyton, what do you think?"

"There's definitely something going on with him and we need to figure out what it is soon," Peyton said. "If he indicts the wrong person, we'll never be able to indict her real killers. He'll lose all credibility. A defense lawyer will tear the case apart."

"He can't do this."

"He can, but we'll do everything we can to stop him." Bianca delivered the words as if she meant them, but she wasn't sure how to get Herschel Gellar to let go of his stubborn fixation on Cyrus Gantry. "Have you talked to Lindsey about helping us out?"

At their last task force meeting, they'd settled on a plan to try to get Lindsey to ask Gellar for an interview. Her cover story would be that the interview was part of the PR piece she and her team had been filming about the DEA, but they would feed Lindsey questions designed to learn more about the motivation behind his singular focus on Cyrus Gantry. They'd chosen Dale to do the ask since she'd not only spent the last couple of weeks with Lindsey and her team, but she'd led the rescue effort when Lindsey had been kidnapped in a botched attempt to leverage her life for the Vargas brothers' freedom.

"Actually, there's something I need to tell you before we move forward with that part of the plan," Dale said.

"Spill," Bianca replied, anxious to know why Dale's face had suddenly reddened.

"Lindsey will do the interview, but I thought you should know she and I…Well, there's more to us than—"

"No way!" Bianca's mind made the leap faster than she could process an appropriate response, but now she recognized the red on Dale's face as a shy blush. That and the stammering delivery of her words told her all she needed to know. "You're a couple? When did this happen? I thought she drove you crazy?"

She started to say more, but felt Peyton's hand on her arm. Peyton shook her head. Dale's face was even redder now, and Bianca regretted her spew of insensitivity. She just never imagined Dale with anyone besides Maria, and she certainly never imagined her getting far enough past the grief of losing Maria to fall in love with someone else. But it wasn't her business either way. She reached over and used a finger to lift Dale's chin. "Sorry about that. You should know by now I'm a bit of a blurter. I'm so happy for you."

Dale offered a thin smile. "Me too. It's new and I'm still getting used to the idea. You two and Mary are the only people who know so far, and until we have a plan for exactly how we want to use Lindsey's skills, I think we should keep it that way."

Peyton said, "I can't promise I won't tell Lily, but other than that, your secret's safe with me."

"Me too," Bianca said and left it at that although she had a million questions. Would Lindsey move to Dallas? Was Dale planning to move to New York? Was everyone she knew going to hook up while she stayed single the rest of her life?

Whoa, that last thought came out of nowhere. Or did it? She'd dated some—as much as having a family would allow, but so far she'd never fallen in love. Part of the problem had been finding someone who didn't mind when her work pulled her away at odd hours or kept her completely occupied, but a big part had been Emma. Not everyone was ready to take on a ready-made family, and she'd always been ultra careful about who she chose to introduce into Emma's life, despite her mother's admonition she was being overprotective. Besides, the main players in her life these days were members of the task force. She considered them family, but definitely not dating material.

"So what do you think?"

Peyton and Dale were staring at her. Damn. She'd completely zoned out. "Sorry, my mind was somewhere else. You mind rewinding a bit?"

Peyton raised an eyebrow, but plunged right in. "I like the idea of Lindsey telling Gellar she's sticking around to do a focus piece on his role in guiding the DEA's investigations. Plays to his ego and he'll love it."

"It's going to drive Diego crazy," Dale said, referring to her boss.

"See, that's the beauty of this plan. Gellar has already disrupted things by dismantling the task force. We get him to throw some more wrenches into interagency relations and something's going to crack. My bet is whatever happens will expose his weakness and tell us what's really going on."

Bianca listened as the plan developed, content to defer to Peyton and Dale for details. Her own role, pretending to gather evidence against Lily's father, would be hard enough. She didn't need to take on the extra work of trapping Gellar into showing his cards.

"And with Bianca watching Jade, we should have our bases covered."

Bianca snapped to. "What did you just say?"

Peyton grinned. "You really did zone out. Dale and I think it would be a good idea for you to cozy up to Jade Vargas. Find out what she knows about her uncles. See how much influence she has over Sophia."

"Define cozy up," Bianca said. Her mind had already wandered to a variety of scenarios, none of which were at all appropriate for an AUSA and a potential witness.

"You know, get to know her. Gain her trust. Get her to confide in you."

Bianca looked at Dale for help. "Isn't this kind of thing more up your alley? You know, undercover agent kind of stuff."

Dale raised her shoulders. "Under other circumstances, maybe." She exchanged a knowing smile with Peyton.

"What's the inside joke?"

"No joke," said Peyton. "It's just we talked about it on the way over and decided you would be the best choice for this particular assignment."

"And why is that?" She looked between them until Dale finally broke.

"We just happened to notice you're more her type. We're pretty sure she thinks so too."

Bianca couldn't stop the flush that flooded her face. Apparently, her pals had noticed the heat between her and Jade when she'd arrived at Valencia Acres. She'd have to be a lot more circumspect if she was going to tag along after Jade, trying to find out her angle.

And there it was. She'd already accepted the challenge. While she pretended to curse Peyton and Dale for sticking her with this particular assignment, she felt a thrill of excitement at the prospect of spending more time with Jade Vargas.

CHAPTER FIVE

The next day, after making a few phone calls, Jade formulated the beginnings of a plan. She went to her closet and slid hanger after hanger aside, intent on selecting the perfect outfit for her outing. She brushed aside cocktail dresses, jodhpurs, and jeans, finally settling on a charcoal gray Armani suit. She paired it with a maroon blouse with a slightly feminine cut, but not enough to detract from the business edge of the suit.

"Going somewhere?"

Jade looked over her shoulder. Sophia was standing in the doorway of her room, dressed for riding. "Yes. I have an appointment downtown. You headed out for a ride?"

"I am and I was hoping you would join me. We still have some things to discuss."

"Maybe later." Jade turned back to her closet, hoping Sophia would pick up on the curt dismissal. She wasn't ready to forgive her mother for entangling their personal and professional business with Cyrus Gantry, let alone a federal prosecutor, but she wasn't in the mood to discuss her feelings right now. Studiously ignoring Sophia's persistent presence, she scoured the closet shelves, looking for the Louboutins she'd purchased to go with her suit. She hadn't worn the designer pumps in ages, but after witnessing how much of a statement Bianca Cruz had made with her high heels the day before, she was determined to find them.

She was certain the box was on the lower shelf, and she shoved aside box after box in her quest. Nothing was where she remembered, and her aggravation grew as she heard Sophia step into the room and sit on the bed. Without looking up, she said, "Is there something in particular you need?"

"I need my family, all of my family, to get along."

"You've got to be kidding." Jade whirled on her mother. "I wasn't gone that long, but you've managed to make a horrible mess of things and now you seem to attribute the consequences to everyone but yourself. You want a discussion? Here's what I have to contribute. Lily Gantry is not your family. She's a product of biology and you barely know her. Cyrus Gantry is not your family. He has family of his own. Tio Arturo and Tio Sergio are your blood, but they believe you've betrayed them. I imagine they would sooner cut you than welcome you into their arms."

She raised her hands against her mother's protest. "I wish you'd severed all ties with them long ago instead of this crazy push and pull between you. Their darkness casts a shadow over everything we do, but inviting federal agents in to take care of the mess you've made with your life puts us all at risk." She took a deep breath. "The truth is I'm the only real family you have, and even that's a stretch considering you barely know me. The fact is I'm fine with our relationship exactly the way it is. We work together and we live together, but let's not try to make it something it's not. You've met Lily and now you want everything to be all daisies and sunshine. That's not real and I refuse to pretend it is."

Jade paused to catch her breath, but before she could start again she caught the haunted look on her mother's face and stuffed the words. She hadn't meant to hurt her feelings. She didn't think she had that kind of power, but the drawn lines and pained reflection told her different. She should apologize, take it back, but there was no way she could reel the words back in. Sophia had made the choices that led them to this place and she would be the one to deal with the consequences. In the meantime, Jade would do whatever she needed to in order to keep the ranch safe from federal agents and her uncles' greedy grasp.

An hour later, she handed the keys to her SUV to the valet at Thanksgiving Tower, marched inside the fifty-story office building, and rode the elevator to the top floor. She'd never been to the exclusive Tower Club, but when the elevator doors opened, it was exactly as she imagined. Clubby, overbearing, opulent. She strode confidently to the maître d' and made a note of his name tag.

"Good afternoon, miss. How may I assist you?"

"Carl, I'm here to see Cyrus Gantry. I understand he's dining here today."

The man made a show of running his forefinger down the sheet of paper on the stand in front of him. She waited, certain she knew exactly what he was about to tell her.

"Hmm, I don't see any guests listed for Mr. Gantry's table. Perhaps you have the wrong day?"

"Every day with Cyrus is the wrong day," Jade muttered.

"Excuse me?"

"Nothing." She leaned forward and concentrated on being more alluring than intimidating, although she reserved the right to switch gears if she didn't get what she came for. "This is kind of a delicate situation. Mr. Gantry asked a 'friend' of mine to meet him here, but she didn't feel right about it. I told her I would check it out first and make sure your discretion was impeccable. So far, I'm very impressed, but here's the thing." She beckoned him forward with a curl of her finger. "Mr. Gantry is expecting me, and if I don't show up, I won't be able to tell my 'friend' that this place can be trusted. Cyrus would hate that and you wouldn't want to be the one he'd blame. Understand?"

Carl's eyes blazed with understanding. Or maybe he was just captivated by the cleavage shot her leaning in had afforded him. "Maybe I could let him know you're here."

Jade nodded. "That sounds like a good compromise." She gave him her name. "Why don't you do that right now?"

Carl meandered through the crowded club toward a door near the rear, disappearing inside a moment later. She didn't understand these membership-only type places, designed to keep people out. In her experience, the people they denied entry were usually the most interesting and accomplished.

Carl didn't keep her waiting long. "Mr. Gantry invited you to join him. Right this way."

Jade followed him on the same route he'd taken a moment earlier, ignoring the admiring glances she received along the way. She'd gladly take money from these people, but she had no desire to break bread with them. When they reached the door she'd seen earlier, Carl stopped and turned to face her. "Shall I announce you?"

She offered him an appreciative smile. "No need. Thanks for your help." She waited until Carl was well on his way back to his station up front and then she pushed through the door, ready to take Cyrus Gantry by surprise.

The door swung wide and she stepped forward. "Cyrus, we need to tal—" The beginning of her lecture fell from her lips and she froze two steps in. Cyrus wasn't alone, and although she'd never met the woman seated next to him, she'd know Lily Gantry anywhere.

Even seated, it was apparent Lily was tall, like her. They also shared long waves of jet-black hair and dark brown eyes. Her skin tone was lighter, but Jade couldn't deny the strong family resemblance. Lily looked so much like Sophia there was no doubt there was blood between them.

For a second, Jade's resolve dimmed and she wished she could slide out of the room unnoticed. She'd been fully prepared to confront Cyrus, but not his other family, the secret, shameful one he and her mother had made. This family had absolutely nothing to do with her, and as far as she was concerned, it didn't exist.

Except it did. Lily was a very real part of her mother's life now. She could accept it or ignore it, but either way the reality affected her, especially since Lily's girlfriend, Peyton Davis, was hell-bent on involving her mother and their ranch in her obsession to put her uncles in prison. She squared her shoulders, assumed a smile she didn't feel, and strode to the table. "Cyrus Gantry, look at you, walking around free and clear as if you haven't done anything wrong. Or maybe it's just they haven't quite figured out what to charge you with." She turned away from his startled face and stuck a hand out toward Lily. "And you must be Lily, the not-quite bastard child of my mother."

She wasn't sure what reaction she'd hoped to provoke from Lily, but she was a little taken aback to see her flinch. "You really had no idea? How is that even possible?" Lily glanced between her and Cyrus, who looked like he wanted to crawl under the table. "For God's sake, Cyrus, did you think your precious Lily and I would never meet?"

"Is someone going to tell me what's going on?" Lily asked, a hint of anger in her voice.

Jade sighed. "Not my job, but someone should probably let you know you're not Sophia's only daughter." She watched as the realization dawned on Lily's face, and continued to watch while Lily turned to Cyrus and shot him a questioning look. "Oh no, he's not my daddy. He's all yours and you are welcome to him. I just came to see him about some loose ends, but it turns out to be rather convenient that you're both here."

Lily shot Cyrus daggers and then turned to face her with a smile that managed to seem genuine despite her obvious stress. "Sit down," Lily said. "If you're here to talk, you may as well settle in." Without waiting for a response, Lily stood, pointed at a chair, and walked to the door of the room. Jade didn't move, curious about what Lily had planned. A second later, a waiter appeared at the door and Lily instructed him to add another set of what they were having to the order. The waiter nodded and ducked out. Lily turned around and fixed her with a stare.

"What?" Jade asked.

"If we're family," Lily said, "you should sit down and break bread with us."

Jade shook her head. "We're not family and I'm not hungry."

"We can talk about that later, but in the meantime, if you have something to say, sit and we'll talk about it."

Jade had to admit she was a tiny bit impressed. Lily came across as unflappable despite the bombshell she'd dropped in her lap. Cyrus, on the other hand, was breathing heavily and his face had flushed deep red. If she didn't know better, she'd think he was having a heart attack. But she didn't care about his health. All she cared about was getting some answers, and the minute she did, she was out of here. If Cyrus needed medical attention, Lily could take care of him. She had no idea what her mother saw in this man, and she had no desire to get to know him well enough to find out, but in the meantime, it couldn't hurt to sit for just a minute.

Once she was seated, Lily joined them back at the table. "Thanks for joining us."

"Don't worry. I won't stay long," Jade assured her. "Cyrus, you mind filling me in on your recent legal troubles?"

Cyrus took a deep swallow of the amber liquid in the glass in front of him before answering. "I wish I could, but my lawyers have instructed me not to talk about it."

"I don't care what your lawyers told you," Jade said, struggling to keep her voice calm. "Did you know that Lily's girlfriend is putting pressure on Sophia to set a trap for Sergio? Do you really think it's a good idea to put everything she and I have worked for in danger when you could just do the right thing? Why don't you step up and admit whatever it is you've done so they will leave the ranch alone?"

"Sophia volunteered to help with the investigation," Lily said. "She wasn't pressured."

"She wouldn't have been so eager to get involved if you hadn't been threatened." Jade made a point of giving Lily a long looking over. "You don't look like you're in any danger to me, and if you are, your daddy here or your prosecutor girlfriend should be able to provide you with adequate protection."

"Peyton would never willingly put Sophia in danger. I haven't known our mother as long as you, but I care about her well-being."

"Let's not pretend we're one happy family. You've known Sophia for what, a month?" She barely waited for Lily's nod before pushing forward. "You have a lot to learn about your new mother, and I'm willing to bet you've got a lot of surprises in store."

Cyrus opened his mouth to respond, but Lily motioned for him to be quiet and reached a hand across the table. "Look, I get that you're angry. I didn't know about you, and you didn't know about me. How about we start from the beginning?"

For a second or two, Jade considered giving in to the plea. Lily's voice was calm and soothing and hinted of possibilities she'd never allowed herself to consider, but she couldn't trust the overture. "See, here's the thing. I did know about you. I've known about you for years. Hard to miss the princess of Dallas society when her picture was splashed all over the society page week after week."

Jade started to say more, but stopped abruptly for fear of revealing too much about herself. She had no desire to bare the insecurities she'd once felt, watching Lily's privileged life play out while she scratched out her own future from whatever was left after her mother shared herself with the rest of the world. Anger coursed through her. She needed to get out of here. She stood and directed her next comment to Cyrus, purposefully ignoring Lily's gaze. "There's nothing else for us to discuss. I don't care how you do it, but get these federal agents away from our ranch." She tossed her head at Lily. "And her girlfriend too, along with the rest of the US Attorney's office. I don't want anyone with a badge of any kind showing her face at Valencia Acres again. Do you understand?"

She'd expected some pushback, but all Cyrus did was nod. She stared him down for a moment to brand his brain with her point before marching out of the room. She could only imagine what was going through Lily's mind, but she did her best not to care.

She'd meant what she said about all of them staying out of her life even if one of the women included in her demand was Bianca Cruz. Jade was no stranger to beautiful women, but the surge of want she'd experienced the second she laid eyes on Bianca was more than arousal—it was dangerous. She had no business entertaining lingering thoughts about a woman who was part of the task force set on putting her business in danger in a probably futile attempt to take down her uncles.

Jade stepped into the elevator and punched the button for the lobby. The car was half full with what she was certain were lawyers and bankers, based on the suits and uptight expressions all ducking her gaze. These people were useful, but they didn't interest her beyond the services they could provide. She preferred the company of people like her, entrepreneurs, people who earned a living by doing something real, not making their way on the backs of others. Law and finance were merely means to an end.

She dug through her bag for the valet ticket for her Range Rover. Sophia had scolded her on more than one occasion about the extravagance, but the luxury ride was a necessary component of the persona she projected. Success breeds success, she quipped the last time she'd been scolded about the expense. She spent her time traveling to shows and races, wining and dining buyers and breeders. Valencia Acres depended on these contacts to stay successful, and while Sophia was good at running the day-to-day operations of the ranch, Jade was the rainmaker in the family.

Family. The word choked out tortured sentiment, a cross between the fond feelings she knew she should have and the reality that she'd been left with only the scattered pieces of loosely connected relations. Her uncles had appeared at all the appropriate moments—baptism, first communion, high school and college graduation—but always in the background, lurking well-wishers, not to be acknowledged, but always noticed. Only her mother had stood by her side, but even so, Jade sensed Sophia had wished for something more, like the life she could have had if Cyrus had had the guts to leave his wife and raise their precious Lily with her. Instead, they'd hatched a soap-operaesque plot designed to buy their freedom from her uncles.

They'd gotten their freedom, but it had come at a price and she'd paid a part of it. The rift between Sophia and her brothers was likely what led to her mother seeking solace elsewhere. She was the product of her mother's search to fill the void. Sophia told her she was a love child, but she didn't believe it since the man who'd sired her had chosen not to stick around, and no evidence seemed to exist to prove she wasn't the result of immaculate conception. Sergio and Arturo attempted to fill the fatherless space, but Sophia's tenuous relationship with her brothers made it difficult for Jade to cultivate any kind of meaningful connection to her uncles.

She walked to the valet stand, making a mental list of what she needed to do the rest of the afternoon, but the meeting with Cyrus and Lily derailed her ability to focus on all the things she needed to do and she found herself wanting instead.

"Jade?"

Jade recognized the voice and spent a moment considering whether she should ignore it. In her current state of mind, she was likely to say things she shouldn't, push boundaries better left in place, but she didn't feel like being cautious, especially not where a beautiful woman was concerned. She turned slowly, taking the time to assume a friendly, hopefully not too feral, smile, and faced Bianca Cruz.

❖

The only thing on Bianca's mind as she crossed the street was the motion hearing she'd just lost and the Russian chicken salad from Cafe Izmir she'd been craving all morning, but the minute she spotted Jade Vargas standing on the street, the object of her hunger took an abrupt turn.

She'd spent the morning in court, distracted more than a little by Peyton and Dale's strategy for her to cozy up to Jade. While her pals were long on plans, they were short on detail about how she should implement their strategy. Stumbling across Jade unexpectedly should have been the answer to her dilemma, but if she didn't handle it right, it could spell disaster. Surely Jade would figure out she had ulterior motives. Why else would she be trying to get close?

Hello? Because she's gorgeous? Bianca shook her head at the distraction. Yes, Jade was attractive. Big time. But Bianca was on a mission that had nothing to do with finding a date even if she had to pretend that's exactly what she was after.

I can do this. Bianca continued walking and repeated the silent mantra several times until she was standing a few feet from Jade who was facing the opposite direction. Before she could analyze the pros and cons, she said, "Jade?"

Although she had the advantage of surprise, she was wholly unprepared for the way her body thrummed with excitement when Jade turned to face her. She stood perfectly still while Jade's gaze swept over her, almost as if she was paralyzed into submission. And she liked it.

"What are you doing here?"

Jade's gruff question broke the spell. Bianca smiled in an effort to show she was harmless. "Just passing by. On my way to a well-deserved delicious lunch after a hard morning getting knocked around…" She paused and made a last-minute change to her choice of words from "in the courtroom" to "at work." No sense reminding Jade she was a prosecutor working on her uncles' case. She studied Jade's tired eyes and the frown creasing her brow. "You look like your morning has been as bad as mine."

A quick smile graced the corner of Jade's lips. "Do you always say exactly what's on your mind?"

Bianca ducked her head. "Mostly, yes. At least when I'm around other adults. I suppose it's because I spend too much time filtering my words for my eleven-year-old daughter and her friends. The strain of making sure I say the right thing seems to disappear when I'm around age-appropriate company."

Ugh. She'd had no intention of letting the "I have a kid at home" information slip so soon. The child card had been a date killer in the past, and there was no sense sharing the bigger pieces of her personal life until she was certain Jade was interested. Granted, she wasn't trying to get a real date out of this encounter, but if she was going to go undercover, she should play the part all the way, right? She looked into Jade's eyes and saw a question there. Uh-oh, first rule of being an undercover agent—pay better attention. "I'm sorry, what?"

"Where did you go just then?" Jade didn't wait for her to reply. "I said, it must take a lot of energy to spend your days prosecuting people and raising a daughter. I assume you have help?"

Hook, line…Bianca resisted grinning at the knowledge Jade Vargas was interested enough to fish around to find out if she had a spouse at home, and took the cue and ran with it. In her very best flirty voice, she said, "Why don't I buy you lunch and tell you all about it?" She watched as Jade's expression morphed from surprise to uncertainty. Worried Jade was about to say no, Bianca tugged on her arm and tucked it in her own. "Come on, I promise it will be fun."

She watched as Jade looked down at her arm and back up again. Gone was the uncertainty, replaced with a cat-like confidence—the kind Bianca wished she had, but only ever pretended to convey. When Jade opened her mouth to answer, Bianca held her breath, convinced even the slightest movement might change the course of this moment.

"Well, if you promise it will be fun, I can hardly say no."

A few beats passed and Bianca managed to resume breathing. "All right then, follow me."

Cafe Izmir was on the next block. Bianca had a million questions she wanted to ask along the way, but resisted the urge, choosing instead to focus on the arm still resting in hers and keeping up with the tall, virtual stranger striding next to her. Jade was dressed in a power suit, an expensive one at that, and Bianca couldn't decide if she was more attractive in this attire or the riding clothes and boots she'd been wearing when they first met.

Damn. What she should be wondering was what Jade was up to, dressed for business, in downtown Dallas, steps away from Cyrus Gantry's offices. She fingered the cloth of Jade's jacket. "This is a beautiful jacket."

"Thank you."

"I guess I didn't picture a rancher wearing a suit like this."

Again the smile played at the corner of Jade's mouth. "A horsewoman, or rancher, as you say, is only one of my personas."

Bianca saw the opening, but she wasn't sure it was time to plunge in yet. Thankfully, they were at the door of the restaurant so she changed the subject. "Here we go. After you."

Jade slipped her arm from Bianca's and Bianca instantly felt the loss. She resorted to conversation to cover. "I hope you like Mediterranean food." She looked at Jade's lips and the idea of garlicky hummus seemed ill-conceived. "If you'd prefer something else, there are a few other—"

"I love it. The spicier the better."

Bianca left the line alone. A few minutes later, they were seated and had placed their orders. Bianca stuck with the chicken salad, but Jade went all out with an assortment of grilled tapas including quail, lamb chops, dolmas, and a side of the garlicky, creamy hummus Izmir was famous for. Now that they were face-to-face with the innocuous topic of food behind them, Bianca floundered around for something to say. "How long have you been raising horses?"

Jade took a sip of water and cocked her head. "We don't actually raise horses. We're kind of like a horse incubator. We stand anywhere between five to seven stallions and we have around a dozen mares at any given time."

"Stand? What does that mean?"

"Horse talk for keep them on hand for stud purposes."

"Interesting."

"You make it sound like anything but."

"Well, I didn't mean to. I guess I'm just curious how it all works."

"Well, unlike thoroughbred horses, most of what we do involves artificial insemination instead of live covers."

"Again with the horse talk. Live covers? Does that mean what I think it means."

"Yes. Live covers are where the horses actually have intercourse. It's required for thoroughbreds, but not quarter horses, though some breeders use that method. Quarter horses are bigger and it can be very dangerous."

"Got it. Horse sex is dangerous."

"You laugh, but it's absolutely true. An aroused stallion will trample anything that gets in his way, and sometimes even the mares are injured."

Bianca watched Jade's face as she delivered the words with a knowing smile. "Duly noted. Don't get between a stallion and a mare. Any other horse tips you'd care to share?"

Jade started to make a smart remark, but the waitress arrived with their food. They both dug in. Her tapas were delicious, but based on her moan of pleasure, Bianca had ordered the best thing on the menu. "What do they put in that sandwich?"

"Sorry," Bianca said with a sheepish grin. "The Eggo I grabbed on the way out the door this morning is long gone and I'm starving."

The mention of the kid-like breakfast food sparked Jade's memory. Bianca had casually mentioned she had a daughter, an eleven-year-old. How was that even possible? "Eggos? Did your daughter make breakfast?" Not very subtle, but it was the best she could manage on the fly.

"Matter of fact, she did. We take turns."

Bianca took another bite of her sandwich, but her eyes offered a silent challenge. Jade decided to bite. "Just you and her? Or does the breakfast making rotation include anyone else?"

"Hmm, sometimes there are three of us." Bianca took another bite and chewed slowly. When she finally swallowed, she took a deep drink of iced tea, and then wiped her lips with a napkin. "But not very often. Only when my mother shows up early to take Emma to school."

Jade wanted to ask more. Where was Emma's dad? Did he show up sometimes too? She'd already taken note of the fact Bianca wasn't wearing a ring, but that fact alone wasn't definitive. What really bothered her was why she cared so much. She'd never cared before if a woman she wanted to bed was attached or not.

But the others were all miles away and you weren't going to be around to see the fallout. True. And the stakes were even higher here. Bianca might not be a cop, but she was associated with them, and in the end she had even more power than her police friends since prosecutors made the final call when it came to whether or not charges would be pressed. Bianca was working on the case against her uncles, and as much as Jade had maintained distance from that branch of the family business, she couldn't help but feel she was being disloyal by lusting after a woman who held sway over her uncles' future.

She resigned to leave her questions unanswered. The answers wouldn't matter anyway because as attracted as she was to Bianca, nothing could come of it. Besides, she didn't want to invite any personal questions Bianca might have. The rest of the lunch was spent discussing innocuous subjects like the mild weather, the new development downtown, and local city politics. The conversation was pleasant, easy, and deceptively safe, and Jade was surprised when she glanced at her watch and realized an hour had gone by. When the check came, she insisted they split it. She didn't need to owe anyone anything. She signed her receipt and rose to leave, but she couldn't resist a friendly, "If you're ever at the ranch again, I'll show you around."

"I'd like that. Very much."

The blaze in Bianca's eyes said there were a bunch more things she'd like as well, but Jade confined her response to a brief handshake before heading to the door. Her invitation might have only been a polite, rhetorical overture, but Bianca's response left her feeling decidedly unsatisfied and wishing for more.

CHAPTER SIX

Bianca looked up at the knock on her office door and saw Peyton staring at her through the crack. "Hey, come on in."

Peyton walked around behind her desk, eyes focused on the large computer screen that took up most of the real estate. "Hmm, these look like bank records. I thought you were doing something a little more riveting since I've been trying to get your attention for the last five minutes."

Bianca stretched her arms and yawned. "I think I might be in a financial coma. I promised Tanner I would go over these records before we meet with the forensic accountant who did the analysis of the Gantry Oil financials, but I swear it's like reading Swahili."

Peyton made a show of turning away from the screen. "Guess I better not get caught looking at any of this, Chinese wall and all."

"Whatever." Bianca minimized the computer screen, but she figured the ship had sailed on completely walling off Peyton from any aspect of the investigation into her girlfriend's father. Someday, if the case went to trial, a clever defense attorney might try to raise the issue of Peyton's involvement in the case as a way to show the US Attorney's office was biased, but they'd have a hard time proving the bias cut against Cyrus Gantry since it was more likely Peyton would help her girlfriend's father rather than try to take him down. If Peyton's family wasn't embroiled in a drilling rights dispute with Gantry Oil, there probably wouldn't be any issue at all. "So, how's life in human trafficking?" she asked, referring to the unit Peyton had been assigned to once Gellar yanked the Vargas and Gantry cases from the task force.

"About what you'd imagine. Horrible. Gruesome facts, not much in the way of evidence to prosecute anyone." Peyton shook her head. "I still can't get that image of all those bodies out of my head."

Bianca nodded, certain Peyton was remembering the bodies that had been found in the back of one of Gantry Oil's semi trucks out near Fort Worth the month before. Poor migrant workers who'd paid money to a coyote to get them safely into the US, had been left to die, locked inside and unable to escape. The truck had been reported stolen long before it was found with its cargo of carnage, but Gellar was still convinced Gantry was somehow involved. She didn't know what to believe, but she'd only had a brief glance at the crime scene photos and she couldn't begin to imagine working trafficking cases every single day. "Sucks you got reassigned."

Peyton looked over her shoulder before saying, "It would suck if we weren't still working together. Speaking of which, I came to tell you we're having an impromptu meeting."

"When?"

"Now. Gellar's headed to a meeting across town. We're having lunch across the street. Dale and Mary are probably already there. Close up whatever you're doing and let's go."

Across the street was a loose term for the Adolphus Hotel down the block. When Peyton and Bianca arrived, they were greeted by the rest of the task force: Tanner, Mary, and Dale, and a surprise addition. Bianca did her best not to fangirl again when Lindsey Ryan shook her hand, managing to utter a simple, "Nice to see you again."

After they ordered, Peyton nodded to Dale who took charge. "I thought it would be a good idea for us to check in," Dale said. "Lindsey has reached out to Gellar about an interview."

"And in the meantime," Lindsey said, "I've primed the pump with a few local sources."

Bianca had a revelation that she delivered with a loud whisper. "You're the source mentioned in the article!"

Lindsey's smile was sly. "I may have channeled a few tidbits to an old pal of mine who happens to be working the crime beat at the *Morning News*, but she did all the digging. I figured giving Gellar the opportunity to respond to the article would give him an extra reason to let me do an interview."

"Brilliant." Bianca reached for some sweetener and added a healthy dose to her iced tea. She brought the glass to her lips and had just taken a sip when Dale asked, "Bianca, want to tell us about your lunch with Jade last week?"

She nearly spewed the tea across the table. She hadn't mentioned the impromptu lunch to the rest of the group. She'd convinced herself her silence was because there was nothing to tell. And there wasn't really. Not related to the cases they were working, anyway. But now that Dale was calling her out about it, she knew there was more to it. Lunch with Jade had been the closest thing to an actual date she'd had in a long time, and she hadn't wanted to make it into something else. "Not much to tell. I ran into her downtown and invited her to lunch. We talked about…" She paused for a second recalling the various topics of conversation. "Horses, food, and, uh, the weather."

"Really?" Dale asked, the inflection in her voice making it clear she wasn't buying it. Dale started to say more, but Lindsey placed a hand on her arm. Bianca watched as Dale flicked a glance back at Lindsey and then softened her tone. "Well, I guess that was a good first start. When are you going to see her again?"

The prospect was inviting, but Bianca was done playing secret spy agent. "Yeah, I'm no good at this. I think we need a plan B." The subject was closed as far as she was concerned, but one detail eluded her. "And would someone mind explaining to me how you even knew I had lunch with Jade?" She made a show of checking the inside collar of her suit jacket. "Am I wearing a tracking device?" she asked, making a direct reference to the week before when Dale had planted a tracking device on Lindsey when she suspected her of nosing around into their investigation.

"You're hilarious," Dale said. "I'll let Peyton fill you in about how we found out about your lunch with tall, dark, and mysterious."

"Jade showed up at the Tower Club where Lily and Cyrus were having lunch," Peyton said. "She warned Cyrus not to let his legal troubles rub off on Valencia Acres, dropped the bomb on Lily that they're sisters, and then stormed out. Lily called me right after she left. I told Mary and…" She stopped and pointed at Mary. "You want to tell the rest?"

Mary nodded. "I happened to be headed out to grab a slice from the place over on Elm and took a detour to Thanksgiving Tower. I didn't expect to see you show up, but when you did, I decided to follow along behind."

"You followed us into the restaurant?" Bianca didn't care so much where Mary had followed her, but she was more than a little disturbed she hadn't clued in to the fact she'd been followed.

"No." Mary shook her head. "I waited outside and then followed Jade when she left downtown."

Bianca still couldn't shake the unsettling notion Mary had had the opportunity to witness her entire interaction with Jade and she hadn't been the slightest bit aware. She took a deep breath to settle her nerves and retraced every detail of the lunch. They'd talked, laughed, eaten good food, but she'd been totally professional no matter how much she'd wanted to be anything but. Her friends had no reason to suspect she'd been doing anything other than the simple task of trying to ferret information from a potential witness. Which was true. Kind of.

To deflect her own dissembling, she asked, "Why didn't anyone mention you'd been spying on me before now?"

"Spied on," Mary said with a grin. "It was just the one time. And we were just looking out for you, I promise." She raised her right hand and looked around the table until everyone else did the same. "We don't know if Jade Vargas is linked to any of her uncles' business interests, so forgive us if we're a little cautious. We didn't bring it up because we figured if you had anything to report, you would've let us know. Anyway, it looked like you did a good job of breaking the ice. That should help you get even closer when you see her next."

"Okay." Bianca looked down as she delivered the simple response, sure that her friends could see through her guise. She supposed it was no more surprising they hadn't mentioned seeing her with Jade than it was that she hadn't told them about the encounter. Still, the whole thing left her feeling unsettled. And now she'd kind of committed to seeing Jade again despite her plan to withdraw from Mission Follow the Sexy Woman.

She could do this. Besides, Jade wasn't really dangerous. Was she? Nothing about their conversation at lunch seemed suspicious. Jade had appeared to be slightly ruffled when they first ran into each other on the street, but after what Peyton said about how Jade had just delivered an ultimatum to Cyrus and run into her half sister, it was kind of amazing that she had seemed as together as she did.

The rest of the lunch was consumed with discussing the evidence Gellar had gathered for the grand jury investigation and Lindsey's plan to help the investigation by interviewing Gellar and other agents and attorneys who might have an inside scoop, but Bianca barely registered the conversation. Jade Vargas—beautiful, intelligent, accomplished—loomed in her thoughts, leaving little room for anything else.

❖

Jade wandered past the perfume counter at Neiman's, lost in thought. After a tedious morning spent with her accountant and banker to discuss preliminary preparation of the end of year financials, she should go back to the ranch. She needed to review the paperwork from her recent purchases with Sophia and give her a list of the contacts she'd made so she'd be prepared when they came calling to purchase breeding services. She needed to plan her next trip and schedule the time in between to maximize networking with local buyers and breeders who would want to line up their services well in advance of spring.

But the trip downtown sparked memories of last week's lunch with Bianca and distracted her from all the other things vying for her attention. She walked through the aisles of the upscale department store, barely noticing the expensive clothes and eager clerks, ever conscious she was a mere two blocks from the federal courthouse. Was Bianca in court right now or was she in her office? Was she thinking of ways to bring down Sergio and Arturo's empire or was she too daydreaming about their pseudo date at Cafe Izmir?

You're being ridiculous. Jade shook her head to clear the distractions. It was completely out of character to let thoughts of a woman burrow past her steely exterior. She'd spent quite a bit of time since last week trying to dissect why Bianca was the exception, but her preoccupation remained a mystery.

She held out a hand to another store employee headed her way. Just walking through the store was a luxury she could ill afford. The numbers from this morning's meetings told her the ranch was doing well, but during this season there was substantially more spending than earning, making purchases of fancy clothes and baubles out of the question.

Jade picked up the Range Rover from the valet and started the drive to the ranch. She was only a block from the valet when her phone rang and she answered via the vehicle's Bluetooth. "I'm on my way home."

"Hello to you too."

Jade modulated her tone. "Sorry, trying to negotiate traffic. What do you need?"

"Are you alone?" Sophia's voice was a near whisper.

"Yes. I'm in the car." Jade almost wished she hadn't answered the phone, but curiosity got the better of her. "What is it?"

"I received a letter from Arturo."

Jade gripped the wheel. Of all the things Sophia might have said, she hadn't expected that. "Has he forgiven you for turning him in to the police?"

"It was more complicated than that."

Jade sighed. "It always is." She drummed her fingers on the steering wheel. "Why are you calling to tell me this?"

"Because he wants me to visit him."

"And you need my permission?"

"Of course not, but I don't think it's a good idea. Federal agents arranged my last visit. I don't think they would like it if I went to see Arturo on my own. They might suspect something."

"And God forbid you cross them."

"Maybe you should go."

Ah, there was the real reason for this call. Jade should've known Sophia wasn't calling for advice, but merely to drag her into her drama. She had no desire to get into all the reasons why this wasn't a good idea so she kept her answer short and to the point. "No."

"Hear me out."

"No."

"Jade, if we don't show up, I worry he will send Sergio to deliver whatever message he has for us."

"Us?"

"We're family. No amount of discord will change that, but do you really want your fugitive uncle showing up here at the ranch, especially when we know we're being watched?"

Jade's first reaction was to say yes. If Sergio showed up, maybe he'd be arrested and they could return to business as usual, but she knew it wouldn't be that simple. A notable arrest at the ranch would bring them all kinds of unwanted publicity. Better she head off whatever Arturo had in mind by going to see him at the prison. She told Sophia she'd consider her request and clicked off the line. She was still driving around downtown, a few miles from the highway that would take her to where Arturo was being held and only blocks from where she'd run into Bianca after seeing Cyrus and Lily the week before.

Cyrus and Lily. She flashed back to the moment she'd walked into the small private dining room at the Tower Club. Lily had been leaning close to Cyrus, telling him something that made him laugh. The father indulging the daughter. Their closeness was cloying, but it stung all the same. She tried to pretend she didn't understand why, but she knew it was the familial connection between them that drew her in and shut her out at the same time. She slapped a hand against the steering wheel to shake away her preoccupation with things she couldn't have. In an attempt to cure her frustration, she made a snap decision.

She punched the button to connect to her phone and asked Siri for directions to the Seagoville Federal Detention Center. The signal was good, and the directions loaded on the screen almost immediately. Before she could give another thought to her mother, her uncles, Lily and Cyrus Gantry, or even Bianca Cruz, she jerked hard on the wheel just in time to make the first right turn of Siri's commands.

❖

Bianca looked at the spread of files on the conference room table and groaned. She had no idea how she was supposed to weed her way through all of this evidence, tag around after Jade Vargas, and still have a life.

You can't.

The ugly thought echoed and, like always, she slapped it away. Her mother would say negativity wouldn't get her anywhere, but she was juggling all the important things and scared that any minute one or more of them would come crashing to the ground, broken and beyond repair. A secret task force, a grand jury presentation, and a clandestine assignment to befriend the niece of two of the most notorious cartel leaders in North Texas—she was overwhelmed just thinking about it and she'd barely scratched the surface.

"Are you daydreaming or just concentrating really hard on that spot on the table?"

FBI Agent Tanner Cohen stood framed in the doorway. Tanner was tall and lanky like Dale and Peyton. Mary was the only one of the group who topped out at a normal height, but Bianca still needed heels to avoid having to always look up. She met Tanner's laughing eyes. "Would you believe both?"

It had been Bianca's idea to bring Tanner onto the task force and she was happy with the results. Tanner had been part of the team of agents who'd served the search warrant on Gantry Oil headquarters at the direction of Gellar, and because of that, Gellar seemed to trust her, a fact critical to their behind-the-scenes maneuvering. Now that it appeared Gellar had decided to trust her too, Bianca knew this time spent working on the grand jury evidence was crucial. She waved a hand at the table full of files. "I'm also wondering how in the world we're going to get all of this done in time. Peyton and Dale have decided they want me to start stalking Jade Vargas."

"Ah, the niece."

"That's the one."

"From what I hear, you've got a pretty sweet assignment."

Bianca couldn't miss the low growl in Tanner's tone or deny the visceral response it elicited, a response she couldn't quite identify. She shoved her emotions aside for the moment. "Oh, sure. That's what you say now until the hot chick in question goes galloping off on a horse and leaves you in the dust."

"Not a fan of horses?"

"I prefer man-made modes of transportation or my own two feet."

"I'm sure you'll figure out a way to make it work." Tanner delivered the words with a sly smile and a knowing wink.

Bianca shoved a stack of files at Tanner. "Quit picking on me and get to work. Gellar wants a report tomorrow, and we need to tell him where things stand. Let's go over the witness list."

They spent the next two hours poring over FBI 302 forms summarizing witness interviews. Tanner and the other agents who'd conducted the raid on Cyrus Gantry's offices, field sites, and warehouses had interviewed dozens of Gantry Oil employees, certain they'd find a disgruntled employee who'd been lying in wait for the perfect opportunity to tank the boss. After reviewing all the 302s, it was beginning to look like their certainty had been misplaced. Bianca tossed a file on the desk. "I don't get it. They all seem to think he's the best employer on the planet. Nobody has anything bad to say."

Tanner closed the file she was reading and slid it back into the pile. "That's what it seems like."

Bianca caught the tone of uncertainty in Tanner's voice. "You think something's off?"

"I'm usually leery about nevers and always. All of these employees were eager to talk to us, and they all had only glowing things to say. A little too good to be true if you ask me."

Bianca nodded. "You're right, but I don't know what to do about it unless you want to re-interview everyone on this list." She paused as she ran a finger down the long list of names. "The real question is why Gellar thinks he has any kind of case at all based on this evidence. He'd have enough trouble trying to make a simple conspiracy charge stick, let alone a murder for hire charge."

"He really thinks Cyrus ordered the hit on Maria Escobar?"

"That's what he says. Didn't you say he's had this evidence squirreled away in his office for days?"

"Under lock and key."

"Are we sure nothing's missing?"

Tanner drummed her fingers on the table. "You know, Counselor, I have to admit, I didn't check."

"Fair enough. It's not like it was scattered on the street. How about we double-check everything against the original logs."

"Good plan." Tanner reached across the table for the evidence log, but before she could start calling out items, her phone buzzed with a text. She read it and, as she did, a slow smile crept across her face.

"What?"

"I just found a way you can do your stalking without having to climb up on a thoroughbred."

"Come again?" Bianca slowly registered the change in subject.

"One of the guards at Seagoville agreed to send me an alert anytime someone shows up to visit Arturo." She showed Bianca her phone. "Guess who showed up this afternoon?"

Bianca looked at the screen, barely able to register the words, but thrilled by them just the same. *Jade Vargas here to see AV.* She glanced back at Tanner who sported a huge grin. "Stop it with the innuendo. If I'm going to do this, I don't need you making it into something it's not. Besides, they're quarter horses, not thoroughbreds."

Tanner waved her hand in the air. "Of course, how in the world could I have made such a silly mistake? I suppose you know all about horses now."

"Shut up." Bianca punctuated the harsh remark with a grin. She waved a hand at the log listing all the files. "Can you check this and then we'll start back tomorrow?"

She barely heard Tanner's yes before she was out of her chair and at the door.

Bianca had just made the turn onto 175 when her phone started blowing up with messages. Taking a page from Emma's playbook, she asked Siri to read the messages out loud to her, but like usual Siri pretended she'd requested something entirely different and started playing a Michael Jackson song from her playlist. Shaking her head, Bianca pulled off the highway and into the parking lot of a convenience store. The first message was from her mother asking if she would be home for dinner. She typed a quick *yes, but can't talk now* to avoid the inevitable string of questions that would follow, asking her what she wanted to eat, etc. Having her parents live close by was a boon most of the time, but the reality of motherhood could be smothering.

The next message was from Gellar, asking for an update on the grand jury work. Doubtless, he'd gone by the conference room and found a spread of files, but no attorney reviewing them. This was confirmed by the next text from Tanner, informing her that Gellar had shown up looking for her. *Told him you were tracking down a witness. For real.* The last line a reference to the fact that "tracking down a witness" was code in the office for out on a personal errand. She was about to call Gellar to ward off his anger, when another text popped up from Tanner.

Source says JV just left Seagoville. Will get you the tape.

Bianca read the text several times while she formulated a plan. Sure, the tape of whatever conversation Jade had had with her uncle was important, but it had nothing to do with why she'd ditched her work and hustled out of the office to try to meet up with her. Bianca had no way of knowing where Jade would go after leaving the detention facility, but if she was heading back to Valencia Acres, there was a good chance she could beat her there. She'd have the hour-long drive to figure out a good explanation for showing up unannounced. She should go back to the office, but she'd promised Peyton she would try to get close to Jade, and if she went back, she was likely to get trapped by Gellar.

The idea of getting close to Jade clearly outweighed the desire to mine for nuggets of prosecutorial gold in the pile of trash Gellar had her digging through. She slipped her phone into the cup holder and got back on the highway in the direction she'd come, determined to make the most of this day.

CHAPTER SEVEN

Jade stood in line with all the other visitors, but was distinct from them by her bearing, her clothing, her expectations. The others shuffled in line or loudly voiced their protestations about being searched. Many were questioned about their choice of dress which violated the posted rules that called for no bare midriffs, no plunging necklines, no sleeveless clothing, as if the mere sight of skin would send the inmates into a frenzy.

She resented all the rules but knew it was pointless to argue. No matter how educated she was or how professionally she was dressed, the color of her skin, combined with her last name and her connection to Arturo Vargas, made her suspect. She might hate that fact, but she was smart enough to realize there was little she could do about it other than quietly go along. Her energy was better spent on more important fights.

Jade only had to wait a few minutes after being seated in the large community room before Arturo showed up with a group of other inmates. While he paused at the door, surveying the room to see who'd come to visit, she took a moment to reflect. She hadn't seen him since the party Sophia had thrown at the old ranch down south for her college graduation. Arturo and Sergio had often shown up for family gatherings when they had lived near the border, probably because they felt safer in those communities, where their people had all the police under close surveillance or on the dole. At the graduation party, her uncles had presented her with a large envelope full of cash, which she was certain wouldn't pass a drug test.

Jade had used the money to make her first big investment—breeding time with a stallion that had won the All American Futurity race that year. The resulting foal had turned out to be the bread and butter for Valencia Acres, Queen's Ransom, and she'd leveraged Ransom's purse into making their ranch the premier breeding facility in North Texas, besting Circle Six.

She'd done quite a bit of research about the Circle Six ranch over the past couple of days. Peyton Davis's family's ranch seemed to be in a bit of trouble. One of her brothers, Neil Davis, had attempted a little leveraging on his own and had signed an agreement with Gantry Oil to allow them to start drilling on the land, an agreement that Peyton and other members of the family denied he had the authority to make. While that litigation simmered its way through the courts, Peyton was still part of the establishment prosecuting Cyrus Gantry even while she was dating Cyrus's daughter. The irony of Peyton Davis acting all law-and-order when she was mired in controversy was almost too much. Did Bianca Cruz understand all the complexities, and was she a part of it?

She wasn't sure why she was so focused on Bianca, but she was and she knew the attraction was a dangerous distraction. Bianca was part of the system that spent so much energy focused on taking things she'd worked so hard to earn. She shuddered as she realized that if Bianca and the rest of her team knew the success of Valencia Acres was founded on her initial investment of a bunch of drug-soaked dollars, they would take every bit of it away from her. And she would never let that happen.

Arturo started walking toward her, but she avoided his eyes, looking instead at the other men in orange jumpsuits filling the room. Each one looked around anxiously before joining his family at one of the tables around the room. She glanced around the room at the mismatched groups of people, the vending machines full of odd food offerings, and thought if they'd been dressed differently, this might have seemed like a family reunion picnic of sorts, but before she could focus too much on the surreal nature of the venue, she heard a low voice speak her name.

"Jade?"

"Good afternoon, Tio," she said, keeping her greeting formal. Arturo looked much as she remembered him, but something was different. Older? A bit thicker around the waist? His expression was defiant, unlike the friendly, smiling, and benevolent uncle of her youth. As an adult, she'd come to know the truth about how her uncles had come by their wealth, but it had never been easy to reconcile what she'd read in the papers with her own experience. Not for the first time, she wondered if any of the emotions he displayed were real or were they all carefully calculated to achieve a particular goal?

Her uncertainty was the primary reason she'd chosen to keep her distance. Which begged the question of why she was here in the first place.

"What are you doing here?"

Arturo's tone was gentle as he asked the question, but Jade found the echoing of her own thoughts disconcerting. She glanced around, but it appeared the rest of the people in the room were engaged in their own discussions and not at all interested in their exchange. "I suppose I had to see for myself what's going on. Take stock. Do you realize how much danger you and Sergio have put the business in?"

"The business?" At first, his reaction seemed questioning, but when realization dawned, his expression reflected disbelief. "Oh, you mean your little ranch."

Jade clenched her jaw. "Yes, the ranch. I've spent everything I have—time, energy, and money—making Valencia Acres a thriving operation. You tried to shoot Sophia and steal Queen's Ransom, and now the feds are crawling all over our business."

He waved a hand in the air. "Sophia can take care of herself."

"And what about me? Do you really want to ruin my chances to make a name for myself?"

"There are many ways to make a name for yourself. You could even make the most of the opportunities you already have with the ranch, but incorporate a little extra to take you to the next level." Arturo leaned closer. "You talk about this horse of yours. He is a fine horse, but don't think for one minute that I don't know where he came from."

Jade's chest felt tight, and she focused all her energy on keeping calm. "I have no idea what you're talking about."

"Oh, right." Arturo pointed back and forth between them. "You think it's in your best interest to distance yourself from your roots, but you're wrong. We can help you. The same way we helped you start your little venture. Your ranch is nothing compared to the empire we've built."

"Empire?" Jade made a show of looking around. "Doesn't look like much up close. Sergio is on the run, and you're locked up. The news is full of the story about how you orchestrated a kidnapping attempt of that reporter. You do realize you're never getting out of here, don't you?"

Arturo lurched forward, his face flushed and eyes bulging. "That's a lie. We had nothing to do with that reporter." He looked across the room, nodding at a guard who appeared to be headed their way.

Jade watched as the guard changed course, and she idly wondered how much influence her uncle had over his keepers. "The details don't matter. You'll have no chance in court."

He waved away her proclamation. "It does matter and we will not be defeated." He dropped his voice to a low whisper. "I'm offering you an opportunity. You went to that fancy business school—you should know the value of opportunity. You are family. It's time for you to start acting like it."

"I make my own opportunities."

"With other people's money."

Jade rubbed the back of her neck. "I'm not having this conversation with you. Sophia and I run a legitimate business. All we want is to be left alone."

"And you came here just to tell me that?"

Jade stared into his mocking face, momentarily stumped at the challenge in his question. Why had she really come? The impetus had been more than Sophia's plea. She'd been plagued with thoughts of family after seeing Lily and Cyrus Gantry in their cozy father-daughter powwow. Had she hoped to find some sort of fatherly advice and unconditional love from her estranged uncle? Was she really foolish enough to believe their blood ties were enough to merit consideration if not counsel? No, she knew better. She'd learned long ago that she was the only person who could or would look out for her own interests. Expecting anyone else to do so ceded power she couldn't afford to lose. Arturo's offer to cut her into his drug business would be viewed by the people in his world as extremely generous, especially considering their estrangement, but to her his help would be a cement collar, pulling her down with him. The money she'd used to fund Ransom's birth may have had its origin in something unlawful, but she'd used it to be self-sufficient. No way was she going to surrender her sufficiency now. She stood up.

"To be perfectly honest, I don't know why I came, but now that I have, I'm ready to go. Leave the ranch alone. It's not part of your empire and it never will be."

She turned to leave, but he risked reprimand from the guards by pulling her back toward him. His words were quick and to the point. "We had nothing to do with that reporter. Our rivals will do anything to put us out of business. If you think your interests are safe and sound because you choose to deny your bloodline, you will be surprised. Watch who you shun or watch your back."

He stepped away as he delivered the last word, a determined scowl fixed on his face. Before she could process his little speech, he'd already crossed the room. He started to walk through the door, but turned and looked her way one last time and then was gone, but not before she caught the hint of a smirk on his face, making her wish she'd never come.

The guard buzzed her out the door, but not nearly fast enough. She walked several steps into the cool afternoon air before stopping. She bent nearly in half with her hands on her knees and took several deep breaths. Tio Arturo, the kind uncle of her youth, was a drug lord, not a doting relative. Expecting fatherly advice from him was not only dumb, but also dangerous, and she was disappointed at herself for thinking this visit would be a good idea. What she needed to do was keep her distance from him, Sergio, and her mother's new law enforcement friends, including Bianca, if she wanted to keep Valencia Acres out of the middle.

❖

Bianca sat in Sophia's kitchen wondering if it would be impolite to ask for a second cup of coffee. So far they'd discussed everything from the weather to world events, but Jade Vargas had yet to appear, and Bianca was caught between giving up or doubling down on the time she'd invested.

Her own mother had phoned during her drive over to say she was expecting her and Emma for dinner. A surreptitious glance at her watch told her she would need to leave in the next hour if she was going to make it in time. Before she could settle on a plan of action, she heard footfalls and looked up to see Jade standing in the doorway to the kitchen. Bianca's gaze swept slowly from Jade's high-heeled black boots to the crisp lines of the charcoal gray suit. Was it possible Jade was even taller than she remembered?

"Jade, come in," Sophia said. "Bianca and I were talking about the horses. Would you like a cup of coffee?"

Bianca watched as Jade stared down Sophia, to no avail. Both women held their own, as if engaged in a silent duel. She stood and attempted to break the silence. "Jade, I was hoping I could take you up on that offer to show me around the ranch."

Jade made a show of examining her from head to toe, and she struggled to remain still, as if any sudden moves might send Jade skittering off in the other direction.

"You're not dressed for horses, and for that matter, neither am I."

Jade's tone was dismissive, and Bianca was tempted to give up. Jade was right. She hadn't planned this out and she wasn't dressed for mucking around with horses. She should tell Peyton this wasn't the job for her and get back to her work at the office. But then Jade walked over to the refrigerator, and Bianca had a brief flash of Jade stepping up into the saddle of the beautiful horse she'd been riding the other day. Suddenly, proper clothes were the last things on Bianca's mind. "I'm not scared of getting a little hay or whatever on my outfit. Are you?"

Jade looked over her shoulder, and now her expression was a mix of amusement and something Bianca couldn't quite read. "Fine.

I'll show you around, but I don't want to hear about it later when you can't get the stains out of your pretty outfit." She tugged two bottles of water out of the fridge and shoved one at Bianca. "Come on." She started walking back through the house in long strides, and Bianca was forced to walk double-time to keep up while her mind rolled the words "pretty outfit" around like they were a treasured prize.

They were halfway across the gravel drive when Bianca lost her footing again on the loose rocks. She scrambled to right herself and was almost standing again when Jade slowed and turned around. Bianca waved her off. "I'm fine." When Jade started back toward the barn, Bianca muttered, "Just need to remember to wear different shoes next time."

Jade held open the door, and Bianca walked through. "Make sure you get a good look around because there may not be a next time." Bianca heard the undercurrent of warning, and she silently cursed Peyton and Dale for this crazy idea. Any goodwill she thought she'd won after their impromptu lunch date the week before appeared to be long gone. If she was going to make it work, she was going to need to melt the thick layer of ice around Jade's personality. Bianca had no idea how she was going to accomplish that, but she figured she should start by talking about something other than the case. "Is this where you keep all the horses?"

"This is the stallion barn. We have five right now, but two more will be arriving in a few weeks."

"Is that where you were? Buying horses?"

Jade cocked her head like she was trying to decide if the question was about more than horses. "I often travel as part of the business. Sometimes to buy horses, sometimes to market the ranch as a breeding facility, and definitely when we are racing one of our stallions."

"And which one was the last trip?"

Jade didn't answer and instead took off walking through the barn. Bianca watched for a moment, unsure if she was being dismissed or simply ignored. When Jade didn't turn back, she decided she might as well follow. When she was close to catching up, Jade stopped abruptly and Bianca had to grab the door of a stable to catch her balance. As she did, she heard a loud snorting and an enormous horse head swung toward her. She leaned way back in a frantic attempt to duck out of the way.

"Hey, hey, hang on there."

Bianca felt the warm embrace and looked up, expecting to see Jade staring down at her, but Jade's eyes were focused on the horse, coaxing him with her soothing, gentle tones. She smoothed her skirt and checked her footing, incredibly conscious that Jade's strong hand was still on her arm. "I'm fine. Don't worry about me."

Jade tossed her an impish smile. "Not very experienced with horses, are you?"

Bianca wavered between honesty and pride before settling on the former. "If by experienced you mean not slightly terrified, no, you speak the truth."

Jade reached in and ran a hand along the horse's mane. Bianca watched the affectionate gesture and couldn't help wishing she hadn't broken the connection they'd shared a moment ago. "He likes you, but I'm pretty sure I'm not his type."

"Anyone who strokes him like this is his type. Ransom's not finicky when it comes to petting. Now, if you wanted to ride him that would be a different story altogether." Bianca shuddered and Jade laughed. "Not big on riding horses?"

"Well, there's the thing where they are so tall." Bianca held a hand up to mark her own height. "People my size weren't meant to be so high off the ground."

"So, you're not big on heights, but I sense there's something else too. Bad experience?"

Bianca looked into Jade's eyes, beyond the playful grin, and saw a hint of concern. Though touching, the genuine interest made her reticence seem silly. "Nothing in particular. A petting zoo experience gone awry combined with a walk the pony around the pole birthday party attraction that turned bad when the pony spooked and ran over the table with the birthday cake."

"Your party?"

Bianca nodded.

"I'm guessing this is a painful memory from your distant past."

"Yes, but losing my favorite cake to a charging pony is kind of an unforgettable experience. The cake was red velvet."

"Red velvet." Jade licked her lips. "Looks like we do have something in common after all."

Bianca watched Jade carefully, certain there was more to this exchange than innocent small talk. At some point in the last fifteen minutes, Jade had decided to treat her like a fellow human being instead of someone interfering with her family's enterprise. What she should do is come up with ways to capitalize on this new mood, but all she wanted to do was bask in the light flirtation. Aside from their lunch, she could barely remember the last time she'd even felt like flirting. Her work and Emma's activities took up a lot of her time, and not everyone was able to respect, let alone understand, those two things would be her first priorities for many years to come.

"What are you thinking?"

Jade's low husky voice was a sure signal real flirtation was happening here, and Bianca was torn. Responding in kind was more likely to garner the kind of information Peyton and Dale were looking for, but she wasn't sure she was prepared to carry it through. She made a split-second decision and answered with words she hoped wouldn't send Jade running. "I was thinking my daughter would love to ride any one of your horses."

A slight pause and then a barely noticeable physical shift and Jade was suddenly a million miles away. Bianca took advantage of the faraway look in her eyes to get a read on what she was thinking, but before she could reach a conclusion, Jade snapped out of it and shot her a smile that didn't quite reach her eyes. "Well, you must have your daughter…?"

"Emma."

"You must bring Emma out to the ranch. We have several horses suitable for young children." Jade barely had the words out of her mouth before Bianca started laughing. "What?"

"I hardly think of Emma as a young child. She's kind of an old soul trapped in the body of an eleven-year-old."

Jade rolled the information over in her head. Some of the same questions she'd resisted asking the week before bubbled up, but she settled on the one that seemed the most important. "Do you think Emma's father would mind if she rode?"

"Let's just say Emma's birth father isn't in the picture."

Bianca's face offered no signal whether this was a good or a bad thing. Jade wanted desperately to know more, but the reality of why Bianca was here in the first place caused her to hesitate. Asking questions invited questions, and no matter what personal tidbits Bianca chose to share, Jade wasn't about to follow suit. She'd already gone further than she intended by inviting Bianca's daughter to come to the ranch and ride.

Maybe it was a good idea. Keep your friends close and keep your enemies closer. The famous mantra was a mantra for a reason. Of the three law enforcement types that had been sniffing around, Bianca by far seemed the least harmful. Why not allow Bianca to get close enough that she could learn more about their ultimate goal? She didn't believe Bianca's sole purpose in coming out to the ranch was for a friendly visit, but if she let her guard down a bit, she might be able to discern exactly what was going on. While she was certain Arturo's admonition to watch her back came from his own innate paranoia, she wasn't convinced he didn't have a point. One thing she had learned from her uncles over the years was no one would make your fortune for you and no one would make sure you got to keep it. She wasn't about to risk what she'd built because Sophia's past indiscretions got in the way, and if sidling up to Bianca was a way to net information she could use to protect the ranch, then it was a small price to pay.

She took Bianca's arm and urged her over to the stall across the way. "This is Juniper. He's a gelding, one of our older horses, small and gentle. He'd be the perfect mount for your daughter." Jade nickered, and Juniper turned toward her, bobbing his head at both of them. Jade watched as Bianca started to reach out a hand, but then drew it back at the last minute. Without thinking, she laced her fingers through Bianca's and raised their clasped hands up toward Juniper's mane. "It's okay, you can touch him. I promise he won't hurt you."

Bianca tentatively spread her fingers and ran them through Juniper's mane, and for a moment, Jade was mesmerized at the simple act, full of naïveté and wonder, and so completely not what she expected from someone with Bianca's occupation.

"His hair is so much softer than I would've thought."

"I brushed him out this morning."

"Do you tend to all the horses yourself?"

Jade spent a second considering whether the question was designed to pry or born of simple curiosity. "No, but I try to check in on each of them several times when I'm home. We have a few farm hands who help out on a regular basis."

Bianca continued to stroke Juniper. "So just you and your mother live here?"

"How about this? I'll answer another question if you answer one for me."

"Sounds fair enough."

"What made you decide to become an attorney?"

"I'm not sure it was just one thing." Bianca gazed up like she was trying to filter through her thoughts. "Promise you won't laugh?"

"Swear." Jade made a show of crossing her heart.

"I had a huge crush on Jill Hennessy, you know, Claire Kincaid from the original *Law and Order*. That started it anyway, but once I got into law school, I knew I'd found my calling."

"Calling. That's an interesting way to refer to it." Jade treaded carefully, not wanting to spook Bianca, but genuinely wanting to know how zealous she was about the work she was doing. "Why prosecution? Why not some other area?"

"I guess I want the world to be a safer place and I'm doing my part, however small." Bianca studied her face. "You don't look like you're buying it."

"I think it's sweet of you to think you're making a difference, but I'm not convinced that's the case."

"And you would make the world a better place how?"

"Why do you assume we need to make the world a better place?"

Bianca didn't hesitate. "Maybe you forgot the part where I said I had a daughter?"

Jade knew the appropriate response. *Children are our future. We must do whatever we can to make the world a better place for them. Children come first.* If she'd experienced any of those societal sentiments in her own upbringing, she might be more inclined to concede Bianca's point, but the simple fact was she was the only one in her life who put her own needs first. She created her own destiny, carved her own future. Children didn't come first. No, they were hindrances, and even if they weren't, their place was deep in the background to keep them from interfering with the needs of adults.

She looked into Bianca's eyes and saw sincerity reflected there. Bianca probably believed her cause was worthy. Someday, sometime, Bianca would realize she would have to make a choice about who came first in order to fulfill her own dreams. Would she choose her daughter, or be like Sophia and take care of herself?

"Bring your daughter over. This Saturday." Jade watched Bianca's expression as she rolled the idea around in her head. At the first glimpse of hesitation, Jade offered, "You obviously trust my mother. Would it help if I promised she'll be here?"

Bianca reached up and touched Juniper's mane again, but her eyes were firmly fixed on Jade when she finally answered. "Okay. We'll come."

CHAPTER EIGHT

Jade watched Bianca's car pull away, waiting until it disappeared before she stepped up onto the porch. The silky glow of anticipation that had prompted her to invite Bianca to return might fade, but until it did she enjoyed the moment of pretending Bianca was an attractive and ready escort instead of a mother on a mission who posed danger to the operation of Valencia Acres.

Sophia looked up from a giant spread of paperwork on the kitchen table. "You went to see him, didn't you?"

"I don't want to talk about it." Jade opened the door to the refrigerator and pretended to explore the contents.

"Don't you want to know how I know?"

"Not really." Jade rubbed her brow and stretched to ease the tension in her neck and back. The rush from Bianca's unexpected visit had disappeared, and in its place, she was left with the eerie reality of Arturo's warning. *Watch your back.* Suddenly, she did want to know more. She turned to face Sophia. "How do you know?"

Sophia held up an envelope, pinched on the very corner edge with her thumb and forefinger. "Because this showed up in the mailbox while you were in the barn." She held it up and shook out a single piece of paper. "Read it."

Jade walked closer and started to pick up the sheet of paper, but Sophia waved her hand away and pointed at the words.

Jade,

Prison visits are nice, but if you really want to live up to your name, there is so much more you can do. Watch for the sign.

Tio Sergio.

Jade read the two lines several times and hoped she was projecting calm, but her insides were swirling with questions. She'd left Seagoville only hours ago. How had Arturo gotten word to his fugitive brother so quickly, and how had Sergio managed to get this message delivered in the same amount of time? There was only one answer. He was close. Very close.

She snatched the paper from Sophia and held it aloft against Sophia's objections. "Why are you so concerned about me touching this? You aren't honestly thinking of turning it over to your friends at the DEA, are you?"

"I hadn't decided yet, but now that your fingerprints are all over it, I suppose that would make things complicated." Sophia looked down at the paper and skimmed the lines. "Do you want to tell me about your visit?"

"Not really."

"I know I asked you to go see him, but you need to be careful. He's dangerous. He tried to steal Ransom and he would've killed Lily and me both if he'd had the chance."

Typical Sophia. Jade was used to the push and pull, but she didn't have to like it. Pure stubbornness kept Jade from responding directly. "Did you see who delivered this?"

"No."

Jade scanned Sophia's face, looking for a clue. A small part of her wondered if Sophia had had personal contact with Sergio. Yes, it was Sophia's action that had sent him on the run, but her mother and her uncles always had a very tumultuous relationship that consisted of on-again, off-again interaction. What had really happened on Sophia's recent visit with Arturo? Maybe he had promised her something in exchange for her help, or maybe she had promised him she would get Jade to help.

Well, if Sophia had made such a promise, she could forget it. Little notes left to threaten and intimidate weren't going to do the trick. She grabbed the envelope with her other hand and strode onto the front porch. Holding the message and envelope over her head, she shouted, "If you have something to say, say it in person or get the hell off my ranch."

She gazed out over the land, but no one appeared to answer her challenge. The ranch hands had gone home for the day, and as far as she could tell, no one was on the receiving end of her message, but delivering the ultimatum made her feel better. She looked at the sheet again and then crumpled it into a tiny ball.

"What did you do that for?" Sophia exclaimed as she stepped up beside her.

Jade looked down at her hand. "What does it matter? You have nothing to gain by turning this over to the feds. You think if you convince them you have something on your brothers, you'll be in a much better position? Don't you realize if they capture Sergio, there's no telling what he might say? If he tells them you helped him out, we could lose everything."

"I haven't helped him."

"But you did believe what Arturo told you about someone else being responsible for the threat on Lily's life. And you avoided telling the feds that for as long as you could, right?" Jade didn't wait for a response before pushing forward. "You really think your new friends are going to interpret everything you do in the best possible light?"

"Lily isn't out to get us."

"But her girlfriend might be. What do you even know about her?"

"Peyton has always been respectful to me, and she comes from a good family."

Jade flinched at the word. "I'm sure it's a fine upstanding family, but don't you see, that just makes it more likely she's going to be suspect of a *family* like ours."

"What do you mean by that?"

"I mean a family that really isn't a family."

"Jade." Sophia's sigh signaled her exasperation.

"Don't Jade me."

"We are a family."

Jade crossed her arms. "That's what you tell yourself and that's fine, but it's not true. You have way too many personal secrets for us to be anything but business partners, and that's fine with me, as long as you're not hiding anything that might disrupt our business." Jade watched Sophia's face, but the all too familiar mask came down as it did each time she referenced the distance between them. She wouldn't get answers today any more than she ever had, and she was disappointed in herself for trying. "Speaking of business, your new friend Bianca is coming by on Saturday and she's bringing her daughter to ride Juniper. I promised you would be here."

Jade didn't wait for a response before striding back into the house and up to her room. The pointless visit to Seagoville, the ominous message from Sergio, the endless argument with Sophia had all combined to wear her down. All she wanted to do now was to be alone and think about her date with Bianca that wasn't really a date because she was bringing her daughter along. And people didn't bring children on dates, did they? Sophia never had. Jade was convinced her stint at boarding school—probably on Cyrus's dime—was more about getting her out of the way than prepping for an Ivy League education. Her mother's actions in sending her away had taught her children were not to be seen or heard.

Damn, how had her mind circled back to Sophia? Jade lay back on the bed and stared at the ceiling, willing her mind to be quiet. A mental image of Bianca with a dreamy look in her eyes talking about making the world a better place did the trick, and she fell into a deep sleep.

Bianca barely had time to set her bag down in the foyer before her mother appeared, sporting a furrowed brow. "Hey, Mom, what's up?"

Her mother placed a finger over her mouth and drew Bianca closer. "Something happened at school. She won't tell me, but she went straight to her room and I haven't seen her since. I even made her favorite for dinner, but not a peep."

"I'll take care of it." Bianca walked through the house until she was standing in front of Emma's closed door. She was tired and emotionally drained. Her bag was full of all the work she had yet to do since she'd spent the entire afternoon chasing Jade around town. And for what? She'd accomplished nothing other than to promise Jade she'd show up this Saturday with Emma in tow, a decision she now regretted. The thick chemistry between them must be clouding her brain or she never would have agreed to bring her daughter to Valencia Acres until they were certain nothing untoward was happening there. Speaking of which, she should check in with Dale and Peyton tonight to tell them about her plans. Perhaps they could arrange for someone to be watching on Saturday, just in case.

She knocked on Emma's door and waited for permission to enter, part of their compromise of privacy, which Bianca tried her best to respect. A few seconds later, she heard a soft "come in" and pushed open the door. Emma was curled up on her bed, staring at her laptop. She wasn't crying, but the red eyes and telltale Kleenex said it hadn't been long. Bianca kicked off her shoes, sat down beside Emma, and pulled her close. "What's up, bug?"

"Nothing." The one word was drawn out long with a sniffle, and Bianca kissed the top of her head. Emma was usually better than most girls her age about not trying to duck affection, but even she had her limits, so Bianca didn't push. Instead she resorted to a familiar method of questioning. "Is it school business or personal business?"

"I don't know."

"Both?"

"Maybe."

"Is it the play?"

"Yes," Emma said, her voice barely a whisper.

"Let me guess. Something about Jack?"

"Mom," Emma said, her voice hissing with exasperation. "His name is Jake."

"Sorry, mom brain. Jake then. What's up?"

"He's dropping out of the play."

"Okay." Bianca paused, certain she was navigating a minefield. "And that's a bad thing because?"

"Mom, seriously. Chelsea says it's because he thinks I'm too young to play Juliet."

"Well, Chelsea often says things that aren't entirely true, but if you repeat that I will deny it vehemently." Bianca scoured her memory for a nugget of helpful information. "Didn't you say Jake is on the basketball team? Maybe the play was interfering with practice or something."

"Maybe, but you'd think he coulda told me."

Bianca nodded, struggling to keep her face fixed in a solemn expression. "He probably didn't think about it. Boys don't always think about things like that, but that doesn't mean they don't have feelings about it. Maybe he was disappointed about not being in the play and isn't ready to talk about it."

"I guess," Emma said, her declaration punctuated with a heavy sigh.

Bianca pushed a strand of hair back from Emma's face. She hated the idea of anything making Emma sad, but knew better than to try to brush by the emotion. Emma always had strong feelings, and that passion, properly channeled, would be a driving force in her eventual success, but along the way it would make for a rocky ride. She wouldn't minimize her daughter's feelings, but she could do something to take her mind off of them. Her regret about accepting Jade's invitation vanished. "I have a surprise for you."

"What?" Emma asked cautiously.

"Would you like to go horseback riding this Saturday?"

Emma's eyes lit up and she jumped off the bed and danced around the room. "You're kidding!"

"Nope. It's for real. I've already met the horse. His name is Juniper."

"Where?"

Bianca hesitated, unsure how to categorize the visit. "It's a friend's ranch." Friend wasn't at all the right word, but anything else was likely to invite more questions.

"And you're going too?"

"I'll take you, but I'll just watch the fun."

"You're not going to ride?"

LETTER OF THE LAW

Bianca contemplated the question. She hadn't asked and Jade hadn't mentioned whether or not she would be invited to ride with them, not that she would've said yes if she had been included. In addition to the birthday-gone-wrong story she'd told Jade, there were a couple of other harrowing experiences as a child with her grandfather's ponies. No way was she going to let Jade witness her clumsy fear of riding on a regular-sized horse, high up in the saddle, unable to control the beast, and completely unsure how to stay on her perch. She looked at Emma and did her best to resist her pleading eyes. "The people that own the ranch only mentioned the one horse, so it might just be you this time, bug, but I promise I'll be there to watch your riding debut."

"What should I wear? I have the boots Abuela bought me last year. Do you think I'll look dumb if I tuck my jeans into them or should I wear them out?"

Relieved that Emma had moved on, Bianca had her own moment of what should I wear before she pushed away the thought. Other than leaving her high heels behind, it didn't really matter since she wasn't getting on a horse no matter how tempting it might be just to get closer to Jade.

A couple of hours later, Emma finished her homework and headed to bed. Bianca sank onto the couch next to her mother and put her feet up on the coffee table.

"*Mija*, put your feet down."

"Mama, it's been a really hard day."

Her mother tapped her shins until she put her feet down. "You want to talk to me about it?"

Bianca turned her head so she could see the expression on her mother's face. She witnessed only concern, but she wasn't in the mood to share. Besides, what would she say? In addition to my regular caseload, my boss has assigned me to charge a man with crimes he didn't commit? Oh, and I've also been tasked with getting close to his mistress's daughter who is drop-dead gorgeous and may be involved with drug lords.

Nope, better to stick with something vague. "Just a lot of balls in the air at work. I can't tell you how much I appreciate you helping out while things are crazy. Papa probably thinks we kidnapped you."

"Your papa is playing cards with his friends, although he calls it a Shriner committee meeting. You know, maybe you could find some nice job at a local firm. You run yourself ragged."

Bianca searched her mother's eyes, now convinced she didn't have an ulterior motive. Still, she did rely on her mother for so much when it came to Emma, and she didn't want to take it for granted. "I appreciate all you do to help. If it's too much, I can make some other arrangements to help out with picking Emma up from school and—"

"Hush your mouth," her mother said. "I love Emma, and the time I get to spend with her is a blessing. I don't want you to regret the time you have to spend away. If it's a matter of money, we can help out."

"No, Mama. We don't want for anything. And if I had one of those nice private sector jobs, I would be bored out of my mind and would probably have to work longer hours. There just wouldn't be as much at stake."

"My Bianca, wanting to save the world."

"As if. I just want to set a good example for Emma. Maybe someday, I'll move into private practice, but I want her to learn the importance of giving back to the community and working for a higher purpose. It's not like you can blame me since I learned it from you and Papa."

A buzzing phone interrupted her mother's response. Both of them reached for their phones, and Bianca groaned when she saw the display on hers flicker with Peyton's name. She punched the button to answer the call and fought to keep the frustration from her voice. "Hi, Peyton. Please tell me you're calling just to say hello."

"Sure, I'll start with that. Hello."

"Hello yourself." Bianca held up a hand to her mother and mouthed "sorry." She walked into the other room. "What's up?"

"Emergency meeting. Any chance you can make it out tonight?"

Bianca looked at the time on her phone. "It's kinda late for a school night, and I mean that literally. Emma just finished her homework and went to bed."

"I promise I wouldn't ask if it wasn't important. We need to all talk before you see Gellar tomorrow. Dale, Tanner, and Mary are all on their way." Peyton paused for a moment. "I guess we could FaceTime you in."

Bianca pictured them all talking about the investigation in between the stops and starts of a buffering Internet signal, and then imagined Emma walking in during the most salacious parts. "No, it's okay. I'll come out there."

"Thanks. We'll see you when you get here."

Bianca hung up the phone, dreading the conversation she was about to have. When she turned to go back into the other room, she bumped into her mother.

"I heard."

"Mama, you shouldn't be listening in on my conversations about work."

Her mother threw up her hands. "Why not when I know it's going to involve me?" She shooed Bianca away with her hands. "Go on."

Bianca drew her into a tight hug. "I'm really sorry. If it weren't important, I wouldn't go. I promise I'll make it up to you."

A few minutes later, Bianca stood in the doorway to Emma's room, captivated by the sight of her daughter sprawled across the bed, sound asleep, with a copy of *Romeo and Juliet* still open on the covers next to her. She turned to her mother who was looking over her shoulder. "I hate to wake her up."

"Don't. I'll be here until you get back. If she wakes up, I'll explain."

"Thanks, Mama. I'll make it up to you."

Her mother waved her hands. "Go, save the world, but don't forget us little people."

❖

Peyton's mother Helen opened the door and ushered Bianca into the house at the Circle Six Ranch. The task force had started meeting at the ranch ever since their boss had officially disbanded the group. Gellar had yet to give a reason for his decision, dismissing any inquiry with a curt, "I have this investigation under control."

But he didn't. While Emma had been doing her homework, Bianca had scoured the files she'd brought home from the office, witness statements, forensic reports, and agent notes. While some of what she'd read implicated Cyrus as a money launderer for the Vargas brothers, she'd found nothing to indicate he was responsible for Maria Escobar's death. Whatever Gellar was up to, it was clear he wanted to put Cyrus Gantry away for life and he would settle for nothing less, even if the evidence didn't back up his claims.

She followed Helen into the kitchen and was greeted by her colleagues. Bianca looked around the table and briefly contemplated her mother's entreaty for her to consider different work. These women had made enormous sacrifices. Peyton left a cush position at the Department of Justice in D.C. to come home to help out her family. Dale had lost her wife to the cartel's violent retribution. Tanner and Mary had both served in the military, yet they'd chosen to continue their public service when their tours of duty were complete. These women had become her family, and the best way to pay tribute to their service was to offer her own. She could think of no better example to set for her daughter.

She slid into a seat. "Deal me in."

They'd developed the cover of a semi-regular card game to hide the fact they were still meeting to discuss task force business. Peyton's brother Neil, who had business dealings with Cyrus Gantry that had led to his own batch of trouble, had recently moved back into the ranch house, which further necessitated the need for secrecy.

Dale deftly dealt five cards to her. "Here you go. We'll wait for you to fold," she said with a grin. "Take your time."

Bianca stuck out her tongue and scanned her cards, wishing they were playing for big money since for once she had a great hand. The game might be a cover, but playing it sparked her competitive nature. After they all placed their bets, Peyton opened the floor to discussion about the Vargas case.

"Bianca, why don't you fill us in on where things stand with the grand jury investigation?"

Relieved Peyton hadn't asked about Jade, Bianca launched in. "Tanner and I have been through all the evidence so far. There's nothing to implicate Cyrus in the Vargas brothers' drug enterprise other than money laundering, but we already knew about that."

"And Cyrus is going to claim he was coerced into letting the Vargases syphon funds through his business," Dale added.

"Not much of a legal defense, but a jury might buy it when they find out he did it to save his daughter from harm," Bianca said before casting a glance at Peyton whose expression had turned stormy. "Sorry, boss. I get this must be hard for you to hear."

"The hard part is not knowing what to do about it," Peyton said. "I'd give anything if Lily didn't have to deal with any of this. When is the grand jury going to hear the case?"

"I get the impression he plans to present in the next couple of weeks. They should no bill on the murder-for-hire charge, but I have no doubt he'll get held over for trial on the money laundering." Bianca watched Dale for her reaction, but she remained stoic. She wasn't sure she could remain so calm if she'd lost her wife in a brutal murder and then found out the US Attorney was trying to pin the blame on the wrong person.

"We're here tonight because Lindsey has an appointment with Gellar tomorrow," Dale said. "He thinks it's a showpiece for *Spotlight America*. Something about top dog crime fighters. I've been working with her on a list of questions, but I'd like to get your input."

"Be careful. Gellar's up to something," Bianca said. "But he's not dumb. If he gets even a hint she's looking deeper, he'll clam up and he might go back to locking up his files."

Dale smiled. "Trust me, Lindsey knows what she's doing."

Bianca poked her friend in the side. "I just bet she does."

"What's that supposed to mean?"

"It means I haven't seen you looking this happy since…" Bianca let the words trail away once she realized her playful banter had stirred unpleasant memories.

Dale shook her head. "It's okay. I am happy. This is not the life I planned, but it's the life I have and it's a good one."

"Pretty understated considering you're now dating a celebrity," Tanner said. "I don't suppose she has any celebrity friends who want the inside scoop on the FBI?"

"Focus, people," Peyton said. "We've got work to do. Bianca, talk to us about Jade Vargas. Mary said you were out there today. Anything to report?"

"So, you're watching me, huh?" Mary nodded and Bianca digested the information. When she'd accepted the assignment to get to know Jade, she hadn't considered that one of the agents on their team would be observing her while she was at Valencia Acres. It made sense, but now her brain was churning as she sorted through every detail of her time there, trying to recollect if she'd done anything stupid. It was pretty likely she'd stared into those deep brown eyes longer than she should, but other than that she'd been completely professional. Hadn't she?

"Looked like you were getting along okay. When are you seeing her again?"

"Well, here's the thing." Bianca hesitated. Now that she'd had time to process Jade's offer from this afternoon, she had doubts about whether she was the right person for the job. "She invited me back on Saturday."

"That's great."

"Not exactly. She invited me and Emma. Well, mostly Emma. You know, to ride horses with her. 'Cause Emma's crazy about horses and I mentioned that, and she ran with it, and I said yes, and now I'm committed to bringing my eleven-year-old daughter to this ranch where God knows what is really going on, and I'm so not the right person for this."

She stopped to get a breath, but before she could start up again, Tanner put a hand on her arm. "Slow down. Let's talk about this."

"Yeah, okay." Bianca looked around the room at the faces of her friends, her skin burning with the flush of embarrassment. Mary, Dale, and Tanner put themselves in harm's way every day, and even Peyton had risked a bullet as part of their investigation, but here she was complaining about having to ride horseback with a potential…Witness? Suspect? She didn't know what she should call

Jade, and she wasn't ever going to know if she didn't stick with the plan and get to know her better. A little discomfort on her part was a small price to pay for the bigger cause. If only she hadn't agreed to bring Emma. "Sorry, guys, I guess I'm just a little freaked out about dragging Emma into this."

"That's fair," Mary said. "Maybe you could call Jade and tell her Emma can't make it. Something about school or some other excuse."

Bianca sorted through her memory of the conversation she'd had with Jade. She'd made it abundantly clear she didn't like to ride. If she didn't show up with horse-loving Emma, there would really be no point in showing up at all. She was either the right person for this or she wasn't. She shook her head. "No, I need to take Emma if I'm going back."

"We've got you covered," Tanner said. "We won't let anything happen to your daughter."

Bianca was certain they would do everything in their power to keep Emma safe, but equally certain they didn't have the power to protect her from her attraction to Jade. She wasn't sure she wanted them to even if they could.

CHAPTER NINE

H ow do you know her?"

Bianca kept her eyes on the road and her hands firmly fixed on the steering wheel as she cast about for just the right mix of truth and fiction. Emma had asked about Jade and the ranch several times since breakfast, and now that they were on their way to Valencia Acres, Bianca had to come up with something to tell her that was both plausible and vague. "I met her through work."

"Oh. Is she a lawyer or a cop?"

"Neither. She's helping me out on a case. I can't talk about it more, okay?"

Emma made a show of zipping her mouth shut. "I get it. Confidentiality and all."

"Right." Bianca hated the lie, but she didn't see a way around it. She'd always made a point of being painfully honest with Emma, choosing to shield her from the things she couldn't discuss rather than risk the strong bond their open dialogue had formed. Which begged the question: why was she dragging Emma out to Valencia Acres where everything about her interaction with Jade was pretense? They were a couple of miles from the turnoff to the ranch; it wasn't too late to turn around.

"That's cool," Emma said. "All I really care about is riding a horse anyway. Marisol rides every weekend. Her dad has three horses and he keeps them in a stable up in Prosper."

Hearing Emma's words, Bianca immediately knew she wasn't about to turn around. Marisol was one of Emma's best friends. Her parents had split up last year, and her father had done everything in his power to make her weekend visits to his place the stuff of legend. Every Monday, Emma had a new story about Marisol's over-the-top weekends, and although her tone always suggested she was merely reporting the facts, Bianca often wondered if Emma envied the fact Marisol had a father who was involved in her life and whether she wished for the things Marisol had and she didn't.

She did her best to provide a good life for Emma. She had extended family, plenty of activities, and she was surrounded by love, but the truth was Bianca's job often interfered with the grander things. They hadn't been on a family vacation in several years, although Emma had accompanied her grandparents to see relatives in San Antonio—a trip Bianca had planned to attend, but had to cancel when a hearing date interfered at the last minute.

She was making too much out of today's plans. Emma would ride a horse around the ring, and she would watch. Emma would get to fulfill one of her dreams and, if she was lucky, Bianca would get Jade to loosen up so next time they were together, Jade might open up about her relationship with her uncles. Satisfied she'd made the right decision and wasn't in danger of ruining her daughter's childhood, Bianca turned the car into the long drive and drove up to the main house.

Sophia was waiting when they got out of the car. Emma didn't wait for an introduction. She stuck out her hand. "Hi, I'm Emma. Are you Jade?"

"No, but I'm her mother." Sophia pointed to the house. "Jade's on the phone, but she'll be right out. Would you like something to drink? Lemonade?"

Bianca watched as Emma shook her head. "If it's okay, I'd like to see the horses. Mom says you have tons of them."

Sophia laughed. "I'm not sure about tons, but we do have a few." She reached for Emma's hand. "Come on, I'll show you around."

Bianca kept her eyes trained on the house, willing Jade to appear until it became clear Sophia and Emma were going to leave her standing there. She tore her gaze away and followed them to the barn.

"We stand five stallions right now. They're all in this barn."

"What does 'stand' mean?"

Sophia looked at Bianca with a hesitant expression. "It's horse talk for how many live here on a regular basis…for breeding."

"Do you have any baby horses?"

"We do have seven foals. They are stabled with the mares in that barn over there," Sophia said, pointing to another barn in the distance. "I'll let Jade show you later."

"Or I can show you now if you'd rather see them before you ride."

Bianca and Emma turned at the same moment and Bianca couldn't hide her sharp intake of breath. Jade stood framed in the doorway to the barn, looking as mysterious as ever with the noon light casting a shadow across her face. Was she smiling? It was hard to tell, and Bianca's attempt to read her expression was thwarted by her visceral reaction to the rest of her. Jade wore a snug-fitting copper colored sweater and curve-hugging camel pants tucked into tall brown boots. Delicious was the first thought that came to mind, followed by pings of warning. *You're not here for her. You're here to find out about her.* She shifted focus to Emma. "Your decision, bug. See horses or ride one."

Emma looked back and forth between them, like she was trying to figure out a secret joke, before she settled on an answer that she delivered directly to Jade. "Ride now, look later?"

"Deal." Jade stuck out her hand. "I'm Jade Vargas, and you must be Emma."

"I am. Are these your horses too?"

Jade nodded. "They are. Sophia and I own the ranch together."

Bianca watched the exchange, enjoying Emma's ability to get Jade to open up. Emma cast a look back at her before venturing a question. "Mom said Sophia's your mom, but her name's Valencia and that's the name of the ranch, but you have a different last name."

"That's a long story. Are you here for stories or horse rides?" Jade didn't wait for an answer before she took off walking. Bianca shrugged at Emma and motioned for her to follow. A minute later, the three of them were standing in front of a room with a sign over the door.

"What's a tack room?" Bianca asked.

"Mom, it's where they keep all the accessories, like bridles and reins and saddles and stuff. Right?"

Emma looked at Jade for confirmation. "That's right," Jade said. "The first step in learning to ride is learning how to care for the tack."

"Cool."

Jade cocked her head. "Really? Most people your age think this part is boring."

Emma folded her arms across her chest. "I'm not most people. Besides, I bet you didn't think it was boring when you were my age."

Bianca watched Jade's face for her reaction, curious to see what insight she offered while she imagined a young Jade Vargas, passionate about horses.

"When I was your age, I didn't have horses of my own," Jade said with a faraway expression. "I was at boarding school. We rode several times a week, but the rich girls weren't expected to do anything other than step into a saddle and ride, and since I was there with them, I was expected to do the same." She didn't wait for a response, pointing to a couple of saddles. "Both of you, grab those and follow me."

Bianca did as she was told, although it wasn't at all clear to her why she was being drafted into duty. Jade filled her arms with equipment and led them out to the ring behind the barn where three horses were waiting. Emma dashed over to the railing and started oohing and aahing over the horses, but Bianca froze. It took her a second to do the math, but even then she was in denial. "Is Sophia riding with you?"

Jade's lips slid into a sly grin, and Bianca shoved the saddle at her. "Oh, no. Not going to happen."

"You trust me to take your daughter riding, but not you? What will you do while we're gone?"

Bianca jerked her chin and waited for Jade to step closer before whispering. "Gone? I figured you would ride around the ring."

"This isn't a child's birthday party. I'd planned to take you both for a real ride. I promise to take you on the easiest trails this time."

Bianca filed away the reference to a future visit, certain she was blushing at the prospect and wondering if her pals could see her discomfort in their telescopic lens. She supposed it was silly to think Jade was going to lead Emma around the ring, but she'd refused to imagine anything else, including the prospect of joining them on a trail ride. She looked down at the saddle in her hands, its weight a symbol of the fear holding her back. She could hold onto it or let it go, but either way she had to make a choice and the surprisingly gentle expression in Jade's eyes cinched it.

Jade walked Descaro along the trail, ever conscious of Bianca's eyes on her. She couldn't decide yet if it was because Bianca wasn't sure if she could trust her with her daughter or if Bianca had other purposes at play. Unlike Emma, who'd taken to her mount like a pro, Bianca might have been a bit clumsy at first, but she was settling in nicely, and Jade was disturbingly distracted by how Bianca on a horse took her captivation to another level.

After delivering a few words of encouragement to Emma, Jade doubled back to ride alongside Bianca. "You're doing quite well for someone who planned only to watch."

"You're very generous. Slow trail rides are probably not your usual fare." Bianca waved at Emma who'd glanced back at them with a wide grin. "She's having the time of her life."

"And you?"

"I'm almost, but not quite, certain I will not fall off this horse, which is a huge step in my equestrian career."

"Let me guess. You had a bad spill once."

"If only it were that dramatic. Let's see, I already told you about the case of the ruined birthday. Are you really going to make me tell about the time a pony decided it was much more fun to run through the fields riderless?"

Emma's voice floated back to them. "Mom, are you telling that story about Brownie? It's so embarrassing."

Jade tried, unsuccessfully, to smother a grin, but when Bianca started laughing, she joined her. "Sounds terribly traumatizing. I'm flattered you trusted me enough to join us on this ride."

"I'd do just about anything to see Emma this happy."

Jade nodded in agreement, but she didn't relate to the sentiment. Sophia likely considered herself a good mother, but Jade couldn't help but think every decision she made was about herself first and Jade second, unlike Bianca who appeared to genuinely care about her daughter's happiness even when doing so meant sacrificing her own comfort. She wanted to acknowledge the difference, but somehow it seemed too personal, so instead she referenced one of Bianca's earlier remarks. "Contrary to what you may think, this is definitely part of my usual fare."

"Pardon?"

"Slow trail rides. Don't get me wrong, I love a fast ride on Ransom, but there's something very comforting about the ease of a leisurely ride, especially along these trails."

"It's definitely beautiful out here."

Jade pulled Descaro to a stop and Bianca's horse, Vega, followed suit. She reached over and grabbed the reins to keep Vega from moving as she spoke and she stared directly into Bianca's eyes. "Yes, it definitely is."

Bianca's face flushed and her lips parted. Jade froze, fearful any sudden movement would spoil the moment, but before Bianca could reply, Emma yelled. "Hey, there's something blocking the path up here."

"Wait up. I'll be right there," Jade called out. She started to nudge Descaro into a gallop, but then realized she was still holding the reins to Bianca's mount. She reached over and placed them in Bianca's hand, giving her a tight squeeze before reluctantly letting go. Did she see a reflection of her own regret in Bianca's eyes, or was she imagining what she wanted to see? She rode off before she could examine the feelings more closely.

"What is it?" she said to Emma as she pulled alongside.

"There." Emma pointed with one hand at a haphazard pile of branches farther up the trail, while she fanned the air with the other. "I think it's a dead animal."

Jade motioned to the reins. "Rule number one of riding. Don't let go of the reins." She smiled to cushion her remark. "It's hard if you're used to talking with your hands. Stay here. I'll be right back."

Jade rode ahead, pulling back on the reins as she approached the mound in the clearing. From a distance, it did look like a large animal had collapsed in a heap, probably dead, judging by the smell, but as she drew closer she realized only part of her assessment was correct. A chill ran up her spine at the sight of a boot poking out from underneath the branches that barely covered the dead body in her path. Her first instinct was to stop Bianca and Emma from getting any closer, but she needed to make absolutely sure whoever this was didn't need her help. She dismounted and whispered to Descaro to stay put.

She circled the pile of branches, noting the leaves were dry and brown. This late into fall, that didn't mean much, but the ends of the branches were smooth, indicating someone had cut them down. Her boots snapped on a stick and she jumped backward. Shaking her head at the imagined fear, she walked closer to the pile and used a bandana from her pocket to tentatively lift a couple of the branches so she could catch a glimpse of what lay beneath.

The naked male torso was marred by a long, deep cut from the base of the throat to the waist. The skin was peeled back, and Jade gagged at the putrid smell of the evisceration. Whoever this was, he was beyond help. Jade shuddered as she imagined the horror of this person's fate.

"Jade!"

The sound of Bianca's voice cut through her contemplation, and she shouted, "Wait there. I'll be right back!" She glanced over her shoulder and, satisfied neither Emma nor Bianca were approaching, she reached to replace the branches, but as she stepped around the body, she accidentally knocked away a bough covering the dead man's face and gasped.

She'd seen this man before. Not recently and not here, but she was certain he was familiar. A friend of Sophia's? One of her uncle's associates? She stared hard as if the effort would force her memory to come up with an answer, but she got nothing. Conscious of the fact Bianca and Emma were waiting and desperate to make sure they didn't witness this gruesome scene, she pulled out her phone and snapped a few quick photos before she mounted Descaro and galloped back down the trail.

"I'm afraid we're going to need to cut this ride short."

Bianca raised her eyebrows and shot a glance at Emma whose face sported a disappointed frown.

Jade tamped down the growing anxiety in her gut and forced a fake smile. "We'll reschedule. I promise." She starting walking Descaro back in the direction of the ranch, but Bianca's voice stopped her. "Emma, I need to talk to Jade for a minute, okay?" She glanced back over her shoulder, and Bianca motioned to her left. Both of them walked their horses over to a cluster of trees. They were barely out of Emma's earshot before Bianca said, "What's going on?"

Jade started to say "nothing," but hesitated at the growing concern creeping across Bianca's face. She wanted to rewind back to just before Emma's discovery, but she knew that moment was likely lost forever. Probably for the best since everything about today was a suspension of reality she couldn't possibly expect to last. "Don't panic, but there's a dead body in the clearing ahead." She watched for Bianca's reaction as dread churned her stomach into knots.

Her eyes narrowed. "Did you say dead body?"

"Yes."

Bianca's attention immediately shifted. She pulled out her phone and held it up in the air. "I only have one bar. Can I use your phone?"

"What?"

Bianca pointed at the device in her hand. "Phone. Yours. Can I use it?"

"No. We'll go to the house and call someone from there." She watched as Bianca thumbed out a message on her phone. "What are you doing?"

"Seeing if a text will go through. Can you take Emma back to the house?"

Jade glanced at Emma who was eyeing them both with burning curiosity, before returning her gaze to Bianca. "We'll all go back. We can use the phone at the house."

"I don't think so." Bianca's phone buzzed. "Hang on."

Jade watched, powerless, as Bianca read the display. "Okay, someone will be here in a minute." She watched as Bianca struggled her way off of her horse and handed her the reins. "I'll be right back." Bianca walked over to Emma and motioned for her to bend down. They exchanged a quick whispered conversation before Bianca strode back toward her.

"What's going on?" Jade asked.

"A couple of federal agents are on their way. Can you contact Sophia and get her to come out here and get Emma?"

"I'll take her."

"I think you better stay."

Jade read the undercurrent of accusation. She'd found a dead body on the property. Of course the cops were going to want to talk to her, but Bianca's sudden shift to authoritarian mode put her on the defense. She sent a quick text to Sophia, telling her to join them on the trail.

"I'm getting the impression you think I have something to do with that." She pointed in the direction of the clearing.

"Just trying to preserve evidence, make sure nothing is disturbed." Bianca said, her voice curt and matter-of-fact. "They're going to want to talk to you as soon as they get here."

Jade started to raise her voice to ask Bianca to explain her basis for the accusing tone, but Emma's voice cut through the air.

"What's going on?"

"Nothing, bug. I have a little bit of work to do with Jade. Sophia will be here in a minute to take you back to the ranch, and one of my friends will meet you there and take you to Abuela's house. Okay?"

Jade watched the exchange, noting the imploring look in Bianca's eyes and the massive disappointment that filled Emma's face. She could totally relate.

A few minutes later, two four-wheelers showed up on the trail, one driven by Sophia and the other held two strangers. Jade had gathered the horses together and whispered assurances she didn't quite feel to keep them calm. Sophia had texted her back to say that federal agents were on her doorstep within minutes of receiving a text from Bianca, which raised more questions than answers. What were these agents doing in such close proximity to the ranch? Was the ranch under surveillance? Arturo's warnings echoed in her mind. Was this part of the enterprise working against him? Who was the body in the clearing? She was desperate now to find out the identity of the man in the clearing, but dared not risk a glance at the photos on her phone until she was away from prying eyes.

Sophia shot Jade an accusatory look, and then helped Emma onto the four-wheeler. Jade watched them go and then turned back to see the taller of the two agents take Bianca aside and engage in a whispered conversation just out of earshot. After much gesticulating, the agent walked over to her, leaving Bianca standing a few feet away. The woman stuck out a hand.

"Tanner Cohen, Special Agent, FBI. You're Jade Vargas?"

Jade ignored the hand. "I am."

"Mind telling me what happened?"

Jade sized her up. Cohen's tone was even and measured, but Jade couldn't read the expression in her eyes hidden as it was behind the reflective lenses of her aviators. Most people Cohen questioned probably melted in the face of her smooth good looks and confident swagger, but Jade was well acquainted with how much insecurity could fit behind a smile. "How about I show you?" She didn't wait for an answer, instead started walking toward the clearing, challenging Agent Tanner to keep up.

"Emma said she saw something up ahead that looked like an animal. I rode to here," she pointed, "and then I dismounted and walked over here." She motioned to a spot next to the body.

"Did you touch anything?"

"I'm not stupid."

"That mean no?"

Jade silently counted to five to keep from spouting off a sarcastic response. She was certain moving aside a couple of branches wasn't enough to contaminate the crime scene, but she didn't want to admit she'd done even that. She didn't know this woman, and this woman didn't know her, but she likely knew her relationship to Sergio and Arturo, and that was going to color their entire interaction. Jade looked around until her eyes settled on Bianca who was engaged in what appeared to be a heated conversation with the other agent, about ten feet away.

"Excuse me."

Jade reluctantly turned back to Agent Cohen. "I moved aside a couple of branches, but I covered my hands with cloth before I did. Other than make sure whoever that is was really dead, I didn't do anything except report what I saw to Miss Cruz. I don't know anything about this body—who it is or why it's here. Is there anything else you want to know?" She'd kept her voice calm, but she could feel the rising fury as she realized her life was about to be turned upside down.

"Wait here."

Jade watched as the two agents huddled around Bianca. Their loud whispers carried in the light breeze and she caught snippets of conversation, but not enough to make sense of why these agents had been so close to the ranch when they'd gotten Bianca's text. After a few minutes of watching their discussion, Jade was over it. This was her ranch, and these people were invading her privacy. They had no authority to boss her around here. If anything, she was the victim, enjoying an innocent ride only to stumble upon a gruesome murder scene.

Murder. The stark reality of what she'd witnessed caused her to buckle at the knees. She turned away from the huddled group and began to tally the specific details of what she'd seen. Whoever had sliced open the man on the trail had covered their handiwork, but the attempt to hide the body had been cursory at best.

"Is there somewhere we can go to talk?"

Jade turned around to see Agent Cohen standing in front of her and Bianca close behind. Annoyed she'd been so wrapped up in her musings she hadn't noticed Bianca and the others had finished their discussion. "Shouldn't you be doing something about," she pointed, "the body?"

"Agent Lovelace will stay here until the other agents arrive. We need to get out of their way. Maybe we could go to the house?"

Jade purposefully ignored Cohen and directed her attention to Bianca. "Probably not a good idea to have this conversation in front of Emma. There's an office at the barn. Let's go there." She turned back to Cohen. "Go on ahead. We'll meet you there. I don't want the sound of your engines to spook the horses."

Tanner looked back and forth between them, and Jade noted the protective look in her eyes. She swallowed the sour taste of jealousy, resisting the urge to throw these interlopers off her property because she feared Bianca would leave with them. She needed at least a few minutes alone with Bianca to sort out where things stood between them. Bianca nodded to Tanner, but Jade waited until Tanner had gotten back on the four-wheeler and started back up the trail before she helped Bianca up on her horse. They were on their way back to the house when she remarked. "Funny how they got here so fast."

"I suppose."

"And to be clear, it's funny peculiar, not funny, ha-ha."

Bianca pulled up on the reins, and Jade stopped Descaro in time to see Bianca's forehead scrunched into a frown. "It can't have escaped you that Arturo was arrested just a few weeks ago while threatening your mother right here on the ranch. There's a strong possibility Sergio could come back to finish the job."

"So you and your friends are only here to protect us, is that it?"

"Is there some reason you would resist our help?"

"For one thing, I didn't ask for your help. And second, it's patronizing of you or anyone else to think you know best how to protect the things I care about."

"Things? Be careful or someone might suspect your motives."

Jade felt the conversation spiraling out of control, but she couldn't help but follow where it led. "What's that supposed to mean?"

A mask fell over Bianca's face and she turned away, but before she did Jade witnessed disappointment laced with regret. She reached out a hand and tentatively stroked Bianca's shoulder. "Hey, what is it?"

"Why did you go to Seagoville earlier this week?"

Her visit to Arturo. She should've known the visit wouldn't be secret, but it hadn't occurred to her Bianca would find out. Her mind retraced her conversation with her uncle. Of course the feds would be keeping a close watch over everything related to Arturo, but she was satisfied she'd neither done nor said anything incriminating. Still, her personal actions were none of Bianca's business and this entire afternoon had been a mistake. She'd let the allure of an attractive woman allow her to forget people would always be out to get her because she was a Vargas.

"Should I call my lawyer?" Jade heard the hint of defensiveness in her voice, and she was surprised when Bianca smiled in response to her query.

"I'm a lawyer."

"Yes, but I don't think you're on my side."

"I'm on whichever side is the right one."

"I think it's amusing that you believe it's so easy to tell the difference." Jade didn't wait for a response before nudging Descaro into a light gallop. She'd found out what she needed. The feds were close by, watching their every move, and they were more interested in getting information than giving it. She'd answer only the basics until she found out more about why they were expending their resources on Valencia Acres. As enticing as Bianca Cruz might be, she'd have to find a different source of information.

CHAPTER TEN

"Mom, I forgot my lunch."

Bianca looked across to the passenger seat of the Miata, a rebuke on her lips, but she stopped before the words came out. Who was she to blame Emma for being distracted? After a weekend with a dead body dropped in her lap, she'd been plenty distracted herself. She pointed to her bag on the floor between them. "Take a five from my wallet and try to buy something semi-healthy with it. Abeula's going to pick you up after practice because I'm probably going to be home late, okay?"

"Because of the dead body?"

"Yep, but that's between you and me. Your grandmother isn't big on dead bodies, especially ones that make me have to work late."

"She only likes the kind of drama on telenovelas, not the kind on the news."

"Exactly." Bianca couldn't help but smile. Emma was full of these nuggets of wisdom, but her insights never failed to amaze.

"Mom, do you think we'll ever get to ride horses at Valencia Acres again?"

She'd been waiting for this question since the abrupt end to their outing on Saturday, but she still didn't have a satisfactory answer. No, was the only response she had, but Emma wasn't the type of kid who would let it go at that. The litany of questions would probably go something like: "Because you think Jade was involved with the body?" "No" "Well, then why? Did Jade do something wrong?" "No" or not that I know of anyway. "Well, then why not?"

She skirted the issue altogether. "I have another friend with horses. How about I check and see if she has one you could ride?"

"So, you and Jade aren't friends anymore? Is it because of the dead body?"

Bianca nearly groaned as her honesty-only policy continued to bite her in the ass. These two seemingly simple questions held layers of dangerous territory. She thanked the universe Emma's school was in sight and settled for the most vague, yet still truthful response she could muster on the fly. "It's all good, but they're going to be busy out at Valencia Acres for a while." She pulled over to the curb. "Don't forget to ask Ms. Cleary for the new practice schedule so I can make plans."

"Sure, Mom." Emma piled out of the car and waved before wading into the crowd. In a few seconds this entire conversation would probably be a distant memory for her as she exchanged stories about her weekend with her friends. But Bianca wasn't as lucky since the events of the weekend were certain to be the hot topic at the office.

She wasn't wrong. Ida, the receptionist aka gatekeeper at the front counter, cornered her the second she walked in. "I heard you found a dead body riding horseback this weekend."

Bianca bit her tongue to keep from saying that actually her eleven-year-old daughter was the one who'd spotted the body first. Instead she shrugged it off. "That's me. Out finding crime, even on my day off. Is Mr. Gellar in?"

"He is, but he's in a meeting. You'll never guess who with."

Lindsey. In the excitement of the weekend, Bianca had forgotten that Lindsey's appointment from last week had been postponed to this morning. She was probably well into her pitch to convince Gellar to be the subject of a feature piece in hopes his grandiose need for attention would allow her to get close enough to figure out what he was up to on the Vargas-Gantry case. Since she wasn't supposed to know anything about the meeting, Bianca said, "I don't have a clue."

"It's the reporter from *Spotlight America*, Lindsey Ryan. She could not be nicer, which I have to say I did not expect at all. Especially after seeing her rip that general apart on live TV."

Bianca nodded at the rest of Ida's remarks, but her brain was whirring on to a plan of action. After spending the balance of her weekend sorting through every detail about the dead body at Valencia Acres, she, along with the rest of the task force, were convinced the murder victim was tied to the men who'd kidnapped Lindsey the week before, especially when the medical examiner had pointed out the Barrio Azteca tattoo on his back. They didn't have much to go on other than they all bore the same tattoos, but somehow it was key to whatever was going on with Gellar.

Bianca was plotting a way to get Lindsey alone while she was here at the office, when she heard the unmistakable rumble of Gellar's voice bellowing down the hall toward her.

"Cruz, come here. There's someone I want you to meet."

Bianca fixed her face into a phony smile and walked to where Gellar stood with his arm wrapped possessively around Lindsey Ryan's shoulders. Good thing Dale wasn't here to witness Gellar's lack of professional boundaries or he'd likely wind up with a black eye.

Oblivious to how his good ole boy ways might offend either one of the women in his presence, Gellar bellowed an unnecessary introduction. "Cruz, meet Lindsey Ryan, crackerjack reporter and brave kidnapping victim. Ms. Ryan, this is Bianca Cruz, she's one of the AUSAs assisting with the Gantry investigation."

Bianca smiled enthusiastically and stuck out her hand, purposefully acting as if she was meeting Lindsey for the first time. Gellar, meanwhile, acted like he and Lindsey were old friends, and based on the way his eyes were glued to Lindsey's body, it was clear he would do whatever she wanted. And who wouldn't? Whether she was standing in front of a tank in Afghanistan or reporting live during an active hurricane, Lindsey was as windswept and down-to-earth as she was captivating and glamorous, completely different from Jade Vargas, whose dark beauty seemed to cloak secrets and mystery.

Whoa, where did that come from? Bianca shook her head, unable to deny thoughts of Jade had been edging into every aspect of her daily routine since they'd parted ways on Saturday. A simple phone call could have netted her real information as opposed to speculation, but every time she'd reached for the phone, her own concerns about boundaries had stopped her. This was no longer a matter of her trying to get close to a woman who might have some contact with her outlaw uncles. After the body turned up on the ranch, everyone close by was suspect until they weren't, and no way was she going to do anything that could compromise the investigation. Until she got an all clear from Tanner and Mary, she had to keep her distance. Shaking away thoughts of Jade, she tuned back into the conversation with Lindsey and Gellar.

"Mr. Gellar," Lindsey said in an extra syrupy tone, "I was hoping I could talk to Ms. Cruz. Perhaps get her perspective as a woman working on such vicious cases. I know a lot of our viewers would love to hear a woman's point of view. You don't mind do you?" She didn't wait for an answer before turning to Bianca. "Maybe we could go get coffee right now. Are you free?"

Bianca didn't look at Gellar before answering, half thinking he'd shake his head no and half because she was scared she might crack up at Lindsey's guise for getting them alone. "I think that's a terrific idea."

Lindsey extracted her way out of Gellar's embrace and locked arms with her. "Perfect. Mr. Gellar, thanks for your time this morning. I think this piece is going to fit in nicely with the other programming the network has planned for sweeps. Once we get all the preliminary interviews done, I'll get my crew back to Dallas, and we'll start filming." She didn't wait for an answer before walking Bianca down the hall. When they passed Ida's desk, her mouth about fell open, but Bianca only smiled.

When they were safely in the elevator, they both busted up laughing. "Do you have to do as much acting for a real interview?" Bianca asked.

"It varies. You'd be surprised how far a little helpless girl act goes toward getting certain people to open up."

"You didn't use any of that action when you impaled General Tyson with his own stupid statements." Bianca said, referring to an interview that had landed Lindsey in hot water with her network and many members of a certain political party.

"That's because he didn't notice me at all. I quickly determined feminine wiles would be wasted on the general, so I merely faded into the background and let him do his thing. Not my fault if his thing turned out to be hanging himself with his own words."

Feminine wiles, wallpaper. Jade wouldn't employ either method. Again with the comparisons.

"Are you okay?" Lindsey asked.

"Sure. Just a lot on my mind." Bianca pushed the button for the first floor.

"Dale said you were at Valencia Acres this weekend when they found the dead body."

"More accurately, I was a few feet away when my daughter saw it." Lindsey's eyes narrowed, and Bianca recognized her going into reporter mode. "I'll tell you all about it, but not here. Okay?"

A few minutes later, they were down the street at the Starbucks in the lobby of the Magnolia Hotel. Once they'd retrieved their orders from the barista, they settled into plush, purple chairs near the back of the shop. Two sips in and Lindsey burst out, "You're killing me. Spill."

Bianca surveyed the room and decided the woman up front with twins in a double stroller had enough distractions to keep her from listening in on their conversation. Still, she kept her voice low. "It's crazy, really. Emma has a thing for horses. I always thought it was the phase most little girls go through. You know, where they draw horse heads on everything and imagine riding off into the sunset with Black Beauty." She took a sip of her coffee and looked up to see Lindsey staring at her with a quizzical expression. "What?"

"I asked you about a dead body, and you're telling me about your daughter's penchant for horses, which is totally cool, but I'm getting a bit of a disconnect. Is everything okay?"

Bianca felt the warm flush of a blush creep up her neck, and she stumbled for a reply. "Sorry, I guess I was just trying to explain why I had Emma with me. Jade offered to take her for a trail ride and I didn't have the heart to say no. I mean I was there too, so how much trouble could she get in, right?"

"And you were there because?"

"I guess Dale didn't tell you that part." Bianca took a deep breath. "She and Peyton had this great idea that I should try and get close to Jade so we could keep an eye on her in case her uncles tried to contact her, so we could figure out what they're up to. I thought it was crazy, and I was right because look what happened. Although if I hadn't been there, who knows if or when the body would have turned up. Anyway, I've made it perfectly clear to them that I am done with undercover work."

"Okay, but has anyone figured out who the dead guy was? When I talked to Dale last night, she said they were still working on it."

"No positive ID yet, but..." Bianca stuttered to a stop. The men who'd kidnapped Lindsey last week were Barrio Azteca, just like this dead guy. She could think of a dozen reasons not to be talking to Lindsey about this, a primary one being the chance it would bring back horrible memories.

"What is it?"

Bianca studied her expression. Lindsey was tough. She had to be or she wouldn't be back at work so soon after what she'd been through: nabbed in a very public venue by heavily armed gang members and held hostage until she was rescued in a hail of gunfire. She'd spent her career embedded with armed forces in desert wastelands, so a close encounter with the local cartel was unlikely to faze her. Suddenly, Bianca felt a little silly for her hesitation. "The guy, whoever he was, was a member of the gang that kidnapped you."

Lindsey shuddered, and Bianca was relieved to see she was human after all. "Of course, it's a huge gang and this doesn't mean he's related in any way."

"I don't believe that, and you don't either judging by your expression."

Bianca averted her eyes, cursing her lack of a poker face, the one litigator skill she had yet to master. "We don't know enough yet. I'm sure Dale and the others—oh shit. Dale's going to kill me for telling you this."

Lindsey reached out and put a hand on her leg. "Dale's not going to do any such thing. She knew I would probably run into you today."

"And she knows me well enough to know I wouldn't be able to keep it from you."

"Something like that." Lindsey leaned back in her seat and took a sip of coffee. "So, tell me about Jade Vargas. What's she like?"

Gorgeous. Striking. Tall. Commanding. Bianca sorted through the adjectives, looking for those that would describe what Lindsey was looking for as opposed to the ones that had distracted Bianca since they'd met. "Is Jade going to make it into your fake story?" she asked, stalling for time.

Lindsey cocked her head. "Too soon to tell, but I'm curious about the woman who makes you blush every time her name is mentioned."

"I thought you reported facts, not fiction." Bianca squirmed under Lindsey's penetrating gaze. "Okay, fine. She's beautiful, and mysterious, and aggravating as hell."

Lindsey laughed. "Sounds a lot like someone I know." She leaned in close, placed her arm around Bianca's shoulders, and dropped her voice to a conspiratorial whisper. "Those are the keepers. Trust me."

Bianca opened her mouth to say no way, not for her, but before she could protest, her phone buzzed with a familiar tone. She reached for the interrupter of all things and read the short message.

Autopsy done. Looks like J's in the clear. Ready to get back at it?

"Everything okay?" Lindsey asked.

No, everything was not okay. Apparently, Dale hadn't taken her seriously when she said she was done with undercover work. Maybe that was for the best because she couldn't deny she was excited about the prospect of seeing Jade again.

❖

At the sound of a car on the drive, Jade walked out onto the porch, wondering who was venturing to the ranch this late in the day. The sun was low on the horizon, and the glow of red against the sky was breathtaking. Everything was bigger and more beautiful here, but as long as the ghost of her uncles haunted this place, it would never truly be home. As soon as she tied up a few loose ends, she'd continue her travels and only come back when necessary to protect and defend Valencia Acres from those who would rob her of what was rightfully hers.

Like a prophecy, Bianca's car emerged from the swirls of dirt kicked up in its wake, symbolic of the chaos she'd brought to the ranch. Bianca was dangerous, and Jade knew she should stay far away from her. Her idea of keeping Bianca close in an attempt to gain information had already backfired. If she'd found the body on her own, which would have inevitably happened, she could have taken her time deciding the best course of action rather than having the cavalry descend on her property to treat it like a crime scene instead of a place of business. She'd had to cancel several appointments with prospective buyers and breeders today while the last of the agents combed through the dirt where the body had been found.

She'd seen enough to know the murder had been carried out by someone well versed in the art of torture. That and her certainty she had met the man before had robbed her of sleep ever since. She'd stared at the photo of the man's face on her phone dozens of times, but she couldn't place it. She'd almost resorted to asking Sophia, but she wasn't quite ready to share what little she knew. She'd figure it out, but right now, she wanted to find out what Bianca was doing back here and dispatch her as quickly as possible, but instead of walking out to greet her, she stayed strategically in place. *She's here because she wants something. Make the woman come to you.*

Bianca stepped out of her car and leaned on the doorframe, one hand blocking the last rays of sun. As she watched, Jade's entire body flooded with warmth, threatening to betray her stoic stance. She wanted to walk over, take Bianca in her arms, and resume the casual, flirty banter they'd shared before a dead body quelled their chance at something more, but her instinct for survival won out. Shaking away the desire, she strode over to Bianca's car. When she reached her, Jade made a show of looking around. "Just you and not a fleet of federal agents?"

Bianca's cheeks reddened slightly. She shut her car door and waved her arms. "Just me. Disappointed?"

"Hardly, but I'm not sure I believe you. Any moment now, I expect a posse to appear."

"Not going to happen. In fact, I'm here to tell you they've finished gathering evidence and you're in the clear."

"You're kidding, right?" Jade studied Bianca's face searching for clues, but all she found was steadfast sincerity. "Did you actually believe for a moment, I would be involved in a murder?" She waited a beat before adding. "And even if I was, that I would have dumped the dead body on my own property and led you and your daughter right to it?"

Bianca shook her head vigorously. "No, no, I'm sorry. Of course, I didn't believe it, but you know how it is, everyone's a suspect until they're not."

A surge of anger fueled Jade's response. "No, actually, I don't know how it is because I've never even had so much as a traffic ticket, let alone been caught up in a homicide investigation. Believe it or not, my only experience with murder is a few random episodes of *Law and Order*. Even on TV, the suspect usually knows he's a suspect. Thanks for the courtesy. You can go now." Ultimatum delivered, Jade turned to leave.

"Wait. Please."

Jade stopped, but didn't turn around. "What?"

"Please look at me. I have something I want to say."

Jade turned slowly, bracing against the impact of Bianca's plaintive eyes. "Say it quickly. I have work to do. Work that your needless investigation has delayed." She crossed her arms and watched as Bianca closed the distance between them with surprisingly long strides. Before she had a chance to back away, Bianca placed a hand on her arm.

"I'm sorry."

She needed to get away fast before the heat from Bianca's touch spurred her to abandon her better instincts. "Fine."

"It doesn't seem fine."

Jade deliberately softened her tone. "It is."

"You were so sweet to Emma. She hasn't stopped talking about the ride since we got home on Saturday."

"It's not every day a kid discovers a dead body."

"That's not it and you know it. She loves all things horse and the ride we took, even though it was cut short, was the highlight of her year. Of course you should know that her highlights tend to only last until the next big one comes along. Any day now, she could meet Zac Efron and then this horse thing will be a distant memory."

Jade couldn't help but smile at the playful tone in Bianca's voice. "She's a nice girl, and she has a natural talent for riding. You should let her ride more often." She watched, curious about the faraway look in Bianca's eyes in response to her statement, wondering what had prompted it. "Did I say something wrong?"

"No, not at all." Bianca looked away as she spoke, and Jade was certain there was some angst there, but before she could ask again, Bianca shook her keys. "I'll be going now. I'm sorry I dropped by unannounced. It won't happen again. Give Sophia my regards and have a good evening."

Bianca turned back to her car and opened the door. Jade knew she should be relieved to know their entanglement had come to an end, but she wasn't. She was disappointed. No, more than that, she was dissatisfied. What had started out as a ruse to discover what the feds were up to had turned into an undeniable attraction, and she questioned the need to let it go. Bianca slid into the front seat and shut the door. She turned the key and checked the mirrors. In a moment, she'd be headed back up the road in a cloud of dust, moving on, never looking back. Jade took a step toward the door, but before she could reach it, Bianca had driven several feet away. To stop her now, she'd have to lunge, wave her arms, or some other extreme action, but to do so would signal more than she was ready to say. Instead, she stayed in place, waved a simple good-bye, and focused on believing Bianca leaving for good was for the best.

CHAPTER ELEVEN

Bianca sat behind the rail, impatiently waiting for the judge to call her case. By her calculation, she should be next in line, but Judge Nivens had taken a couple of cases out of order, so the entire docket was up in the air. She flipped through her file in an effort to make the time pass faster, until she heard Peyton whisper, "You look like you'd rather be anyplace but here."

Peyton and Tanner had slipped into the row behind her. "True. It's career day at Emma's school, and at the rate things are moving here, I'm going to be the poster child for the bad parent society."

"You here for a detention hearing?" Peyton asked.

"You bet. If they ever call the case, it should be quick. Defense doesn't have grounds to contest, and I'm sure they're only putting on a show for the family." She motioned to a motley group sitting across the room.

Peyton reached for the file. "I'll handle it." She used her other hand to wave Bianca off. "Go be a role model for kids."

Bianca spent a split second considering the offer before she decided to accept. She handed over her file and rushed out of the courtroom and into the elevator. As the doors closed, a hand reached in to stop them and Tanner joined her. "You following me?"

"Actually, yes," Tanner said. "I need to talk to you. How about I give you a ride to Emma's school and we can talk on the way?"

Bianca's stomach churned as she wondered what was so important it couldn't wait, but she deflected by saying, "Only if you agree to stick around for show-and-tell. I'll get extra special mom points for bringing an FBI agent to career day."

Tanner shrugged. "Sure, why not."

They agreed Tanner would bring her car around while Bianca ran by her office to pick up her bag. She'd barely rounded the corner into the suite, when Ida called out to her.

"Mr. Gellar is looking for you and you have a package." She reached under her desk and produced a medium-sized rectangular box. Bianca thanked her, tucked the box under her shoulder, and practically jogged to her office, hoping she'd be lucky enough to avoid Gellar.

No such luck. She'd just crossed the threshold on her way back out when she saw him heading her way.

"Miss Cruz, a moment please?"

Resigned to the encounter, she prayed it was quick. "Sure." She backed up and invited him into her office, but remained standing.

"I thought you were in court this morning."

"I was, but the docket was running long and I need to be somewhere, so Peyton is filling in for me." She didn't plan on filling in more detail, but his raised eyebrows said she better. "My daughter's class is having career day, and they asked me to speak."

"Really."

His tone told her it wasn't a question and he wasn't happy, but there was absolutely no way she was going to disappoint Emma. "Yes. It's important. One of those goodwill things." She cast about for a way to reach his opportunistic mind. "The kind of thing a reporter like Lindsey Ryan would think made you a superior public servant. You know….if she knew you encouraged your employees to get involved with local schools."

His face morphed through a full display of emotions from a furrowed brow of disbelief to nodding assent. "Actually, that makes a lot of sense. Maybe I should go with you. Wouldn't that be an excellent surprise for the kids?"

Like they'd even know who you are. She scrambled to find a way to keep him at bay. "Actually, that's a great idea, but you should go when you can be in the spotlight. I know they've got a pretty full lineup today, and they would definitely want to set aside an entire slot just for you."

"Good point." He rubbed his hands together. "If we set it up in advance, Lindsey can have time to get a crew together to film it for her story."

Bianca resisted the urge to shake her head and started edging away from him, anxious to get to Tanner's car in time to make it to Emma's school. "This won't take long, I promise. I'll be back this afternoon."

"Good, because I want to talk to you and Agent Cohen about where things stand with the grand jury witnesses."

Great. A few minutes later, Bianca was outside the building and Tanner pulled up alongside. She climbed into the front seat of Tanner's SUV and tugged on her seat belt.

"You can set your stuff in the back if you want."

Bianca looked down at the box in her lap. "I meant to leave this back at the office, but I got waylaid by Gellar. I don't have a clue what it is." She examined the outside of the box. No name and the address was a P.O. box. "I'm opening it. Hope I don't blow us both up." She didn't wait for a response from Tanner before tearing into the box to find a book and a slip of tan linen stationery.

"What is it?"

"Hang on." Bianca zoomed to the signature on the page before she began skimming the short note written in flowing fountain pen script.

I'm sorry our ride ended in such an abrupt manner. Please give Emma my regrets and this small offering from one horse lover to another.

Sincerely, Jade Vargas

Sincerely? And not just Jade, but Jade Vargas, as if there were some other Jade she'd been riding horses with lately. Could she be more impersonal? Bianca started to shove the contents back in the box, but the title of the book caught her eye. *Misty of Chincoteague.* She pulled it closer and tugged open the cover as fond memories of the first time she'd read the story rushed through her. Though the book had never inspired her to want to be a horsewoman, it had captivated her with its romantic tale of two kids trying to tame a wild horse and her colt. She ran her hands along the script, noting the slightly yellow pages and the uneven edges. She flipped through the pages and glanced at the copyright. A first edition. Collector's piece.

"Is that *Misty of Chincoteague*?"

Bianca held it up for Tanner to see. "It is."

"I had a copy of that book when I was a kid. Read the covers off of it."

"This is a first edition."

"You a collector?"

"Nope, but Jade Vargas must be. She sent this for Emma."

"You're kidding."

"Nope. Mushy note and everything."

"Hmmm."

Bianca shifted in her seat. "What's that supposed to mean?"

"It's a pretty nice gift. Sounds like Jade may have a thing for you. Maybe it's time to resume your role."

"Not going to happen. I'll leave it to you and your pals to do the fancy undercover work. I'm not cut out for it. Besides, the gift is for Emma not me, and I've already spent too much time away from home. Gellar has made it clear he wants us focusing on the grand jury investigation. Between trying to steer him clear of indicting Lily's father for murder and my regular docket, I have enough on my plate."

"Speaking of that, there's one witness I think we should talk to again, but it's kind of a delicate situation."

"Spill."

"It's Neil Davis."

"Peyton's brother? Delicate is an understatement."

"I know, which is why I'm talking to you about this and not any of the others."

"What's your theory?"

"I don't know that I have one, but things don't add up. Supposedly, Gantry gave him a big wad of cash to get him to sign over drilling rights, but the money disappeared in no time. I don't think Neil spent any of it on the Circle Six, and I'm wondering where it went. Plus, I don't think it was the first time Gantry paid him money. Something else was going on between these two, and I'd like to know what it was."

"Are you starting to think Gantry really was involved in Maria's death? And do you think Neil had something to do with it?"

"No. I mean, I don't know." Tanner tapped her fingers on the steering wheel. "I think we need to explore every angle, and since Gellar expects us to be talking to witnesses, it's the perfect opportunity to do just that even if we aren't predisposed to finding the conclusion he wants us to."

Bianca's stomach knotted at the prospect of looking closer at Peyton's family, but Tanner was right. If their only conclusion was Neil and Gantry could be eliminated, then the effort was well worth it. "Okay, I'm in, but we're going to need to come up with a game plan for dealing with Peyton if she finds out we're doing this without telling her."

"It'll be fine." Tanner pointed at the package in Bianca's lap. "You plan on giving that to Emma or sending it back?"

Bianca stared at the book, torn between honesty and caution. "I'm not sure. It's seems like a harmless gesture, but…"

"But it feels weird to accept a gift when you think there might be strings attached?"

Was that it? Did she think letting Emma keep the book would somehow obligate her to Jade? It was just a book, albeit expensive, but Jade had seemed genuinely interested in Emma and her passion for horses. She'd seen firsthand the way both their faces lit up as they discussed the horses, the ranch, the ride. Before they'd run across the body, it had all seemed very idyllic. Why couldn't she just accept Jade might have no ulterior motive for the gift?

Because this job makes a person suspect everything and everyone.

It was true. She'd become a much more cynical person during her stint prosecuting cases than she used to be, but cynicism afforded her protection, security for her and the people she loved. But it was only a book, the non-cynical side of her argued. Surely, accepting it was a harmless act even if it kept her connected to Jade. Right?

❖

"Jade, it's for you." Sophia's voice carried from the kitchen into the sitting room at the front of the house.

Jade looked up from the spreadsheet open on her laptop and wondered who was calling her on the home phone. She hadn't bothered to reconnect with anyone she knew locally on a personal level, and even if she had, the possibilities were few. Between boarding school, college, and travels, she'd spent little time making friends in the area.

Sophia appeared in the entryway. "Are you coming, or should I tell her you're not interested in taking her call?"

"I don't suppose you asked who's calling?"

"I did not."

Jade swore she spotted a slight grin, but it was gone before she could analyze it. Sophia was up to something, but she wasn't in the mood to play games. She'd spent the last several hours poring over the numbers for the ranch, trying to squeeze every dollar she could find for the few horses she planned to purchase at auction in the next few weeks. The exercise was akin to working a Rubik's Cube, but she could never seem to get all the sides the same color. Maybe a break was exactly what she needed. "I'll be right there."

She walked into the kitchen, wondering if they were the last people on earth to have a landline phone, let alone one that was attached to the wall instead of a cordless unit. Sophia liked the charm of the old phone and had declared it indestructible, a theory Jade often wanted to disprove. She lifted the receiver from the countertop and leaned against the cabinet. "This is Jade."

"I have someone who would like to talk to you." The words were followed by the sound of paper crinkling and a loud whisper. "Settle down or I'm going to hang up. I told you I would, just wait."

Jade almost laughed out loud at Bianca's background conversation. "Is everything okay over there?"

"Everything's fine," Bianca said. "Hold for your caller."

The next voice Jade heard was decidedly younger. "Jade?"

"Yes?"

"It's Emma. You know, from last Saturday."

"Hi, Emma. How are you doing?"

"Great actually. Mom brought home the book you sent. It's amazing! I'm going to read it a bunch of times so when I get my first horse I'll be ready for anything. Thanks!"

Jade could hear the exclamation points and she found the enthusiasm contagious. "You're welcome. I remember when I got my first horse. There's nothing quite like it."

"Was it Ransom?"

"No, Ransom came later." The sting of how she'd come to purchase Ransom didn't lessen how she felt about him, but she glossed over it all the same. "My first horse was a Chestnut gelding and his name was Otto. He was a gentle beast, perfect for learning the ropes."

And completely unlike Ransom who was as fearless as he was handsome. If she'd had her way, she would've chosen to start riding on a horse like Ransom. Her uncles would have let her, but Sophia had insisted on the safer choice. Jade had hated her for it at the time, certain she was missing out on the excitement of riding a headstrong stallion, but looking back, she realized she was a better horsewoman because she'd had the chance to acquire her skills slowly and carefully rather than while hanging on for dear life. Emma should have that same opportunity.

"Otto. That's a funny name."

"It is, but he was a great horse. He died a few years ago and I still miss him."

"Maybe next time I see you, you can show me a picture of him. Hang on."

Jade stayed on the line, trying to interpret the muffled sounds on the other end. A few seconds later, Emma was back. "Sorry about that. I need to go do my homework, but Mom wants to talk to you. Thanks again, Jade. See you soon."

Jade barely had time to process Emma's prophecy about a future meeting before Bianca's soft voice tickled her ears.

"She might be a little excited," Bianca said.

"You think so?"

"You didn't have to do that, you know."

"The book?" Jade asked. "I wanted to. I remember being over the moon the first time I rode a horse. I instantly knew there was nothing better."

"Nothing, huh?"

"Well, you know…" Jade stumbled for a response. She hadn't anticipated this conversation might involve flirty banter and she was caught off guard.

"Sorry, I was kidding. But seriously, thank you for the ride last weekend and the book. I think she's already read it twice through." A few beats of silence passed and then Bianca added, "Well, I better go make sure someone is actually doing her homework and not sneaking another read of *Misty*."

"It was the least I could do. Especially since the ride was cut short. After what happened, I doubt you'll want to bring her back here ever, although, it's too bad because it's really the perfect place for her to learn to ride." Jade couldn't seem to stop the torrent of words designed to keep Bianca on the line. Why was she so drawn to this woman, and how could she manage to see her again? "Hey, I have an idea."

"Yes?"

Jade plunged forward before she could second-guess her plan. "I'm meeting a man in Canton this Saturday about a couple of horses he has for sale. The meeting won't take long, and it's First Monday Trade Days, so there's the flea market." Jade's words skidded to a stop and she took a breath to force herself to slow down. "Anyway, I thought Emma might enjoy tagging along."

"Just Emma?"

Jade heard the grin in Bianca's voice and played along. "Well, I suppose you could come too, if you'd like. I know horses aren't your thing, but there's plenty of other stuff to do, and maybe—"

"Yes."

"Excuse me?"

"I said yes. Now, I think it's customary for you to work out the details about how we get there and all that. Text me?"

Jade agreed, still digesting the fact she'd asked Bianca out and she'd said yes. After they exchanged cell numbers, she hung up and pondered her newfound impulsive side, hoping it wouldn't get her into trouble, but not entirely caring if it did.

❖

Friday afternoon, Bianca was sitting at her desk deep into a case file when Tanner appeared in the doorway. "Is it time already?"

"Yep. He should be there any minute. Your boss is headed back to the office, so we need to bug out now if you want to avoid getting waylaid."

Bianca grabbed her bag and followed Tanner out of the office. It was two p.m. She told Ida she was headed out to talk to a witness, not caring if she thought that was code for happy hour. She'd rather Ida or anyone else who heard, think she was going out for drinks instead of where she was really headed.

Once she and Tanner were in Tanner's SUV she asked, "Does anyone else know we're talking to Neil?"

"Not yet. Let's see what he says and then we can decide if we want to let Dale and Mary in on it."

"But not Peyton?"

Tanner shot her a surprised look. "I thought we discussed this."

"You did, but I haven't fully processed it yet. I don't like keeping secrets from the rest of the team."

"Don't think of it that way. Think of it like you're protecting Peyton and helping the case by keeping conflicts out of it. You know as well as I do that if she gets involved and he gives us something good to go on, a defense attorney is going to jump all over that. It could cost a conviction."

"You're right, but until we know who we're likely to convict, it's a little hard to make that call."

"Having a case of selective prosecution?"

Bianca bristled at the implication. "You can call it that if you want, but there are times the net gets cast a little too wide in my opinion. I thought we were united on that front."

"We are. I was only making an observation. I don't think Neil had a tangible connection to Maria's death, but I'm hoping he can shed some light on helping us find Sergio Vargas since he's had some association with him in the past. Neil might not even know he has helpful information. I just want a chance to talk to him."

"And you need me here because?"

"Gellar's on a warpath. At some point he's going to find out we looked at Neil, and two of us saying he has nothing to do with Maria's death will be better than just me. I don't trust that guy."

"Neither do I. How did you get Neil to agree to meet?"

"You don't want to know."

"Seriously?"

"I might have intimated Cyrus flipped on him and it would be in his best interest to get out in front of it."

"So you lied to him."

"I did. You have a problem with that?"

She didn't, in the abstract. She was well aware agents lied to potential witnesses all the time to get them to open up, but Neil was Peyton's brother, and despite their estrangement, Bianca felt lying to him was a betrayal of her loyalty to Peyton. What she really wanted to do was call Peyton and ask her opinion, but that would defeat the purpose of keeping her out of the loop. Damn. She was probably just overthinking it. "No, we'll do this your way." She changed the subject. "Any ID on the body from Valencia Acres yet?"

"Yep. Hector Villegas, a lieutenant for Barrio Azteca. Long record, but we haven't found anything yet that connects him directly to the Vargases, and we still don't have any idea how he turned up at Valencia Acres. Too bad your little undercover assignment got cut short."

"What? Oh yeah." Bianca spent a split second debating whether she should let Tanner know she had plans with Jade for the next day. If she'd made the plans in order to keep an eye on Jade, she should definitely tell Tanner and the others, but she hadn't. Tomorrow was about Emma and horses and a good time. If she told Tanner, she would tell the rest of the team and they'd probably send someone to follow them around. But she and Emma were headed to a flea market, and there would be thousands of people around. The likelihood she or Emma would be in any danger was remote at best, and she wasn't interested in having her every move watched. She settled on a vague response. "I'm not really cut out for undercover work anyway."

A few minutes later, they arrived at the restaurant where Neil had agreed to meet them. While Tanner parked the car, Bianca set the ground rules. "I'm going to follow your lead on this, but don't get too far into the whole Cyrus flipped on him thing. I don't feel comfortable with it, and I have a feeling it could come back to bite us."

"You're the boss." Tanner offered a mock salute.

Bianca recognized Neil from one of her visits to the Circle Six when she spotted him sitting at a table in the back of the diner, pretending to read the paper. His shifting eyes and nervous tics told Bianca the newspaper was no more than a prop. She followed Tanner to the table and watched their initial exchange.

"What's she doing here?" Neil asked Tanner. "I thought this was a one-on-one."

"She's a prosecutor," Tanner said in an even tone. "She's here to make sure I don't make you any promises I can't deliver. I figured you'd want the reassurance."

"I've seen her at the ranch. She's one of Peyton's pals."

"We've both been out there. You just haven't seen me." Tanner sat in one of the chairs with a view of the door and motioned for Bianca to take the seat across from Neil. "Aren't you even a little bit interested in why your sister's been hosting a group of federal agents and prosecutors so much lately?"

Bianca sucked in a breath and felt a kick from Tanner under the table. Was Tanner about to let Neil in on their secret task force? What in the hell was she thinking? "Agent Cohen, may I have a word with you?"

Tanner kept her eyes on Neil. "It's okay. He knows all about what we're up to. Don't you, Neil?"

Bianca swiveled her head between them, trying to get a read on what was happening. She was still running through a list of possibilities when Neil spoke.

"Yep, I do, but I don't know why you're bothering."

Bianca abandoned all pretense in favor of getting information. "What's going on? I mean what do you think you know?"

"I know my sister won't let anything go if she thinks she's right. You all aren't really playing poker. I figured it out the second time you were out there. While Peyton was in D.C., we put in an extra storage closet to keep medical supplies for dad. It's upstairs in between Zach's and Mom and Dad's bedrooms, right above the kitchen. We didn't spend a bunch of money insulating the damn thing, and you can stand in that closet and hear everything going on in the kitchen."

"So you've been crouching in the closet upstairs while we're there, listening to every word we say?"

"Only after I figured it out. Peyton's always assumed I was in my room, which I was the first time you all had one of your meetings, but I went to get something out of the closet and…you know how it is when someone's talking about something really juicy. Hard to ignore. Anyway, from then on, when I saw you all show up, I made a point to check out what was going on."

Bianca turned to Tanner. "When did you figure this out?"

"Last time we were there. I needed to use the bathroom before I left, and Mary was hogging the one downstairs, so I went upstairs. I saw Neil here coming out of the closet. He was acting all shifty, and I thought it was strange so I waited until he was out of sight and I slipped in there. I could hear every word the rest of you were saying."

Bianca had a dozen questions, starting with why Tanner hadn't told the rest of the group about her discovery and why she'd chosen to confront Neil today instead of when she'd figured it out, but what she really wanted to know was what Tanner was up to right now. She didn't know Tanner as well as the others who'd been working on the task force longer, but she knew enough about Tanner's reputation and work ethic to know she wouldn't have arranged this meeting without having devised some strategy for using Neil's spying to their advantage. "So, what's your plan?"

"I'm glad you asked. Neil, you've heard what we're up to. How would you like to work for the good guys and get back everything you've lost—your drilling rights, your reputation?"

Neil held both hands up. "Just so you understand, I don't think Cyrus Gantry would've gotten involved with the Vargases except under duress."

"I'm sure you know by now we're not focused on Cyrus Gantry. We've got our sights set elsewhere." Tanner turned to Bianca. "If Neil can help us break this case open, are you on board with helping him out?"

She should say no. Or at the very least, take some time to think about it. Peyton would be furious if she found out they were negotiating with Neil behind her back, not to mention Gellar would go ballistic if he learned anyone associated with Gantry was getting a deal without agreeing to testify against him. But Tanner seemed so confident Neil could help them, and Tanner was the only one on the team who didn't have a direct connection to any of the Vargases' victims. Dale had lost her wife, and Mary was Dale's best friend. Cyrus Gantry was practically Peyton's father-in-law. Maria Escobar had been a mentor to her and she'd come to care for her very much. Tanner had no such connections, which allowed her to remain objective.

An image of Jade flashed in her mind and a shiver of desire coursed through her. Perhaps they all needed a dose of objectivity right now, especially since her own efforts to get inside information had resulted in an inability to separate personal from professional. She threw up her hands. "Fine. Let's try it, but if anything goes wrong, we're all going down together."

CHAPTER TWELVE

Jade attributed the lack of conversation in the car to the early hour. When she'd shown up at Bianca's house that morning for the trip to Canton, it was clear Bianca and Emma were not morning people. Both of them were sleepy-eyed and neither was ready to go. She'd lounged in the kitchen with a cup of coffee while waiting for them to finish preparing for the trip, but she was the one who wasn't prepared when Bianca walked in, an adorable cross between preppy and edgy, dressed in skinny jeans, red Converse, and a lightweight, tan V-neck sweater over a white oxford button-down shirt. Jade stood when she walked into the room.

"Sorry we're taking so long," Bianca said. "I know you're probably on a schedule."

Jade licked her lips. "It's fine. We have plenty of time. Where's Emma?"

"We were doing battle over a piece of toast. Should she eat it or should she forego all form of nutrients that could be referred to as breakfast? It's our new thing. I highly recommend it for anyone who has an unruly kid living in their house. I won, by the way."

"I have no doubt." Jade scrutinized Bianca's face, noting prominent worry lines. She wanted to know their source but didn't feel like this was the time or place to ask. Instead, she elected to stay on safe ground. "Do you need help with anything?"

"No, she'll be done in a sec and we can get going." Bianca stopped like she was considering her next words very carefully. "She's really looking forward to this."

Jade sensed an undercurrent, but she couldn't put her finger on exactly what Bianca was trying to convey. "And you are looking forward to this?"

"I am. I hope it's okay that I invited myself."

"Wouldn't have it any other way." Jade could tell Bianca wanted to say more, but the moment passed when Emma came barreling down the stairs.

"I'm ready!"

Jade watched while Bianca surveyed Emma's wardrobe, signing off on the jeans, sweater, and checkerboard Vans. "Grab a jacket," Bianca told her.

"Mom, it's not even cold out."

"Not sure how you know since you haven't been outside yet."

"It's supposed to get colder later," Jade chimed in, holding up her phone as proof of a reliable source. "Probably a good idea."

"Okay," Emma said agreeably. Jade shot a look at Bianca who rolled her eyes.

They were near Terrell on I-20 when Jade asked, "Anyone hungry?"

Emma spoke up first. "No way. I'm having a funnel cake for breakfast. Did you know there are over a dozen funnel cake stands at the flea market?"

Bianca shook her head. "Guess the piece of whole wheat toast I forced her to eat will be the only healthy food she gets today. The girl is convinced we're going to a cross between the state fair and horse heaven."

"Well, it kind of is," Jade said. "The breeder we're going to see has quite a few horses, and I have my sights set on a couple of his mares. We'll meet with him first and then we can walk the flea market and get as many funnel cakes as we want."

Emma threw a fist in the air while Bianca sighed with resignation.

"I can't believe neither of you have ever been to Canton," Jade said.

"Crazy, right?" Bianca said. "I guess the idea of traipsing around outside looking at other people's odds and ends never really appealed to me. No one told me there would be funnel cake."

"Travesty."

Thirty minutes later, Jade pulled off the highway and they sat in a long line of cars, waiting to enter the enormous parking lot near the original flea market location. She paid the attendant five dollars and followed his directions about where to park. After they climbed down from the SUV, she opened the back and pulled out a rolling cart. "Emma, you want to be in charge of the cart?"

"Sure!" Emma grabbed the handle, and Jade showed her how to unfold the sides to form a wagon. Once she got it rolling, she took off for the gate to the market grounds.

"You think we're going to need that?" Bianca asked.

"Maybe, maybe not," Jade said. "But I can guarantee if we don't bring it, you will need it. Happens every time." She locked arms with Bianca and whispered in her ear. "I can tell this isn't your thing, but I promise we'll have fun. Trust me?"

Bianca stopped in place and looked up into Jade's eyes, her expression probing, curious. Jade felt the heat of her inspection in every cell of her body, and only Emma's presence kept her from pulling Bianca into a kiss. A deep, probing, all-consuming kiss. Instead she settled for brushing a hair back from Bianca's eyes and letting her hand linger longer than necessary as she repeated her question, "Trust me?"

Bianca's eyes fluttered as if the words had broken a spell. "Yes, matter of fact, I do." She shook her head. "Now, come on and lead us to the funnel cakes."

"I should've known that look of desire was about sugar."

"As opposed to?"

Emma's voice carried back to interrupt their exchange. "Mom, Jade, I'm starving!"

"Be right there," Bianca yelled before turning back to face Jade, her expression transforming from playful to serious.

"What is it?"

"I'm not sure. I mean I enjoy being with you, and I'm looking forward to today, but…"

Jade's gut clenched as she contemplated the possibilities, but she headed off whatever Bianca was about to say with a playful,

"This might be a world record." At Bianca's puzzled expression, she pressed on. "Fastest end to a first date ever. Should I give you a lift back home or do you want to rely on the kindness of strangers?"

"Please. I fully expect you to treat for the funnel cake. But seriously, is this really a date? I kind of thought this was you being nice to Emma, you know, because of your shared love of all things horse."

"Couldn't it be both?"

"It could. It's just…"

"Spill."

"I don't go on a lot of dates. A heavy caseload and Emma occupy most of my time. And speaking of Emma, I'm usually pretty careful about who I invite into our lives."

Jade stiffened, and she braced for rejection. "And a woman whose family has close ties to crime doesn't meet your strict criteria. If that's the case, then what am I even doing here?"

"Wait. I didn't mean it that way. What I'm trying to say, really poorly, is I usually don't introduce people to Emma unless I'm fairly certain they're going to be sticking around for a while."

"Is that so?"

"Yes."

"And have there been a lot of those people?"

"No, actually not."

"So, this is new territory?"

"Yes."

"It is for me too," Jade said. "So, what do you say we take this…whatever you want to call it, one step at a time?"

"Okay, that sounds like a good plan."

Jade looked down at their hands, fingers laced together. Everything about the connection felt right, sure, and strong, but Bianca's words prompted her to release the connection. "Not sure if we should be holding hands on this not quite a date thing."

"Me neither, but I want to."

"Me too."

"Mom!"

Bianca sighed. "Seems someone else's hunger is going to rule this day." She tapped Jade on the shoulder and then took off running. "Last one to the funnel cake is a rotten egg."

Jade stood still as she watched Bianca chase after her daughter. They were both so vibrant, so enthusiastic. Had she ever had this much fun with her own mother in between boarding school stints and summers in Mexico with her cousins? If she had, she couldn't remember. Emma was the center of Bianca's world, but Jade had always revolved around the edges of Sophia's life, close enough to see in, but not enough to feel like she was truly on the inside. If Cyrus had had the balls to leave his wife back when Sophia found out she was pregnant with Lily, she was certain she would never have been born.

But she had been born. She didn't know her father, her mother was preoccupied with her love child with Cyrus, and her uncles were on the run from the law. The rest of her so-called family was in Mexico, living a life connected to crime, as far removed from her own well-bred, well-educated upbringing as possible. She'd never been a part of their lives, and she never wanted to be.

Bianca slowed her pace and looked back over her shoulder, waving for her to join them before placing her arm around Emma and pulling her close in a display of affection Jade couldn't possibly relate to. Jade crossed her arms tight against her chest. She wasn't a part of her own family, but in this moment, she wanted desperately to be a part of Bianca's, and the realization filled her with both hope and sadness.

❖

"At some point I might need something to eat that isn't composed entirely of sugar," Bianca said as they walked through one of the large open air buildings in the middle of the flea market. Jade was grinning at her. "What?"

Jade pointed to one of her packages that had escaped the cart. "You dropped something. Again."

"This cart is smaller than it looks," Bianca protested. "Seriously."

"Well, that might be, but it looks like it's getting a bit heavy."

Bianca ducked her head as Jade pointed at the overflowing cart. "Okay, okay. I was wrong about the whole flea market thing. I had no idea there would be so many craftspeople here selling original pieces, but in my defense, Christmas is just around the corner and now I'm almost done with my shopping."

Emma tugged on the cart and made a show of groaning at the weight. "You did go a little crazy, Mom."

"Don't even start with me about crazy, you who ate two funnel cakes all by herself." She touched Emma's forehead. "What's that I see? More powdered sugar?" She ruffled Emma's hair. "I bet we'll be finding it for days."

"Mom!" Emma drew out the one syllable in a mock show of horror.

"How about I run this back to the car and then we can find you both some real food?" Jade said, placing a hand on the cart handle.

Bianca looked down at Jade's hand next to hers, more conscious of the closeness of their bodies than coming up with an answer to Jade's question. Every little shift between them brought the most delicious friction.

"What do you think, Mom?"

Emma was standing with her hands on her hips and, based on the knowing grin Jade shot her way, Bianca was certain her question alluded to a piece of conversation she'd missed entirely. Rather than admit she had no clue what they were talking about, she answered with a vague, "I'm not sure, bug."

"She zoned out," Emma explained to Jade. "She does that. Mostly it's because she's thinking about work stuff. Mom has a really important job."

Bianca offered Jade a pained smile while she contemplated Emma's easy summary of why she was distracted. *Job.* The one word had the potential to be a complete buzzkill to the wonderful afternoon they'd shared. If she let it. She'd managed to put aside all thoughts of the task force, the upcoming grand jury, and Tanner's plan to use Neil Davis as a confidential informant, which was pretty amazing since all of those things had combined to keep her from getting any sleep the night before. At this moment, all she cared about was her desire for more days like today. It had been one of the best family outings she'd had in a long time, and any distraction she experienced was due to the many stolen glances and semi-accidental touches between her and Jade the entire day. She was hyperaware of how the heat of attraction robbed her of the brain power she needed to focus on basic tasks, like keeping up with a simple conversation, but for Emma's sake, she had to try. "All right, I promise I'm not thinking about work or anything else. What's the question on the table?"

Emma glanced at Jade before she started talking. "Jade and I are going to take this stuff to the car while you wait for us over there." She pointed at a group of picnic tables in a grove of trees. "When we get back, we'll go in search of real food, you know, the kind without sugar. Okay?"

"I can go with you."

Jade squeezed her hand. "We got this." She leaned in close and whispered, "Rest up for the next round."

Jade's tone was suggestive, and Bianca was incredibly conscious of her quickening heartbeat. Maybe a few minutes' break would allow her time to pull herself together because right now all she wanted to do was tug Jade closer and run her tongue along Jade's full and super sexy lips. She spent a moment luxuriating in the fantasy before Emma's voice crash-landed her back in reality.

"Mom!"

Bianca shook her head, unsuccessful at dislodging the daydream, but desperately attempting to multitask. "Yes, you can go, but stay with Jade and do whatever she says, no questions. Got it?"

Seconds later, as they walked away, Jade shot a grin over her shoulder, and Bianca melted. Her words to Emma echoed in her head. If Jade asked for something more, would she be able to follow her own advice?

❖

After they loaded the packages into the car, Jade led the way through the crowd while Emma kept up a running list of horse-related questions. Had she been this enthusiastic about anything when she was Emma's age?

She had, but she hadn't had anyone to share in her passion. Sophia loved horses, but more as a business venture than anything else. The other girls at boarding school took for granted their relationship to the proud beasts, most of them having had access to expensive mounts their entire lives. Not one of them possessed the same sense of wonder and awe at the fact that these huge, beautiful creatures allowed them to sit on their backs and pretend they were in charge.

But Emma was different. She possessed the right mix of respect and awe that would make her an accomplished horsewoman, and Jade was committed to giving her the opportunity if Bianca would allow it. Her mind started whirring with ways to convince Bianca to bring Emma back to the ranch for riding lessons, fully aware her goal was twofold.

This day had been perfect, from the easy laughs they'd shared to the slow burn of desire flickering between her and Bianca. If Emma hadn't been present, Jade was certain she would have found a way, even in the sea of people, to grab a private moment and give in to the persistent desire to kiss Bianca's alluring lips. But as much as she wanted the intimate touch, she wouldn't have traded Emma's presence for the opportunity. The realization confused her—it wasn't like her to let anything get in the way of taking what she wanted. As she tried to sort out the mixed feelings, she felt someone grab her hand and looked down at Emma's small hand nestled in hers. Jade squeezed Emma's hand and smiled down at her, but before she could say anything she felt a tap on her shoulder.

"Excuse me, Jade Vargas?"

She didn't recognize the man standing behind her. She smiled politely. "I'm sorry, do I know you?"

"Not personally, but I'm here on behalf of a friend."

Jade kept her smile in place for Emma's sake, but an instant wave of dread flushed through her. The stranger was taller by a few inches, with dark skin and jet-black hair. Despite the cool fall air, he was dressed in warm weather clothes, khakis and a short-sleeved guayaberas that showed off thick arms with well-sculpted muscles and the trail of a tattoo snaking up the side of his neck. Jade swallowed against the sour taste in her throat and resisted the urge to grip Emma's hand tighter lest she scare the girl. Whatever this man wanted, she would handle it alone.

She injected her voice with calm. "Oh, right. Hang on a minute." Jade bent down to Emma. "I need to speak to this gentleman…" she tried not to gag at the word, "alone for a minute." She pulled out a five-dollar bill and pointed at a lemonade stand a few yards away. "Why don't you get your mom a fresh lemonade and we'll surprise her with it?"

Emma glanced between her and the man, but thankfully, she didn't ask any questions. Once Emma was well on her way to the lemonade stand, Jade turned back to the stranger. "Who are you and what do you want?"

"Who I am isn't important. I'm here to deliver a message."

Jade resisted the urge to look in Emma's direction. "Spit it out."

"It's simple. Your family is counting on your loyalty."

Jade glared at the man, anger rising at his vague proclamation. "Well, I have a message for you. Tell my uncles I reserve my loyalty for those who earn it, not those who make threats."

He shrugged. "You'll do what's asked of you." Before she could respond, he pointed over her shoulder. "Looks like your little friend is on her way back. She seems like a nice girl. You seem to care about her."

Jade turned to see Emma walking toward them, holding an enormous cup and wearing a huge grin. She forced a return smile while she replayed the man's words in her head. His tone had been light and easy, but there was no mistaking the ominous undertone. She looked back at the man. "Leave now," she hissed.

He grinned. "We'll be in touch. Tomorrow."

And then he was gone, lost in the sea of people just as Emma appeared at her side. "Was that a friend of yours?"

"Not really." Jade kept her eyes on the crowd, not entirely convinced the man wouldn't reappear. "I don't know him, but he knows one of my relatives." Finally satisfied he was really gone, she looked down at Emma. "All set?"

"I bought the biggest one they had. Mom loves lemonade."

"Good job." Jade paused, certain about her next move, but a little unsure how to approach it. "Hey, Emma?"

"Yes?"

"Your mom's pretty protective, right?"

"That's for sure."

"I'm thinking she might not be too keen on me letting you go off to hunt for lemonade while I talk to some stranger, so maybe we don't mention it. Is that okay with you?"

"Sure."

Emma's response was quick and easy, and within a few steps she'd probably forgotten all about the man, but as they walked back toward the grove where they'd left Bianca, Jade's excitement about seeing Bianca again was tempered by the acute awareness of the secret that now existed between them.

CHAPTER THIRTEEN

Bianca leaned her head against the passenger side window, letting the bright lights from the other cars on the highway wash over her as she reflected on the day. She couldn't remember the last time she'd spent an entire day having fun. No signing on to the Internet for a few minutes of research, no scribbling notes for a hearing, not a single phone call from work, official or unofficial. Her mind was free and full of decidedly personal thoughts. She glanced over her shoulder at Emma who was fully engaged in a text conversation with her bestie and then risked a longer look at Jade.

A week ago, she wouldn't have imagined Jade Vargas, Wharton grad, ranch owner, niece of drug lords, running around with her at a flea market. But despite her preconceptions, Jade had patiently stowed her packages, found the best funnel cake stands, and sent her and Emma into gales of laughter as she modeled a half dozen crazy felt hats from a costume vendor. The three of them had had a wonderful time, and as the Range Rover sped back to Dallas, Bianca regretted every mile marker signaling the end of their day.

The gentle touch of Jade's hand on hers pulled her out of her thoughts. She linked her fingers with Jade's, mildly conscious that if Emma scooted forward, she might see them touching. She wasn't sure she cared. She just didn't want to let go.

"Did you have a good day?" Jade asked.

Bianca started to answer, but Emma beat her to it. "I had the best day ever. Well, except for actually riding horses like we did at your ranch. Mom says I can't ride Juniper again, but she might be able to find me another horse to ride at someone else's ranch. Jade, maybe you could come along?"

Bianca silently cursed Emma's lack of a filter and shot Jade a plaintive smile. "Hey, bug, how about you finish enjoying this day before you start planning your next outing?" She squeezed Jade's hand before she let go and turned in her seat. "And maybe we can work something out about Juniper."

Emma squealed and pointed at her phone. "Awesome. I was just telling Marisol about the horses we saw this morning. She's jealous because her dad's out of town and she didn't get to go riding this weekend." Her phone buzzed in her hand. "She wants to know if I can spend the night?"

Jade laughed. "Does she always have this much energy?"

"You have no idea," Bianca said. "Bug, I think you've had a full day already. Besides, it's kind of late."

"Uh, Mom, it's barely six o'clock and we're only a few miles from home, right, Jade?"

Jade held both hands up in the air. "Not fair dragging the family friend into a debate with your mom."

Bianca looked back and forth between them. She wasn't used to the recent time change that made it dark so early. Emma was exaggerating. It was after six, but still early. If Emma spent the night with Marisol, and Jade was up for it, they could grab a nice dinner, sans junk food. An evening out after a full day of play was such a foreign concept, if she didn't know better, she'd think she'd been body-snatched. What surprised her most was how much she didn't want this day to end. She made a split-second decision to go all in. "Jade, do you have plans tonight?"

Jade raised her eyebrows. "Matter of fact, I don't."

"See, Mom, you'll have someone to keep you company. Can I text Marisol and tell her I'll be over as soon as we get home? Her mom's ordering pizza."

"Yes, text her. But tomorrow you have to come right home when I say and do your homework and learn your lines for the play. Okay?"

Emma answered with a frantic head nod while she furiously punched away at her phone. Bianca watched her for a second and turned back to Jade. "Were you just being nice or are you really up for spending the evening with me?"

"I wasn't being nice," Jade said, flashing a suggestive smile. "Do you have something in particular in mind?"

"Let's square away the kid and we can make plans."

"Fair enough."

When they arrived back at Bianca's house, Emma packed a bag in record time. "I can drop her off and be right back," Bianca said.

"That's silly. My car's out front. We can go together and then figure out our next move."

Bianca was torn. She wanted to be with Jade, but exactly how that would play out was another matter. The fridge was full of groceries and she could cook them dinner here, but a home cooked meal didn't feel quite special enough. It had been so long since she'd had a real date night, she wasn't sure how they were supposed to go. She was pretty certain spending the evening here, with Emma's schoolbooks scattered across the kitchen table and her parents down the street and likely to drop by with no notice, wasn't a great start. Maybe she should let Jade take the lead. "Okay, that works."

Emma bounded down the sidewalk with Jade while Bianca locked the front door. As she turned the key, her hand twitched at the sound of a familiar voice. She turned to see her mom and dad standing next to Jade and Emma. Desperate to get to them before her mother started firing off a barrage of questions, Bianca knocked over one of the flowerpots next to the door.

"Bianca, are you okay?" her mother called out.

"I'm fine," Bianca answered. *I would've been more okay if you'd showed up five minutes later*. She walked quickly and carefully to close the distance between them, offering Jade an apologetic look.

"Emma was introducing us to your new friend," her mother said while her father merely nodded. "She said you were in Canton today and that you're going out tonight."

"Did she?" Bianca gritted her teeth and forced a smile. "Well, allow me to do my part. Mom, Dad, this is Jade Vargas. Jade, my parents, Lourdes and Rey Cruz."

Jade smiled and did a mini bow that appeared to delight her mother. "Jade Vargas, pleased to meet you."

"Do you work with Bianca?" her mother asked.

"Mom, maybe we can visit another time. Emma's spending the night with Marisol, and her mother has dinner waiting."

"Fine. I can tell when you're trying to avoid me."

"And I can tell when you're trying to guilt me into telling you things." Bianca leaned close and hugged first her dad and then her mom. "I promise I'll fill you in later," she whispered in her mom's ear.

Marisol's house was less than a mile away. Once Emma's bouncy energy was gone from the car, an awkward silence settled in.

"Are you hungry?" Jade asked.

"I could eat."

"That's persuasive."

"I'm sorry. I'm not so good with this."

"This being…" Jade tapped her fingers on the steering wheel.

"Making the plans, knowing where to go."

"Ah, I see. The woman, she likes to be romanced instead of the other way around?"

Bianca play slapped Jade. "That's not fair. It's just been a while."

"Okay, how about this? I'll take the lead this time, and next time you can be in charge."

"You can take the lead, but rest assured, I'll always be in charge."

"Oh, is that so?"

"Mostly. Now where are you taking me? Someplace causal I hope since you wouldn't let me change clothes."

"I know just the place." Jade turned onto the highway and headed toward downtown while Bianca tried, unsuccessfully, to get her to reveal their destination. Finally giving up, she settled back in her seat, content to enjoy the ride.

❖

Jade drove like her destination was a given, but she was making things up as she went. Despite the easy back and forth flirting that had gone on all day, at no point had she imagined having the opportunity to spend an evening alone with Bianca. The prospect was enough to block out the dread that had churned in her gut since the run-in with one of Sergio's henchmen at the flea market. She'd deal with her uncle's demands tomorrow, but tonight she would make the most of her time with Bianca. Eager not to waste the opportunity, she raced through a mental inventory of possibilities.

Truth was she didn't do a lot of dating, if the activity she usually engaged in with beautiful women could even be called dating. She especially didn't go out in Dallas, preferring to save her trysts for when she was away on business. But there had been a couple of occasions she'd agreed to meet a prospect for drinks in a hotel lobby, and one thing had led to another. She could take Bianca to her usual "grab a drink and get a room" spot because this was no different from all those other occasions, right?

But it was different. Bianca wasn't the kind of woman who would let a couple of cocktails and bar snacks be a prelude to a main course of all-night sex. Bianca was a mom and a good one, judging by the interactions Jade had witnessed all day. Bianca was the kind of mom who taught her daughter to respect and be respected, likely something she'd learned from her own mother. The kind of woman that required substance and romancing before she fell into bed with someone she barely knew.

Jade shook her head. Her usual mode of operation was useless tonight, which left her searching for a place that wouldn't send the wrong signals and respected Bianca's desire to keep it casual. Before she could think the idea to death, she signaled a lane change to catch the next exit. She knew exactly the place to go.

A few minutes later, she pulled into a circular driveway and stopped in front of a valet stand.

"You're taking me to the Stoneleigh Hotel?" Bianca asked.

"Not exactly." Jade motioned to the eager valet that they would be a minute. "We're actually going across the street to the

Stoneleigh P, but I'd rather valet than try to park this beast in that cramped parking lot."

"It's like you're speaking a foreign language. What's the Stoneleigh P?"

"And you call yourself a Dallasite? Have you seriously never been there?"

Bianca stuck out her tongue. "I've never been to this hotel, but I know it's one of the oldest in Dallas. And expensive. And I'm totally not dressed to eat at any restaurant inside."

"Then it's a good thing we're headed across the street. You made me promise casual, and I'm keeping my promise." She ran her hand down Bianca's arm, her thoughts anything but casual. "Trust me?"

"I'm too hungry not to."

Jade hadn't been here in a while, but it was exactly as she remembered, a rustic space outfitted with pool tables, a huge neon Lone Star Beer sign behind the bar, and packed full of people enjoying good food. Later, when they'd demolished a plate of nachos, Bianca tilted her bottle of Modelo at Jade and nodded her approval. "This was perfect."

"No, what was perfect were those chicken nachos."

"I wasn't talking about the beer. I was talking about this whole day. Emma's probably going to keep her friend Marisol up the entire night talking about everything she did."

Jade took a sip of beer, measuring her thoughts. "I'm glad Emma had a good time."

Bianca reached across the table and lightly stroked her hand. "Emma wasn't the only one who had a wonderful day. I can't remember the last time I had this much fun."

Jade wound her fingers through Bianca's. "I'm glad. I wanted today to be perfect. I wanted…" She let the words trail off rather than speak her insecurities out loud. She wanted Bianca to see her as more than the niece of a fugitive, a conduit to his capture. Jade recalled the stories about Pablo Escobar and how the DEA had tracked him though his family. His family had been blindly loyal, oblivious to the atrocities committed by the cartel king. Unlike them, she'd never been blind even if she had chosen to overlook the evil deeds of her uncles in favor of her own pursuits. But she didn't want to admit any of this to Bianca, so she changed course. "What I mean is, I'm glad Emma had a good time, but it was just as important to me that you have a perfect day too."

"Mission accomplished." Bianca ducked her head. "I didn't expect to like you so much."

"I guess we did have kind of a rocky start."

"You were protective of Sophia. I get it."

"I was protective of the ranch. It's all I have."

Bianca heard the defensive undertone and weighed whether pushing the point was worth the possibility Jade might shut down. But this day had been all about breaking boundaries, and she couldn't resist pushing through the wall Jade had erected around the topic of her relationship with Sophia. "When did Sophia tell you Lily Gantry is your sister?"

Jade's eyes narrowed. "Wow, you don't pull any punches do you?"

"Sorry. Well, not really. If I want to know something, I ask."

"How does that work for you in the courtroom?"

"Sometimes great, sometimes not so much. I'm working on subtlety, but I didn't figure you for the type that would prefer I dance around a subject instead of getting to the point."

"Touché."

"Do you intend to answer me or just admire my directness?"

Jade set the beer down and drummed her fingers on the table. Bianca employed one of the techniques she'd learned from Peyton, which was to stay silent until the other person gave in and spoke first. After what seemed like forever, Jade finally said, "She never told me, at least not on her own. I figured it out, and she confirmed. Cyrus didn't stop seeing her even after my uncles made her give up the baby. He stayed away for years, but then he came back and he's been a regular visitor as long as I can remember." She stared off into the distance. "I found Lily's picture in his things and that's when I figured it out. Sophia admitted the truth when I confronted her."

"How old were you?"

"Thirteen."

"That's a lot to digest at any age, but especially in the tumultuous teens." Bianca waited a few beats and sorted through the dozens of questions on her mind. "Do you think Sophia was seeing Cyrus when she was with your father?"

"I have no idea." Jade rubbed her arms. "The man who got my mother pregnant left before I was born. That's what Sophia says anyway. I have no idea if he even knows I exist."

Bianca's heart ached for Jade. "I'm thinking you and Sophia have had a lot to overcome."

Jade's laugh was bitter. "You assume either of us wants to overcome anything. More like we've agreed to accept the nature of our relationship. We're business partners who happen to be related by blood. We're both good at what we do, and running the ranch together allows us to play to our strengths, but there's nothing more." She finished her beer. "You look shocked. Let me guess. You and your mother are the best of friends."

Bianca fiddled with her napkin, reluctant to compare her situation with Jade's, but her brutal honesty deserved the truth in return. "Definitely not best friends, but we're very close. I don't know what I'd do without either of my parents. They weren't happy when I announced I was pregnant the week before I was supposed to start college. Even less so when I said no way in hell was I going to marry the father. But they were there for me every step of the way. Without them, I would've had to drop out of school, and I'd probably be working at McDonald's. Even now, mom pitches in whenever I have to work late or on the weekends." She gathered the now torn shreds of napkin into a ball. "Don't get me wrong. Sometimes it's a little suffocating since they live down the street and, as you saw, they have a habit of dropping by whenever, but on balance I wouldn't change a thing."

"You're lucky."

"I am." Bianca reached her hand across the table. "But not just because I have helicopter parents." She gazed intently at Jade, willing her to feel the sincerity behind her remark. Jade met her eyes and opened her mouth to reply when the waitress appeared at their table.

"Get y'all another beer?"

Jade raised her eyebrows, and Bianca wavered between not wanting a beer, but wanting to prolong the evening. Jade took her hesitation for a no and told the waitress to bring the check.

When they walked out of the restaurant a cold breeze greeted them. "I didn't think it was supposed to get this cold until early next week," Bianca said.

"It wasn't." Jade slipped out of her jacket and placed it around Bianca's shoulders.

"Thanks, but what about you?"

Jade locked arms with her. "This will keep me warm."

They dodged cars and dashed across Maple Avenue toward the big, beautiful hotel with its livery of valet drivers waiting to bring cars around in record time. With every step toward the building, Bianca felt the distance growing between them. In a few minutes, they'd be in the car, driving through the dark night back to her house. Would Jade walk her to the door or merely sit in the idling car until she was safely inside? If only her parents didn't live right down the street, she'd invite Jade in, maybe even ask her to stay— anything to prolong the evening, to keep this connection. But she wasn't ready to answer the questions that would come the next day when her mother knocked on the door to ask why Jade's SUV was parked outside her house.

Jade released her hand and started toward the valet. Bianca had a moment to make a decision, but she didn't need the time because she knew exactly what she wanted. "Jade?"

"Yes?"

Jade turned and Bianca was struck again by her beauty. The night air whipped Jade's jet-black hair into sexy waves, and Bianca wanted to drown in the smoldering pools of her deep brown eyes. "I don't want this night to end."

"What are you saying?"

For a brief moment, Bianca hesitated while the needs of her body competed with the pull of responsibility. Emma, her parents, her job—each in turn had claimed all her energy and passion, but tonight she craved more, and with Jade so close, so irresistible, she was ready to break the pattern. She wasn't sure what she would do if this gorgeous woman turned her down, but deep-seated longing urged her to take the risk. *If I want to know something I ask.* "What do you say we get a room?"

❖

Jade barely heard a word the front desk clerk said. Something about reward points, amenities, and an exorbitant rack rate, but none of it mattered. She tossed her credit card on the counter and willed the guy to move faster. She'd pay any price, and the only reward or amenity she needed was standing beside her.

Finally in the elevator, they rode to the tenth floor with two other couples who chatted incessantly about the dinner they'd just shared. Steaks and wine. Lots of wine judging by the red faces and slightly too loud voices. Bianca tugged on her hand, and when Jade looked down they shared a grin.

The room was far away from the elevator, and when they finally reached it, the card key wouldn't cooperate. With each flicker of the red light, Jade began to feel as if being alone with Bianca was a quest full of obstacles to overcome.

"Here, let me try," Bianca said, placing her hand over Jade's and slipping the key from her grasp. One smooth motion later and the green light signaled they were free to enter.

"You're good at that." Jade led the way into the room.

"I'm better at other things," Bianca said with a sly grin.

"Is that so?" Jade asked the question seductively, but now that they were on the precipice of intimacy, she wanted to make sure Bianca wasn't regretting her impulsive decision. "Are you sure this is what you want?"

To answer, Bianca pushed her gently back against the bed, and once Jade was seated, Bianca moved between her legs. Face-to-face, they were so close Jade could barely breathe. She was used to being the one in charge, calling all the moves, but Bianca's confidence and command was more exciting than wielding her own power. "Show me."

Bianca's kiss was soft at first, and Jade let her eyes flutter shut, content to relax into the slow pace, the silken touch, as Bianca's lips traced her mouth with light brushes and gentle nips. When Bianca's tongue glided past her lips, Jade groaned with pleasure as the actual experience of kissing Bianca topped all of her imaginings by far. She opened her eyes to see Bianca gazing intently at her, her eyes dark with need.

As the kiss intensified, Jade's skin burned hot and her clothes hugged tight. Too tight. Skin, she needed skin. Hers against Bianca's—smooth, wet, hard, soft. She craved every possible sensation with an immediacy that was undeniable. When they broke for air, she slid her hands underneath Bianca's sweater and growled, "Off, please."

Bianca took a step back and teased, pulling the sweater and shirt up just enough to show her bare waist. "You want me to take my sweater off? Is that what you want?"

Jade tugged on the sweater and pulled her back into her arms. She leaned close and whispered against Bianca's neck in between a trail of kisses. "I want you to take it all off. I want to see you naked, to feel you against me. You're making me crazy."

"Well, we wouldn't want you to go crazy." With a flourish, Bianca pulled the sweater over her head and tossed it on the bed beside Jade.

"More."

Bianca slowly unbuttoned her shirt, shook it off her shoulders, and let it fall to the floor.

"More," Jade said.

Bianca shook her head. "Nope. It's your turn."

Jade wasn't sure she could stand, but she managed. She shucked off her boots and then reached for her fly. Before she could unzip her jeans, Bianca's hand was on hers.

"Let me."

Jade stood still, praying her knees wouldn't lock, while Bianca took an excruciatingly long time to unzip her jeans and shimmy them past her hips. Assuming the more submissive role was making her insanely hot, and the surge of wet heat between her legs left her wondering how long she could last without release. "Again with the crazy."

Bianca's smile was cocky. "According to plan." She raked her fingers over Jade's panties, teasing the skin beneath. Bianca moaned as her fingers stroked slowly at first and then with a steady rhythm. Jade threw her head back and bucked her pelvis into Bianca's hand. This time it was Bianca who whispered. "I have a feeling you like to be in charge."

"Mostly," Jade gasped. "But I'm not complaining."

"You're so hot like this."

"Like what? Jell-O?"

Bianca's laugh was low and sexy. "Loose, free, like you don't have anything on your mind other than feeling good."

"So good. Amazing." Jade could barely form the words, and then Bianca slipped her fingers past the fabric and pressed against her sensitive folds.

"You're so incredibly wet. I wonder if I'm as wet as you."

Jade arched against her touch, but even in her heady haze, she heard the cue. "Let's find out." She stepped back but not out of reach and pulled off her shirt and then tugged at Bianca's pants. She couldn't completely undress her without breaking their connection, so she murmured in Bianca's ear. "Your turn. Pants off, please."

Bianca used her free hand to finish undressing, and then Jade leaned back against the bed and pulled Bianca on top of her. "You are amazing. This feels amazing." She ran her fingers over Bianca's breasts, watching her nipples harden with every pass until she couldn't take it anymore. She took first one then the other into her mouth, teasing them to hard points with her tongue. With each stroke, Bianca intensified her touch, rubbing Jade's clit with the pad of her thumb. "I want to feel you inside me."

Bianca raised her head and gave her a slow and lazy smile. "Oh you do, do you?" She punctuated the words with kisses along Jade's shoulders, dipping down to her breasts. Jade arched into her mouth and moaned as Bianca's tongue flicked her nipples in a steady rhythm. When Jade began to shake with the first wave of orgasm, Bianca slowed to an excruciating stop.

"You're the one who's amazing," Bianca whispered against her throat, her tongue trailing up Jade's neck and back down to lips as she entered her with first one finger and then another. Her mouth returned to Jade's breasts as she pumped her fingers in and out, maintaining pressure on Jade's clit. Jade's head swam at the divine onslaught of sensations ravishing her entire body, and she barely heard Bianca say, "Are you ready to come or should we wait?"

Desperate to hold on to the delicious climb, Jade tried to hold off, but for once in her life, more was driving her excitement than sexual release and she was powerless to resist. "Can't wait…" Jade gasped as she bucked off the bed, unable and unwilling to stem the tide crashing through her. "Please don't stop." Her entire body shook as the intense orgasm roared through her.

When the vibrations subsided, Jade lay spent with Bianca's fingers still inside her, her thumb still resting against her swollen clit, eliciting tiny aftershocks. "Oh my God."

Bianca nipped at her shoulder. "You okay?"

"Okay doesn't even begin to describe what I am."

"That was pretty amazing."

Jade rolled over to face Bianca, surprised at the look of wonder reflected in Bianca's eyes. She shuddered at another aftershock and pulled Bianca's hand from her clit, kissing each fingertip. "You. You were the one who was amazing. Are you always this commanding?"

"I don't know." Bianca watched Jade's eyes widen, knowing the brief answer wasn't going to suffice. "It's been a while. And there's not a lot of privacy at my place, with a kiddo needing help with her homework and parents who love to drop by without notice to 'help out.'" She exaggerated the air quotes, and then regretted the negative impression. "Don't get me wrong. I love my life and the people in it, but this," she waved her hand around the luxurious hotel suite, "is not my normal."

"Hmmm."

Bianca studied Jade's thoughtful expression, but she couldn't get a read on what was going on behind those soulful eyes. "Now you're thinking you just bedded the boring mother-type and how do you escape?"

Jade answered by pulling her close for a long, toe-curling kiss. "Not even close. After that orgasm, I'm barely able to put two thoughts together, but knowing that full command mode isn't the norm for you kind of makes me feel special. Is that silly?"

Bianca breathed deep as relief flooded through her. From the moment she'd asked Jade if they could get a room, to her snap decision to take the lead once they were alone, she'd been a bundle of nerves. Jade struck her as sophisticated and experienced, and her gorgeous good looks likely netted her plenty of attention everywhere she went. Making Jade feel special made Bianca feel like superwoman. "Not silly at all. Actually, the only thing I'm feeling right now is incredibly aroused."

"Good."

Jade punctuated the word with another searing kiss, and every nerve ending in Bianca's body hummed with anticipation. Touching Jade had left her taut, wet, and ready, and she didn't have to wait long before Jade's mouth and hands were everywhere, touching, probing, stroking her arousal to a fever pitch. Willing herself to believe the future held many more moments like this, Bianca ceded command in exchange for the euphoria of Jade's hungry touch.

CHAPTER FOURTEEN

Jade rolled over and slapped her hand on the nightstand, willing the noise to stop so she could return to her dream. The darkness of the room thwarted her efforts, and she struggled to switch on the light, immediately feeling slight movement to her right. Bianca was sleeping, her hair rumpled and the sheet barely covering her chest. Jade sighed with relief. Not a dream after all.

She located her phone and squinted at the display. Five a.m. She didn't remember setting an alarm. It was the weekend and she didn't have anywhere she needed to be. Five o'clock was early any day of the week, let alone Sunday, but a closer examination revealed the noise wasn't an alarm, it was an incoming call from Sophia.

"Hello?"

"Jade, where are you?"

She glanced again at Bianca, willing her to remain asleep. Sophia's urgent question was loaded, and Jade wasn't ready to share this, whatever this was. "What's wrong?"

"Something terrible has happened. Wherever you are, I need you to get here quickly. Please."

Jade wanted to write the call off to unnecessary hysteria, but despite all the drama in her life, Sophia wasn't prone to theatrics. Jade flashed on the face of the man who'd confronted her yesterday at the flea market, and a wave of nausea coursed through her. She pressed for details.

"Not over the phone. Please just get here right now."

"Okay, I'll get there as soon as I can."

Jade disconnected the line and set her phone on the nightstand, her mind reeling with possibilities. When she looked back, Bianca was staring up at her with sleepy eyes.

"Was that the front desk calling about a noise complaint?"

Jade couldn't help but crack a smile. "A little too late for that. Although I have to say, I enjoy your, how should I say this, expressiveness?"

Bianca raised a hand and swatted at her, which caused the sheet to fall down and expose her breasts. Jade sucked in a breath, instantly aroused and disappointed she had to leave. She traced the curve of Bianca's breast before pulling the sheet up and tucking it in around her.

"Uh, not to tell you how to do things," Bianca said, "but I think you're supposed to expose the skin, not cover it up."

Jade bent down and kissed her on the lips, a sweet, lips only kiss. "Sorry, dear, but I have to go. There's some trouble at the ranch and Sophia needs me."

Bianca shot up. "What kind of trouble? Do you need me to call someone? Did you tell her not to touch anything? Is she okay?"

Jade regretted not thinking of another excuse for her early morning departure. How funny that she felt the need to think of any explanation at all since she usually made it a habit to slip out while her assignations still slept. But Bianca wasn't like the others. She actually wanted to see her again, and how she handled this moment might be the tipping point for their future. She forced her features into what she hoped was a nonchalant expression. "It's not like that. Probably something with one of the mares. Several of them are pregnant. I didn't get into the details because I was trying not to wake you, but now that you're up, how should we handle this?"

Bianca looked confused for a moment and then realization dawned. "Oh, right. You drove."

"I could run you home, but it's super early. Why don't you go back to sleep and order a decadent room service breakfast when you wake up? I'll arrange for a car service to get you home."

Bianca waved her off. "Don't be silly. I'll get an Uber. Go, do horsey things." She drew her lips into a pout. "If you must."

Jade pulled her close and wound her legs through Bianca's. "I don't want to go."

"And I don't want you to, but I get it." Bianca looked up and stared intently. "Really, I do."

"Thank you," Jade said. "For this. It was…you were… amazing." She eased away, silently cursing Sophia for interrupting her time with Bianca. This hotel room was an oasis, and she feared if she left it, she might never get this feeling back.

❖

"It's the house at the end of the street on the right. The one with the burgundy shutters," Bianca said, pointing before she realized the driver's GPS was already telling him the exact same thing. It was still early and her brain was fuzz, but in a good, "I don't remember the last time I had that much sex in one night" way. Totally worth the morning walk of shame.

But she had no shame about the night she'd spent with Jade. If anything, she was proud she'd suggested the hotel and initiated the amazing sex. Her only regret was the abrupt end to their perfect night. In her fantasy, they'd woken in each other's arms, ordered room service, fed each other bites of French toast, and slowly licked away drops of syrup that happened to fall astray.

You're being silly. She was. A little. She would've had to get up early no matter what to make sure she was home when Emma returned. Now, she'd have a bit of alone time to enjoy the memories of last night before real life kicked in. She wondered what Jade was doing right now.

As if in answer, her phone buzzed. Her heartbeat quickened as she unlocked the screen to read the text. But it wasn't from Jade.

Where are you?

Her mother. Bianca set the phone back on the seat, not ready to start a conversation that would probably result in an invitation to breakfast. She'd walk down to their house later, when she was ready to enter reality. As they pulled up to the house, her phone buzzed again.

Call me. ASAP

This one was from Tanner. Bianca's heart started beating quickly again, but from anxiety this time, not arousal. Something was wrong, but before she could process the instinct, the driver pulled in front of her house. She jumped out of the car and hurried to the door, fumbling for her keys, but the door swung wide before she could find them.

"Where have you been? I was worried sick. Where is Emma?"

Bianca held up a hand at the rush of words. "Mama, slow down. Nothing's wrong. I was out with a friend, and Emma's still at Marisol's house."

Her mother heaved an exaggerated sigh of relief. "Okay. I'm sorry. I was so worried when I saw neither of your beds had been slept in and your car was in the garage, but neither of you were here." She stepped back from the door. "Come in. I'll make you some breakfast while you tell me all about your new friend."

Bianca resisted the urge to make a smart remark about being invited into her own house, but she held her tongue. "Mama, I have to make a call. For work. It's important. How about you go home and I'll come over and fill you in?"

Her mother narrowed her eyes. "Promise you're not just blowing me off?"

Bianca drew a finger across her chest. "Cross my heart."

"Fine. Breakfast will be ready in thirty minutes. Don't be late."

Bianca waited until her mother had cleared the sidewalk, and then she took out her phone to call Tanner. Two more texts had come in from Tanner.

Are you okay?

We need to talk. Urgent.

She punched the number and Tanner answered on the first ring. "Where are you?"

"That seems to be a popular question this morning. I'm home now, wondering why you're blowing up my phone."

"Are you alone?"

"Yes. For now. At some point Emma's probably going to show up, tired and grouchy from staying up all night at her friend's. You're scaring me a little. What's up?"

"I'm coming over. Be there in five minutes." She clicked off the line before Bianca could protest, and in more like two minutes, Bianca heard the doorbell. Tanner strode into the house.

"How did you get here so fast? Don't you live in Oak Cliff?"

"I came by earlier, but you weren't home, so I went around the corner to grab some coffee."

Bianca yawned. "Too bad you didn't bring me a cup. Any particular reason my house is such a hotbed of activity this morning?" At Tanner's puzzled look, she said, "Never mind. Come in the kitchen. We can talk in there."

She motioned to Tanner to sit while she put on a pot of coffee. It was pretty clear whatever was wrong meant she was going to miss breakfast at her mother's. She should have ordered room service at the hotel like Jade had suggested, but she'd been restless after Jade left, and enjoying the luxury didn't feel the same without her there to share it.

"Bianca, I need you to look at this picture."

Tanner's expression told her it wasn't the first time she'd asked. Her brain really was mush. If she was going to keep having mind-blowing sex, she'd have to do crossword puzzles or something to keep her mind sharp. "What?"

Tanner shoved a mug shot into her hand and pointed at the picture. "This guy. Did you see him yesterday?"

"I'm not following. I was in Canton yesterday."

"Yes, I know."

Realization dawned. "Who followed me?"

"Mary and I took turns."

"You don't need to follow me with Jade anymore."

"Please just look at the picture."

Bianca stared at the photo. The dark-skinned man was distinctive. He had carefully coiffed hair, a tattoo of a snake on his neck, and eyes that gleamed with hate, but she didn't recognize him. She handed the photo back to Tanner. "Never seen him before."

"Where did you say Emma was?"

"At a friend's house." Bianca set her coffee down on the counter. "I'm not answering another question until you tell me what's going on. What does this guy have to do with Emma?"

"I'm not sure." Tanner's face was a scowl. She jabbed at the photo. "This guy. His name is Enrique Garza, but he goes by Razor. He's an enforcer for the Vargases. He was in Canton yesterday."

"Okay," Bianca said, drawing out the word. "There were a lot of people there. Maybe it was a coincidence."

Tanner pulled out her phone and held it so Bianca could see. "It wasn't."

Bianca reached for the phone, her hands trembling. Fear made it hard for her to focus, and she had to stare at the photo for a while to make sense of what she was seeing. Against the backdrop of a teeming crowd, Jade stood with her hand raised like she was trying to make a point. Although the man she was speaking to was turned slightly away from the camera, there was no mistaking the tattoo on the side of his neck, but any shock she experienced at seeing Jade engaged in conversation with a killer for the cartel was nothing compared to the horror that gripped her when she saw Emma standing in the background, looking up at them with a curious expression.

She shoved the phone at Tanner. "We need to find my daughter. Right now."

Jade pulled up in front of her house and looked around. The ranch was as quiet as she would expect on a Sunday morning. Sophia's "emergency" had better be worthy of leaving Bianca naked in bed. She'd spent the entire ride home planning ways to see Bianca again, soon.

She'd barely reached the porch when the door flew open and Sophia rushed toward her, looking like her world was lost. "What is it?"

"Oh, Jade, I'm so sorry. I have no idea when it happened. I was home all night and didn't hear a thing."

Steeling herself for overwrought drama, Jade grabbed Sophia's shoulders. "Tell me what's wrong."

"Ransom. He's gone."

The words were few and simple, but Jade couldn't process why Sophia was so over-the-top upset. One of the hands had probably left the door to his stable open by accident. Definitely bad to have their prime moneymaker loose on the property, but not the end of the world since the ranch was fenced. Stallions were prone to wander, especially with mares nearby. If that was the case, then why was Sophia here in the house and not out searching for him?

She should grab one of the other horses and head out now. He probably hadn't gone far. She'd start looking near the barn where they kept the mares and foals. "We'll need to go together. It's probably going to take both of us to get him in."

Sophia appeared puzzled at first, but then she shook her head. "He's not lost. He's gone. Ransom's been taken. Sergio took him."

Jade's knees buckled. The words the stranger had spoken to her yesterday roared in her ears. *Your family is counting on your loyalty. We'll be in touch. Tomorrow.*

Tomorrow had come, and Jade knew deep in her soul, Ransom's kidnapping was a message from her uncle. Overwhelmed with anger and helplessness, she slammed her hand on the porch railing. Ransom wasn't just a horse or the symbol of her success. He was the only living being that loved her unconditionally.

She didn't need to read the terms on the note Sophia had found nailed to the stable to know she would do whatever it took to get him back.

CHAPTER FIFTEEN

Bianca pressed the doorbell for the third time. "If someone doesn't answer in the next three seconds, I'm going to need you to pry, kick, shoot—whatever you have to do to get us in there."

Tanner motioned to her hand. "Check your phone again."

They were standing in front of Marisol's house. When Bianca hadn't been able to reach either Emma or anyone at Marisol's house on the phone, she'd insisted on driving directly here, and Tanner had come with her. Now they were here and they still had no more information about Emma's whereabouts. Bianca's fear was escalating into full-blown panic.

"Where are they? Why aren't any of them answering their phones?" Bianca heard the crack in her own voice. She had to pull it together if she was going to find Emma. "Tell me again about this guy. Razor? Tell me what you know."

Tanner grimaced, but Bianca pressed her. "I need to know. I need to know everything. Do you know what he said to Jade? Were either of you close enough to hear?" She dreaded the answer. She'd been so careful not to bring anyone into Emma's life that might disrupt the careful world she'd built for them, but her attraction to Jade had caused her to cast aside her caution, and now Emma was in far greater danger than the possibility of being hurt by a breakup. Oh God, what had she done?

The rumble of a car engine sounded behind them, and they both turned. Bianca blinked against the bright morning sun, but even in the glare she recognized Doris Lopez, Marisol's mother at the wheel. Bianca gripped Tanner's arm to ground her swirling emotions. The car pulled into the drive, and Marisol hopped out with Emma on her heels. At the sight of her, Bianca sagged against Tanner as the adrenaline she'd been riding for the last hour flooded out of her system.

"Hi, Bianca," Doris said. She looked at Tanner and back to Bianca. "Is something wrong?"

Bianca tried to speak, but she couldn't find the words to voice her relief. Instead, she pulled Emma into her arms and kissed her on the head. Tanner looked between her and Doris and took charge.

"I'm Tanner, one of Bianca's friends. From work." She emphasized the last word like it was code. "I need to talk to Emma for a minute. Do you mind if we come inside?"

Doris's expression went from puzzled to knowing in the span of a few seconds. "Oh, okay, sure." She led them into the house and pointed out a room just off the foyer before leading Marisol off to another part of the house. "Let me know if you need anything."

Bianca, still holding Emma's hand, sank into a chair while Tanner shut the door. She covered her mouth, torn between relief and anger she'd been worried in the first place.

"Mom, what's wrong?"

Bianca took a deep breath and kept her tone measured and even. She didn't want to frighten Emma, but she did want to make it clear this scare could have been avoided. "Where's your phone?"

Emma reached for her pocket and her face scrunched into a frown. "I must've left it upstairs in Marisol's room."

"What's the rule?"

"Phone privilege comes with responsibilities." Emma recited the words in a dull singsong. "I know, I know, but we were with Ms. Lopez. She offered to take us to the Original Pancake House, but she said we had to hurry or there would be a big line, and I barely had time to get dressed. You know how I love pancakes, and they have the best bacon."

Bianca held up a hand to stop the ramble. "It's okay, but, bug, the rule's important. I need you to keep your phone with you.

Always." This was the moment she should list the reasons why, but speaking her fears out loud seemed like tempting fate. She settled on a simple, "Promise me."

"I promise." Emma pointed at Tanner. "Who's your friend?"

Happy to change the subject, Bianca said, "This is Tanner Cohen. She's an FBI agent and she's working with me on a case. Tanner needs to ask you some questions, okay?"

"Me?"

"Yes, you," Tanner said. She stuck out her hand, and Emma shook it with enthusiasm. "We can use all the help we can get when we're working on a case. I understand you were at the flea market in Canton yesterday."

"Yep. You wouldn't believe all the stuff Mom bought. And we got to see horses. They were—"

"Emma," Bianca interrupted. "Let Tanner ask her question, please."

"Sorry."

"It's okay. Sounds like a fun day," Tanner said as she pulled out her phone. "I'm going to show you a picture, and I want you to tell me if you remember seeing this person yesterday."

Emma identified Razor. "That's Jade's friend."

At the pronouncement, Bianca exchanged a pained look with Tanner and pressed a palm to her head. Tanner stuck her phone back in her pocket. "Did she call him a friend?"

"I'm not sure." Emma scrunched her face into her thinking really hard expression. "She said he knew some of her relatives, or something like that."

Tanner smiled and encouraged her to continue. "Do you know what they talked about?"

"Uh-oh." Emma stared at the floor as she shifted in place.

"What's the matter?" Bianca asked.

"Nothing. It's just, Jade asked me not to tell you she talked to him because she let me go get lemonade while they were talking. She didn't want you to be worried about her talking to strangers."

Bianca tried to sort through Emma's recollection. It didn't completely make sense, but she got the gist and it left her fuming.

Was the entire trip to Canton yesterday a cover for a clandestine meeting between Jade and this enforcer for her uncles? What was the point of taking Emma along?

Bianca couldn't think of any rational reason, and her mind dove down to dark places. Jade had suggested she stay behind while Emma accompanied her back to the car. Bianca flipped through every detail of the day before, looking for clues. Clues she should have seen in the moment. Clues that would have warned her that the sweet tenderness of the lover she'd been with the night before was only a façade, and her decision to expose her own vulnerabilities had been nothing more than weakness she could no longer afford.

❖

"The note says no police." Jade loosened her grip on the single sheet of paper and let it fall to the table. They'd been sitting in the kitchen for the last hour while Jade made Sophia recount every detail of the morning's events. How she'd had a light breakfast and coffee, and then walked to the barn to pull a saddle from the tack room for an early morning ride. The door to Ransom's stable had been wide open, and the piece of paper in front of her now had been nailed to the wall. Jade had read the words dozens of times, hoping each time they would say something different.

"Peyton can help us," Sophia said.

"She can't."

"You don't know that."

"Peyton and her friends are the ones who got you into this mess." Jade stabbed at the paper. "It was their idea for you to offer Arturo a way to launder his and Sergio's drug money. But your brothers are smarter than the feds. They knew if they threatened Ransom, they could get us to work for them without involving the feds."

Sophia sat silently while Jade stared at the paper one more time.

Jade,

Valencia Acres is now a Vargas family business. My associate, Razor, who came to see you yesterday, will deliver specific instructions and you will follow them exactly. Rest assured, you will be well compensated and you will be protected. If you have any doubt, you should know that the body you found last week was a man who intended to do us all harm.

I know this means of assistance was originally Sophia's suggestion, but we will do this our way, not hers. You must make sure she does not talk to any of the federal agents she has befriended.

To ensure you comply, we will hold Ransom until we are satisfied you have our interests at heart. Don't worry. He will be safe as long as you accept your role in this family.

Jade swallowed against the sour bile that rose in her throat. The note wasn't signed, but it didn't need to be. She recognized the writing from the last note Sergio had sent. Besides, who else could it be? It sickened her to realize her uncle, her flesh and blood, was threatening Ransom.

The crunch of tires on gravel rousted her from her thoughts. Sergio said Razor would visit soon. Was he driving up to the house right now? Her mind raced, searching for a strategy that would stall his mission until she could figure a way out of this mess.

She looked at Sophia whose face flushed with guilt, and her fear took off in a different direction. "Who did you call?" Jade asked, rising from her chair.

"It was instinct," Sophia cried out. "She knows what he's like. She was there when he first threatened the ranch and Ransom."

"Instinct! Your instincts are what got us in this mess in the first place. If it wasn't for you, we would still live in the valley, but no, you had to move north to be near Cyrus and your love child. You've antagonized your brothers with every decision you've made. You accuse me of not caring about my family, but you're the one who's torn our family, such as it is, apart."

An image of Bianca's mother hugging Bianca and Emma close flashed in her mind and filled her with longing. She'd never had that kind of connection with Sophia or anyone else in her family and she never would. "Because of you, I have no real ties to any of my blood relatives." She motioned between them. "Our only connection is business, and if anything happens to Ransom, if this ranch becomes a pass-through for the cartel, then we are done. Over."

"Hello?"

Jade turned to see Lily Gantry standing in the doorway to the kitchen.

"Sorry," Lily said. "No one answered the door and Sophia's message sounded urgent."

"It wasn't," Jade said. "Please go." She watched with growing irritation as Lily looked at Sophia for confirmation. When Sophia didn't immediately back her up, Jade grabbed Sergio's note from the table and strode out of the house.

She stood in front of Ransom's stable. The day was sunny, crisp and cool, a perfect day for a ride. Sometime in the early morning hours, she'd fantasized about bringing Bianca to the ranch today and showing her all her favorite spots. They'd have a picnic lunch in the meadow near the north ridge, and in the privacy of that distant place, relive the intimacy of last night, this time in the light of day.

She'd been stupid to fantasize. The moment her uncle's associate had approached her in Canton yesterday, she should have distanced herself from Bianca. She was a good woman, a good mother. Jade had nothing to offer her or Emma except the dangerous entanglements of her sordid family.

"I'm sorry about your horse."

Jade whirled to find Lily standing behind her. "Why did you come?"

Lily cocked her head as if surprised by the question. "Because Sophia called. She sounded very upset."

"I have things under control, so you can go."

"Do you?"

Jade bristled at the presumptive tone of Lily's question. "How is it any of your business?"

"Because Sophia is my mother and you are my sister."

"On paper maybe, but those words don't mean anything."

"If that's how you really feel, then I'll accept you don't want my help, but you're not the only one at risk. Sophia has a lot to lose, and I'll do whatever I can to help her."

"You're going to tell Peyton about this, aren't you?"

"We don't keep secrets."

"If you really want to help, you should stay out of it and stay away from us."

"I know you think that's right, but I don't agree. You need family right now." Lily held up a hand as Jade started to protest. "I know what you're going to say, but family is as much about choice as it is blood. I grew up thinking none of the family I knew were blood relations, but we loved and supported each other, good and bad. I didn't have to try to find Sophia, but I wanted to know more about the fabric of who I am. Now that I know her, I choose to accept her as part of my family. I choose you too, if you'll have me. We could all use more people who choose to be with us. Take it from the Love Child."

Jade couldn't help but feel a tinge of respect in response to Lily's self-deprecating smile, but she wasn't ready to accept things could be so simple. "We're different people. Different worlds."

"It doesn't have to stay that way."

Jade leaned against the stable and closed her eyes, remembering Bianca, just as she'd left her this morning, tangled in the sheets, sleepy, naked, beautiful, and sweet. For hours, they'd connected, and not just sexually. For the first time in her life, she had made love to another woman and imagined possibilities for the two of them beyond the four corners of a bed. That Bianca had a child, that she was dedicated to sending Jade's uncles to prison, that their lives up to now could not be more different—none of those things had seemed insurmountable, but now, in the light of day, Jade knew their differences were tall walls topped with jagged glass. Even if they could get to the other side, they'd be too scarred to heal.

CHAPTER SIXTEEN

Monday morning, Bianca pulled into the long line of cars in front of Emma's middle school and resisted the urge to stand on the horn.

"Mom, it's okay. You can drop me here."

Here was about twenty-five yards from the door, but it wasn't close enough. She'd deliberately driven Emma to school this morning, despite the fact her mother had volunteered to help out. She was fully aware she was being overprotective, but after yesterday's scare, she needed to watch Emma walk through the doors or she wouldn't be able to focus on anything else the rest of the day. Tanner and Mary had assured her they would have someone on campus keeping an eye out for the next few days.

Once Emma was safely inside, Bianca drove downtown, dreading the day ahead. Gellar had sent a couple of emails yesterday asking about her progress with the grand jury prep, and his escalating tone signaled he was going to be all over her the minute she got to the office. She was tempted to finally tell him he didn't have a case, but Tanner had talked her down from that plan. What they needed was a diversion. Something to distract his attention. She'd left a message for Lindsey last night, hoping she might be able to cook something up to get Gellar to focus on something other than his witch-hunt, and she still held out hope Lindsey would come through.

Jade had called three times before she'd stopped counting. Her messages were simple enough. *I had a wonderful time. I miss you.* That kind of thing. The third time she saw Jade's number, she blocked it. A small part of her felt bad about not telling Jade why her communications weren't welcome, but it was overshadowed by the need to make a clean break. Clean break or not, she hadn't been able to quell the persistent ache from Jade's betrayal. Her mind was cluttered with questions. She'd made it clear from the start how important Emma was to her, so why had Jade put her in close proximity to a killer? Why had she trusted Jade in the first place, especially after she'd always been so careful to shield Emma from the dark side of her job? No matter what the question, the answer boiled down to one simple fact. She'd let her attraction to Jade blur the lines between what she knew was right and what made her feel good. The realization left her feeling not only betrayed but stupid. Gellar wasn't the only one who needed a distraction.

Ida greeted her as she walked in. "Tanner's in your office." She lowered her voice to a whisper. "And Mr. Gellar is looking for you."

Bianca mouthed thank you and took the long way to her office so she could grab a cup of coffee. She'd need all the fortification she could get today. Her plan was thwarted when she found Gellar in the break room with Lindsey Ryan. For Lindsey's sake, Bianca managed a semi-enthusiastic, "Good morning."

Gellar frowned in her direction. "Where do things stand? I plan to present to the grand jury by the end of the week. I hope you and Agent Cohen were working hard this weekend to make sure we're ready."

If she'd been alone, she was pretty sure the harsh reminder of how she'd actually spent her weekend would have caused her to burst into tears. As it was, all she wanted to do was get some coffee, hole up in her office, and wish away this entire investigation. No, that wasn't true. Sunday morning, as she lay in the tangled sheets of the bed she'd shared with Jade, she would've told anyone who listened that she'd never work on the weekend again. Now she was more determined than ever to prosecute every member of the Vargas organization and she'd work round the clock to make that happen.

Gellar was waiting on her response, and she settled on a half-truth. "I did work with Agent Cohen over the weekend. We have a few more pieces of evidence to run down, but we should be able to meet with you midweek to review everything."

"Good," he grunted before turning back to Lindsey all bright and smiley. "Ms. Ryan, I prepared a list of people you should talk to about my accomplishments. I think you'll find all of them are willing to meet with you at your convenience."

I just bet they are. At this rate, Lindsey would get so bogged down in Gellar's PR parade, she'd never have time to do any real digging, which was probably exactly what Gellar had in mind.

Gellar motioned for Lindsey to lead the way out of the break room, but she hung back and placed an arm on his shoulder. "Herschel, do you mind if I meet you in your office? I need to ask Bianca a question." In response to his raised eyebrows, she lowered her voice and said, "It's private. You know, a girl thing."

Gellar pursed his lips in distaste that he tried to cover with a hearty smile. "Of course. Take your time. I'll be down the hall."

He delivered the last words while on the move and seconds later was out of sight. Bianca nearly choked from laughter. "Girl thing? Ewww. We're never living that one down."

"It worked didn't it?" Lindsey handed her a cup of coffee. "I heard you had a rough weekend."

"Guess I have no secrets." Despite the flicker of annoyance, Bianca knew she was fortunate to have such loyal and protective friends.

Lindsey held up her own coffee. "Can we take these back to your office? I have something to tell you, and I promise it's not a girl thing."

The word *office* triggered her memory. "Oh crap. I just remembered Tanner's waiting in my office."

"Good. She'll want to hear this too."

Once they were safely behind the closed door of Bianca's office, Lindsey started talking. "I know you probably think I've been jacking around with this assignment, but I've been doing a lot of work in the background."

"Hey," Bianca said. "No one's questioning your methods. I mean you're essentially doing us a favor."

"Except I kind of have a personal interest, you know, having been kidnapped and held at gunpoint and all."

Lindsey delivered the remark with a smile, but Bianca felt like a dumbass. She was acting like her world had ended because she'd made love to a woman who wasn't who she thought she was, but others had suffered far worse fates as a result of their involvement in this investigation. "I'm sorry. I'm not usually this insensitive."

"It's okay. Really." Lindsey placed a hand on her arm and gave it a gentle squeeze. "So, here's the deal. I've been doing a bit of digging into your boss's affairs. Have either of you been to his house?"

"I have," Bianca said. "He had a get-together there when Peyton transferred in from D.C."

"I don't suppose he took you on a tour of his bunker?"

"Bunker?" Tanner asked. "Like a root cellar?"

"No," Lindsey said. "Like a wait out the apocalypse kind of bunker, complete with generators and safes and anything else a person hiding out might need."

"Well, that's weird," Bianca said. "But I'm pretty sure it's not illegal."

"It's not, but there's more." Lindsey pulled a thin notebook out of her purse and thumbed through the pages. "He has over twenty bank accounts. At different banks."

"Again, not illegal, but definitely suspect. Speaking of illegalities, I'm not going to ask how you got that information."

"Good plan. And I only know about the existence of the accounts, not balance information or if other people are listed as account holders."

Bianca pointed at the notebook. "You mind sharing those account numbers? Tanner and I can get the missing pieces, and it'll be easier if we don't have to start from scratch." Lindsey tore a page out of her notebook and handed it to Tanner. "Anything else?"

"Maybe." Lindsey flipped to another page. "He makes a lot of trips to Denton, a few times a week. Does he have a kid in college up there or something?"

Denton was in another federal district, about forty miles north of Dallas, and home to two universities. Technically, neither Gellar nor his staff had jurisdiction in that area, although when the task force was in operation, they'd been allowed to liaise agents and AUSAs from adjacent districts when necessary. "His kids are grown and neither of them live around here," Bianca said. "Any idea exactly where he's going on these trips?"

"It varies, but it's always someplace near the UNT campus. Last Friday, he was at some place called the Mellow Mushroom."

"I know that place," said Tanner. "It's a student hangout. Not at all the kind of place I'd expect to see Gellar."

"What do you make of it?" Bianca asked.

"Not sure yet," Tanner said. "But I want to do some digging. I came by so we could go talk to the witness we spoke with last week. Maybe while we're out we can run down a couple of these leads."

Lindsey looked back and forth between them. "I'm hearing code for 'wait until the reporter leaves the room to discuss all the details.'"

Bianca looked at Tanner who gave her a subtle shake of her head. She knew Tanner was talking about Neil Davis. If it were up to her, she'd tell Lindsey about Neil and how he'd decided to cooperate with their investigation, but it was clear Tanner didn't think they should share everything at this point. Cop DNA, but Lindsey wasn't just any reporter. Maybe Tanner was right to want to keep a lid on their plans until they knew if Neil's help was going to lead to any actionable evidence. In any case, she wasn't in a position to question Tanner's judgment since she'd exhibited a pretty poor ability to tell the difference between people who could be trusted and people who were using her. "Sorry, Lindsey. We're just following up on a couple of things and we don't even know if they're going to pan out yet."

Lindsey laughed. "No worries. I'm helping you out, not the other way around. I don't expect to be deputized. Seriously, I'm fine. Now I'm going to go pretend I enjoy hearing Gellar talk about himself while you two solve crimes. Let me know if you think of anything else you need me to do."

After Lindsey left, Bianca asked Tanner, "What's your plan?"

"Grab your stuff. We have a meeting with Neil."

"I'm not sure how that helps us figure out what we're going to tell Gellar when he asks about the grand jury prep."

"It doesn't, but if we dig up something, we might be able to distract Gellar from his deadline."

Bianca wasn't convinced anything would distract Gellar from his mission to put Gantry behind bars, but maybe staying busy would help distract her from thinking about Jade.

❖

Jade stepped out of the bank and put up a hand to block the sun. In her mission to remember every detail of Razor's instructions, she'd forgotten her sunglasses. Blinded by the glaring light, she didn't see Peyton Davis and the woman with her until they were right next to her.

"Hey, Jade, you remember me and Agent Nelson, don't you? Have a minute to talk?" Peyton asked.

Jade recognized Nelson as one of the agents who'd shown up at the ranch the day she'd first met Bianca. She kept walking. "Leave me alone."

"No can do," said Nelson. "Don't worry, we've checked to make sure no one's watching this particular stop on your tour of banks. I think by now, they've figured out you're going to do what they want."

Jade slowed but didn't stop. Obviously, Peyton and Nelson had been watching her all morning as she'd gone from bank to bank, opening new business accounts for the ranch, according to the instructions Razor had delivered. At each bank, she made a cash deposit, just under ten thousand dollars. Valencia Acres now had five new operating accounts, all to be used to launder drug money under the guise of ranch business. Each bank was a small local bank, and the bankers at each of them had greeted her like she was an old friend. She had no doubt future cash deposits wouldn't raise suspicions at these hand-picked banks, and she planned to play along just long enough to coax her uncle into believing he'd brought her into the fold, if Peyton and her pal didn't spoil her plan. "You have no idea what I'm doing. I'm a business owner, conducting business. If you have a warrant for my arrest, take me in, otherwise, leave me alone."

"Jade, please talk to me."

Jade stopped, stirred by the note of sincere pleading in Peyton's voice.

"You may not want to have anything to do with Lily, but she's worried about you and she asked me to talk to you, to see if I could help." Peyton didn't wait for an answer before continuing. "Surely you know how it is when the woman you love asks you for something."

Jade opened her mouth to deliver a sharp retort, but choked. Was Peyton deliberately provoking her? Had Bianca told her friends about their night at the Stoneleigh? Had she shared the intimate details of their lovemaking?

Jade's stomach roiled at the idea these strangers who already knew so much about her private life, might also know she'd been cast aside. Bianca hadn't answered her calls or returned any of her messages. The last time Jade called she was greeted by a busy signal and then abruptly cut off, which she was certain meant Bianca had blocked her number.

It was probably best. She didn't need to drag Bianca into the mess that was her life now. She supposed Bianca had made the same decision after Lily reported what was happening at the ranch. Her fleeting glimpse at what a relationship could be like was over. "Unlike you, I make my own decisions, not because a girlfriend asks me to intervene."

"Maybe you should be a little more attentive to your girlfriend's needs," Agent Nelson said. "You could start by not meeting with your uncle's top enforcer in the presence of her daughter."

Jade's heart sank as she remembered Emma's face when Razor had approached them. Curious but distrustful. So whatever she'd imagined about why Bianca hadn't called her back, it was worse than she thought. Bianca wasn't just avoiding her because the ranch was once again a crime scene. Bianca thought she'd put Emma's life in danger.

All she'd done was try to escape the dark shadow of her family for a single day, but like always, the shadows found her and staked their claim. Bianca would never believe she hadn't willingly spoken with Razor. Especially not now that she'd done the first task on her uncle's list. "Please tell Bianca I'm sorry. I would never willingly put her or Emma in danger."

"Tell her yourself," Peyton said. "Come with us." She waved an arm toward the bank. "This isn't you. You're not a drug dealer. Tell us everything you know, and we'll make sure you and the people you care about are safe."

For a second, Jade was tempted. She could turn over Sergio's instructions and the book of false account ledgers Razor had left in the night and let someone else worry about taking down the enterprise that tainted everything she'd worked so hard to earn and the happiness she sought.

If only it were that simple. Peyton would keep Bianca and Emma safe even if she didn't cooperate with their investigation, but what about Ransom? As valuable as he was, she had no doubt Sergio would slit his throat in an instant if he thought the feds were on to him. If she agreed to cooperate, Bianca would never see her as anything more than the niece of drug dealers and a witness in a case, and Ransom would surely die. And what if Razor decided Bianca was still important to her? The idea she might put Bianca and Emma in danger was unthinkable. She might not be able to change what Bianca thought of her, but she would do everything in her power to walk away and make sure no one else was harmed in the process.

❖

Bianca sat across from Tanner at the Mellow Mushroom wishing she wasn't working. If she wasn't working, she could order a beer. Or maybe three beers. And a shot.

Tanner had called Neil and told him to meet them here instead of the original meeting place so they could cross two things off their list. While they waited for Neil, Bianca looked around at all the college kids who were doing nothing more than hanging out. She wasn't that much older than they were, but she couldn't relate to their experience at all. Her college days had consisted of coming home to a toddler who demanded her full attention until bedtime, which is when she finally got to put in the hours of study she needed to graduate at the top of her class.

Bianca didn't regret a single thing about having Emma in her life, but she couldn't help but wonder what her life would have been like if she'd shown up at college like these kids, unencumbered with preconceived ideas about what was expected of her. Would she have dated more? Would she have met someone like Jade? Had Jade partied her way through school or had she been ultra-studious? They hadn't reached the topic of college, and now it seemed they never would.

Neil appeared at the table, interrupting her thoughts. He barely had time to sit down before Tanner held out her phone. "Take a look at this guy and tell me if you recognize him."

Neil scrunched his forehead and studied the picture. "Yeah. He works for the Vargases. I don't know his real name, but I think he goes by Razor."

"You think?"

"I'm pretty sure. He's not the kind of guy you want to know, if you get my drift."

Tanner shook her head. "As if any of these guys are great company to keep. Do you know him well enough to reach out and try to set up a meeting?"

"Definitely not. Almost all my dealings were with people a little lower on the food chain. I met Arturo and Sergio a couple of times, but that was just part of the vetting process. Those guys like to know who they're dealing with. Word is, if you get to know this dude," he pointed at the picture on the phone, "your days are numbered."

Bianca shuddered at his words, the image of Emma standing less than a foot from Razor burned into her brain. "Do you have any idea how we can find him?"

"Sorry. I can try to set something up with one of my old contacts, but chances are none of them know where to find any of the higher-ups. They'd have to go through some pretty elaborate messaging rituals to get in touch."

"Okay, if we think of something else, we'll let you know." Tanner held her hand out for her phone. Neil started to hand it to her but stopped and stared at the screen. "Who's this guy?"

Tanner took the phone from him. "You're kidding, right?"

"No, I've definitely seen him."

Tanner held the phone up so Bianca could see. When Neil touched the screen, he'd flicked to the next picture, a photo Tanner had taken of Gellar's official portrait. She'd snapped the picture as they'd left the office today so they could show it to some of the staff here at the bar. "You recognize him because your sister works for him. That's Herschel Gellar, US Attorney."

Neil reached for the phone, and Tanner let him have it. Bianca and Tanner both watched as Neil stared at the picture. "No. I mean, I guess you're right about who he is, but where I saw him, well, he wasn't on the job. It wasn't long before Peyton came back from D.C."

Bianca glanced at Tanner who was patiently waiting for Neil to get to the point, but she couldn't stand the tension. "Spit it out."

Neil pointed at the picture of Herschel Gellar. "This guy. He was arguing with Sergio. Told him if he didn't stop working with Gantry, he was going to take him down."

CHAPTER SEVENTEEN

Jade ran her fingers over the bound ledger Razor had left at the ranch, satisfied a simple touch wouldn't reveal the slim GPS chip she'd slid between the backing and the cover. She'd ordered several of the chips after her last lost luggage debacle, but she'd never imagined using one of the handy devices to track down her fugitive uncle.

She slipped the ledger into the tan waterproof duffle bag she'd found it in and rode the four-wheeler out to the clearing where she and Emma had found the dead body only a week ago. She stuffed the bag in the hollow of the tree on the north side of the field as she'd been instructed. At first she'd thought Razor had been stupid to leave the cash and documents here, but now it made perfect sense. Now that the clearing was no longer a crime scene, the likelihood federal agents would be back was slim.

The spot where the body had lain had already reverted back to its natural state—pine needles, leaves, and random pieces of tree limb—as if nothing bad had ever happened here. Sergio's letter said the man had been killed for their protection, but why did she need protection from a man she didn't even know? Now she wished she'd asked more questions when she'd had the chance—the identity of the man, the status of the investigation, the connection to her uncles. All this information seemed important now, but a week ago, she couldn't be bothered other than to wish the federal agents off her land. She knew why she hadn't asked, even if she didn't want to admit the truth. Her ability to compartmentalize the evil world of her uncles from the one in which she grew up to be a well-educated, successful owner of a legitimate business had been perfected over many years. Now it was almost as if she didn't recognize when the worlds collided.

From the moment she'd met with Arturo at the prison to Razor's appearance in Canton, she'd been on a clear course toward disaster, no matter how much she tried to deny it. Peyton was right when she'd said the life her uncles had chosen wasn't one she wanted, but it wasn't up to Peyton or anyone else to wrest her freedom from its knotted ties to her heritage. She'd blown her chance with Bianca, but if she was ever going to find happiness, she had to break free. And she had to do it her way.

Back at the house, she took the copies she'd made of the ledger and the bank deposits, along with a jump drive containing photos of the stacks of bills she'd deposited into the accounts, and sealed it in a box. She had just started writing the note to accompany the box when her phone rang. Sophia. She considered not answering. She wasn't in the mood to talk. She wasn't in the mood for anything other than a stiff drink.

Four, five, six rings. On the seventh ring, she gave in to curiosity and answered.

"Jade, where are you?" Sophia asked, her voice loaded with anxiety.

"At home. Where are you?"

"Broken down on the highway. One of the tires blew out."

Jade breathed a sigh of relief. She imagined something far worse. "Call Triple A."

"I called. They said it would be two to three hours before they could get someone out here."

"And you don't have a spare?"

"I do, but it's pitch-black out here. I can't change it myself, and frankly, I don't feel safe standing on the side of the highway in the dark all alone."

Jade started to make a smart remark about how Sophia might be better off calling one of the men in her life, but she stopped.

Sophia needed help and she'd called her, trusting her to take care of things. She could reject the overture or she could embrace the opportunity to try to salvage some sort of relationship with Sophia. "Okay, I'll head out in five minutes. Where exactly are you?"

"Um…hang on."

While Jade waited on the line, she finished the note and stuck it in the envelope she'd taped to the box packed full of the evidence of Sergio's scheme. She had time to stow the box and find her keys before Sophia returned.

"It's kind of in the middle of nowhere. I'm texting you the GPS coordinates from my phone. You should be able to plug those in and it'll get you right to me. Thanks!"

"Okay," Jade said, but she didn't really mean it. Something was off. "What are you doing in the middle of nowhere?" She waited but heard nothing, and a glance at her phone told her the call had been disconnected. While she was staring at the screen, a text popped up with the promised coordinates. Deciding she was overthinking things, Jade grabbed a jacket and headed to her car.

❖

Bianca pointed at the chart on the refrigerator. "This is the practice schedule. Emma should be done by seven thirty. Promise you'll be there early to pick her up."

Her mother waved her off. "I've picked her up from soccer practice before. I think I know how to do it."

"Just promise me." Bianca could tell her mother thought she was going crazy. She was probably right, but she was still overly cautious where Emma was concerned. Soccer practice, with a slew of kids, several coaches, and a group of overly interested parents, was likely the safest place for Emma. She should be there too, but after the bomb Neil had dropped earlier today, she'd called a meeting of the task force and they were all gathering at the Circle Six tonight.

"I promise. Now, I want you to promise me something."

"Sure. Anything," Bianca said, anxious to get on the road.

"Dinner Friday night at our house."

Friday. Friday was the day Gellar planned to present his case to the grand jury. Depending on how long they met, she might be trapped at the office later than usual. "I'll do my best."

Her mother grabbed her by the shoulders. "I need you to do a little better than that. It's an important night."

Bianca looked at her mother's eyes and knew she was missing something. She started a mental inventory of important dates, and it didn't take long for her to realize her mistake. "Papa's birthday. The big Six-O."

"I talked to you about it several weeks ago."

"I know and I'm sorry. I'm a little distracted lately."

"Is it your new girlfriend?"

"What?"

"What was her name?" her mother asked, her question purely rhetorical. "Jade, that's it. She's pretty. Very polite. Emma can't stop talking about her."

Whoa. Bianca held on to the kitchen counter to steady her balance. The onslaught of Jade-related information was like a sucker punch to the gut. "Jade is not my girlfriend."

"Well, it's okay if she is. You deserve to be happy."

"I am happy." Bianca rubbed the back of her neck to try to stave off her irritation.

"Good. You should bring her to the party. We can get to know her better."

Bianca suppressed a groan. "I have to go. I'm going to be late. Don't forget—"

"I know, I know. Be at the field early to pick up Emma."

Several traffic snarls on the drive to the ranch only ramped up Bianca's frustration. She knew her mother meant well, but her comments about how much Emma liked Jade were alcohol in a fresh wound, made worse by the fact she couldn't share the reasons why she'd never see Jade again. By the time Bianca turned onto the two-lane farm road several miles from the entrance, she'd spent an hour and a half cursing her decision to bring Jade into her life, but she felt no better for it. She was so caught up in her misery, she almost didn't see the person ahead of her, standing close to the road.

Bianca slammed on the brakes and then cautiously eased forward, barely able to make out the form of a woman standing with her hand up to block the glare of her headlights. Was that...it was Sophia. What was she doing out here in the dark?

Bianca waved and then pulled her car in behind Sophia's big SUV. She hopped out and walked toward her. "Are you okay? Can I help?"

Sophia pulled her aside. "I'm fine. I was at the ranch. Lily wanted to show me the house she and Peyton are renovating. Blew a tire on my way out."

"And you're trying to change it yourself? In the dark?" Bianca pulled out her phone. "Let's call Peyton. I bet she can help." She started to punch the numbers, but Sophia placed her hand on the phone to stop her. At that moment, a familiar voice called out. A voice she hadn't expect to hear again. "The spare is fine. I'll just need you to hold the light and I can do this."

The clink of metal, the crunch of boots on gravel—Bianca heard each sound. Any moment Jade would appear from behind the car. She had only seconds to get away, but she was paralyzed in place.

"What are you doing here?"

Jade's voice was soft and full of gentle surprise. Bianca tried not to, but she was unable to resist looking into her eyes. Reflected in the headlights, they were as beautiful as she remembered, still deep and soulful, but everything else had changed. No longer would Bianca let those eyes or anything else about this dangerous woman captivate her. The price was too high, for herself and for her daughter. "I think a better question is, what are you doing here?"

Jade's brow furrowed and she pointed at the lug wrench in her hand. "I think it's kind of obvious. Sophia called me because she broke down, so I came to help."

"Where's your car?"

Jade gave her a puzzled look, but she pointed toward Sophia's SUV. "I parked over there on the shoulder so I could shine my headlights on the tire."

That explained why she hadn't seen the Range Rover on the drive in, but that didn't answer all her questions. "And it's just a coincidence you're less than a mile from Peyton's ranch?" Bianca didn't try to hide the suspicion in her words, but when Jade's only response was to glare at Sophia, she was confused.

Sophia threw up her hands. "I promise, it is a coincidence. Jade didn't know where I was. She's never been to the Circle Six."

Bianca looked at Jade for confirmation, but Jade's head was down. Bianca clenched her jaw, determined not to go to her, though the urge was strong. Maybe this was a coincidence, but maybe it was also an opportunity to tell Jade how she felt about everything that had happened between them. Out of the corner of her eye, she saw Sophia slowly edge away. Now was the moment. She only needed to open her mouth and let the words tumble out, but as she moved to do exactly that she froze. All the feelings she had experienced for Jade—excitement, hopefulness, affection—were still there, but they were too twisted up with anger to give any one of them a proper voice. This chance meeting wasn't a sign of anything. It was only an inconvenient coincidence. The smartest thing she could do would be to walk away. She turned to go.

"Wait. Please."

Bianca stopped but didn't face Jade. "There's nothing left to say."

"And yet, we haven't really said anything."

"You've made your choice. You know I can't be with you if you choose this life." Jade's hand on her arm was warm and inviting and threatened her willpower, but she resisted the urge to lean in. "Don't."

"Please, just look at me. For a minute, and then I promise I'll leave you alone."

Bianca steeled her resolve and looked up into Jade's eyes, guarding her heart against whatever she had to say.

"I would never willingly have put you or Emma in danger."

"And yet, you did."

Jade flinched, but she didn't let go. "I've never felt this way."

Bianca resisted asking her to explain, preferring instead to believe Jade meant anything other than the intimacy they'd shared. She'd never felt this way either, but apparently falling in love meant soul-ripping pain.

Falling in love. The phrase tumbled out of her brain so naturally, but she'd never spoken those words aloud to anyone and she wouldn't now. What she had felt for Jade couldn't be love. If it was love, it would be strong enough to keep Jade from the strong pull of the dark world her uncles had created. What they'd shared had been sex, nothing more. The rest was a fantasy.

"I have to go."

Jade released her arm and stepped back, her face a mask with no affect. Bianca left without saying good-bye to Sophia, not trusting herself to be in Jade's presence for another moment.

When she walked into the kitchen at the Circle Six, her friends were already seated around the table, cards dealt, ready for their pretend poker game. She slid into the seat next to Tanner who leaned over and whispered, "Should we tell the others there's really no point in pretending to play poker anymore?"

"In a minute." She'd known if they were going to share the information they'd learned earlier in the day, they'd have to break the news to Peyton that they'd found a way to use Neil's penchant for spying to their advantage. But after the surprise encounter with Jade, she wanted to delay the confrontation as long as possible.

"Are you okay, Bianca?" Mary called out from the end of the table. "You look pale."

She mustered a smile. "Pale? Have you looked in a mirror, lately, *gringa*? In the dictionary under pale, there's a picture of you." The group laughed, and Bianca relaxed into the friendly atmosphere. "Tanner, have you told them everything and claimed all the glory or did you save some for me?"

"I filled them in on what Lindsey told us, but saved the rest for you."

Bianca set her cards on the table and told the rest of the group about their trip to the Mellow Mushroom. "Several of the employees confirmed they'd seen Gellar there often and as recently as last week. Sometimes he's by himself, but sometimes he meets people there."

"Any ideas about who he's meeting?" Dale asked.

"We got some pretty generic descriptions, and it sounds like sometimes he's met with a variety of people. Tanner's going back with some photos to see if any of the employees can make an ID."

"Be careful," Peyton warned. "If he goes there often, you don't want to risk running into him." She leaned back in her chair. "I think it's time we started looking more closely at Gellar's dealings."

"How would that work?" Bianca asked.

"I'm not sure," Peyton said. "Officially, we can't open an investigation into an attorney, especially not one in Gellar's position without permission from Main Justice."

"But you know people there," Dale chimed in.

"Sure, but they're going to want more than vague facts like he has an underground bunker and a bunch of bank accounts. We need to know more about what goes on at that bunker and what kind of money is flowing through those accounts, but to get that information, we need to take some official action, like with subpoenas and such. See the problem?"

"I do," Bianca said. This was the moment she needed to share what she and Tanner had been up to with Neil. She looked over at Tanner who nodded. "There's something else," Bianca said.

"Spit it out."

No matter how many times she practiced the words in her head, she knew Peyton was going to be pissed, so Bianca opted just to blurt the words. "Tanner and I have convinced Neil to cooperate with us. We thought it would help us get a lead on Sergio Vargas, and it may, but more importantly, I, I mean we, think Gellar may be involved in exactly the kind of activities he's trying to indict Cyrus Gantry for."

"And you thought talking to Neil without telling me was a good idea?" Peyton asked with a sharp edge in her voice.

"Hear me out." Bianca relayed what Neil had told them at the restaurant about witnessing Gellar arguing with Sergio Vargas. To Peyton's credit, she appeared to be listening with an open mind.

She couldn't imagine what it must be like for Peyton to know her brother was working with drug dealers while she had spent her career fighting crime. What kind of circumstances made half of a family respectable and the other half bad news?

An image of Jade's pained expression popped into her head, and Bianca had a revelation. Maybe a childhood spent being cast aside by her mother had caused Jade to seek acceptance from her uncles. If Jade was choosing to align with them, maybe her choice hadn't been easy. Still, Bianca couldn't help but wish Jade would choose her instead.

CHAPTER EIGHTEEN

Jade heard the knock at her bedroom door but ignored it. Again. It was Wednesday afternoon and she'd managed to avoid having any meaningful interaction with Sophia since they'd returned to the house after her encounter with Bianca on the road outside Peyton's ranch.

"I need to talk to you," Sophia called out.

"I'm busy."

"What could you possibly be doing in there for the last day and a half? I promise this will only take a minute."

Jade looked at her phone. According to the app, the ledger hadn't moved from where she'd left it in the clearing. She'd been glued to the phone since she'd returned to the ranch Monday night, ready to move at a moment's notice. She wasn't entirely sure what she was going to do once the ledger started moving. It wasn't like she could chase whoever retrieved it down with a horse trailer and rescue Ransom all on her own, but she'd remained dressed and ready the last two nights just in case. She started to tell Sophia to go away again, but the door creaked open before she could speak.

Sophia's eyes were red and her face was drawn. Jade wanted to take pleasure from her disarray, but she was too worn out to feel anything other than remorse about how she'd handled her opportunity to set things right with Bianca. She'd had the opportunity to plead her case, but she'd only managed vague overtures. Bianca wasn't going to give her a second chance, which meant it was time to turn her focus to taking back her life.

Sophia was still standing in the doorway, just another reminder of how complicated her life had become. "Come in, but only for a minute."

Sophia walked to the edge of the bed and sat on the corner. "I know you're mad at me. I should've told you where I was when the car broke down."

"Did you plan for me to run into Bianca?"

"No."

Jade heard the note of genuine surprise and realized the accusation was a little crazy. "Then why didn't you tell me? Did you honestly think I wouldn't come get you if you told me where you'd been?"

"I suppose I didn't want to tell you I'd been visiting with Lily and Peyton. In fact, I tried to reach Lily first, but when she didn't answer… Anyway, I know how hard all of this has been on you. I want to have a relationship with Lily, but not at your expense." She reached over and pushed back a strand of Jade's hair. "I never meant for things to be like this."

Where once she would have pulled back at the uninvited display of affection, Jade found her mother's touch strangely comforting. "I don't begrudge your relationship with Lily. Hell, I understand. If you had to do it all over again, maybe you would've chosen differently."

Jade let the words hang in the air. She didn't need to say the rest. It had always been painfully obvious Sophia regretted the fact she hadn't defied her brothers and kept Lily when she had the chance. For the first time in her life, Jade tried to imagine the amount of courage it would have taken for a young, pregnant, unmarried Sophia to stand up to her powerful older brothers.

Who are you to judge? Unlike Sophia, she'd been raised with privilege. While at the time she'd hated the isolation of boarding school and far-away universities, looking back, Jade could see how the experiences Sophia had provided equipped her with enough confidence and perspective to see a life outside of her uncles' control. Did it really matter that Sophia had been able to provide those things because of the generosity of her lover?

If she was going to completely sever any relationship with her uncles, maybe it was time to also leave behind the notion Sophia had ruined her life. What Sophia had done was make choices based on love, something Jade had always disparaged because love was something she didn't care about. But that was no longer true. Suddenly, she cared very much about love and she knew exactly why. The question was whether she was going to follow her mother's path and risk anything for a chance at love or continue to wallow in the belief her heritage made her unlovable?

"Your phone's buzzing."

"What?" Jade looked from Sophia to her phone as her brain shifted gears. She stabbed at the screen and it came to life. The ledger was on the move.

She jumped off the bed. "I'm sorry, but I have to go." She looked down at Sophia. For the first time in her life, she had so much she wanted to say to her mother, but like always their timing was off. She walked over to the closet and pulled out the box she'd packed Sunday night. She set it on the bed. "Will you hold onto this for me?" She paused, trying to decide how to phrase the next part so as not to set off alarms. "I've been doing a lot of thinking lately and I'm ready to make some changes. This box is for Lily. If anything ever happens to me, please make sure she gets it right away."

"Jade, what's going on?"

"Nothing. Just please promise me you'll give it to her. Okay?"

Sophia ran a hand over the top of the box, her fingers pausing over the envelope with Lily's name printed in neat letters. "Okay, but when you get back, I'd like it if we could talk some more."

Jade bent down and kissed her mother on the cheek. "That sounds good."

❖

"No offense, but you're kind of grumpy today."

Bianca shot a fierce look at Tanner who was sitting at the other end of the conference room table. "You ever notice how when someone says no offense, they're about to say something that's going to piss a person off?"

Tanner grinned. "I think you just made my point." Her grin faded into a look of concern. "You want to talk about it?"

Bianca tossed a file on the table and huffed into a chair. "Let's see. We're supposed to meet with Gellar in two hours, and we don't have a clue what we're going to say to him. All I can think of is hey, you're crazy to think Cyrus Gantry had anything to do with killing Maria Escobar and by the way, isn't it true you have a money laundering scheme of your own going on? But that's probably not going to go over so well."

"Is that all that's on your mind?"

"That's not enough?" Bianca knew her stress about meeting with Gellar was magnified by the constant mental replay of every moment of her meeting with Jade on Sunday night. The encounter haunted her because, instead of closure, all she walked away with were raw nerves. Everything and everyone agitated her, and her work, which she'd always been able to count on as a reliable source of distraction from her personal life, had failed her miserably.

It was her own fault for letting the boundaries between personal and professional come crashing down. Had she really expected to survive the falling debris unscathed?

"You can talk to me, you know."

Bianca looked into Tanner's kind eyes. "You're very sweet, but we have enough going on without mixing in my personal drama." She opened the file in front of her and pretended to read the words in the report, but Tanner wasn't letting go.

"It was a lot to ask."

"What?"

"The rest of us have been doing this for a while," Tanner said. Bianca raised her eyebrows in question. "You know, getting close to suspects, witnesses. Makes you forget how hard it is to shut off your feelings when you really get to know the person you're investigating. There's no shame in how you feel."

Bianca gave up pretending to work and put her head on the table. "Devastated. That's how I feel. How did I let things get so out of control?" She looked up at Tanner. "How did you know?"

"I've seen it before. Maybe you remember Peyton ripped me a new one for asking Lily a few questions during the agency raid on Gantry Oil. You think she might have been a little conflicted?"

"But this isn't the same. Lily wasn't helping her father launder money or anything else illegal. But Jade…"

"Go ahead and finish that thought. Do you really know what Jade is doing?"

While Bianca cast about for an answer, Jade's words echoed in her head. *I would never willingly have put you or Emma in danger.* Bianca had parsed the words a million times, but in this moment she saw them in a new light. *Willingly.* Jade was acknowledging she had put them in danger, but denying she'd intended to do so. Bianca's mind raced through every fact they'd managed to gather about the Vargas brothers. Dozens of operatives at all levels of the cartel did their bidding. Maybe some were acting of their own free will, but Sergio and Arturo had the kind of power to threaten others into doing their will. If they could exert that kind of power over strangers, why not their niece?

"You know they took her prize horse, right?"

Bianca shot up. "What? Ransom?"

"Yes. Sometime during the night on Saturday, he disappeared from the stables at Valencia Acres. Sergio had a note delivered to Jade basically telling her he was going to use the ranch to funnel money for the cartel."

"Why didn't anyone tell me about this?"

"Dale and Peyton didn't want to upset you by piling on. They figured it was enough that Emma had been put in potential danger."

Bianca raised her voice. "I'm not some weakling you all have to protect. I'm perfectly capable of taking care of myself." She spoke the words with confidence, but if her impaired judgment was any standard to go by, she wasn't entirely sure it was true. She'd been so quick to assume Jade had made a choice to work for her uncles, but she hadn't had a choice at all. Bianca remembered the first time she'd seen Jade with Ransom, more concerned about his comfort than impressing her. Jade loved that horse and she would do anything to protect him. She doubted Jade's loyalties were confined to horses alone.

She reached for her phone. Ninety minutes until Gellar showed up wanting them to make the impossible happen. All she wanted to do was call Jade and let the rest fade away.

"Go ahead. Call her." Tanner pointed at the files on the table. "It's not like we're going to make this mess into an indictable case in the next hour."

"Stop reading my mind." Bianca gripped her phone in her fist but didn't dial. "I don't know what to say to her."

"You'll figure it out."

"How'd you get so wise?"

Tanner shrugged. "I'm not. But I do know chances have a way of disappearing if you don't grab on."

Bianca jumped as the phone in her grip began blaring the obnoxious ringtone Emma had set for Lourdes. "Sorry," she said to Tanner. "Hi, Mama. What's up?"

"Don't panic."

Bianca's heart raced. "What is it?"

"Papa and I were out running some errands and we had a little accident."

"Are you okay?"

"We're both fine, but the car is being towed. The tow truck driver is going to take us home, but I don't think we're going to be done here in time to pick up Emma from school."

Relief that her parents were okay was quickly replaced with anxiety about logistics. Emma's school let out in half an hour. Bianca had plenty of time to make it to the school grounds if the meeting with Gellar weren't eminent. "I'll figure something out. I'm just glad you're okay."

She hung up and started assessing her options. She called Doris, Marisol's mother, but got her voice mail. A lot of the kids walked home from school, but she wasn't ready to let Emma be that exposed so close to the incident with Razor. She knew she was being overprotective, but she couldn't help it.

"What's up?"

Bianca reached for her bag. "I have to pick Emma up from school. If luck and traffic are on my side, I'll be back just in time to tell Gellar we have diddly-squat."

"We still have an agent stationed near the school. I could call him and ask him to pick her up."

"I'm not entirely sure I want to explain to my daughter how it's not okay to talk to strangers, but feel free to take a ride from this random guy. Besides, Emma's smart. If she finds out someone's there keeping an eye on her, she's going to ask a lot of questions I'm not prepared to answer."

"Fair enough. Go. I'll cover for you if Gellar shows up early."

Bianca raced to her car and made it out of downtown in record time. Emma's school was in a weirdly zoned area of East Dallas where rundown convenience stores shared street space with spacious historic homes. She'd chosen to purchase a home in this part of town because it was where she'd grown up and it was close to her parents. When she'd been a kid, she'd longed for the cookie-cutter sameness of the suburbs, but now she appreciated the eclectic neighborhood where she could buy *paletas* from vendors on bicycles.

When she arrived at the school, the front drive was crowded with buses waiting for the final bell to ring. She could pull in behind them, but her tiny car would be hidden amongst the cluster of SUVs jockeying for space. She did some fancy jockeying of her own and managed to score a parking space in the lot on the west side of the building. When she heard the bell ring, she sent Emma a text telling her where she was parked and urging her to hurry. While she waited, her thoughts turned back to Jade.

Tanner was right—she didn't know for sure whether Jade was involved with her uncles. All she did know was no other woman had ever affected her the way Jade had. Bianca's first instinct when she found out Ransom was missing was to go to Jade and soothe her pain. The idea of never talking to her again, never making love again, was unthinkable. Somewhere along the way, without looking for it, without meaning to, she'd fallen in love with Jade Vargas, but she wasn't sure what to do about it.

What had Tanner said? *Chances have a way of disappearing if you don't grab on.* Maybe it was time to grab on.

❖

Jade stopped at the light and checked her phone again. The blinking dot representing the ledger was still on the move. She'd followed its path from the ranch, and now it looked like it was heading south on Central Expressway. She checked her gauges, thankful for a full tank of gas since she had no idea where this pursuit would end. When the traffic light changed, she followed the beacon and merged onto the highway.

As she drove, her thoughts were torn between this cat-and-mouse game and her conversation with Sophia. Their talk had left her feeling vulnerable, but for once she didn't shy away from the emotion even though vulnerability hadn't worked out so well for her lately. No, that wasn't right. She'd let her guard down with Bianca and she'd never experienced greater pleasure, both physical and emotional. Exposing her feelings wasn't what had sent Bianca running. Bianca had done what any mother should at the hint of danger to her child—eliminate the threat. The only way to get Bianca to let her back in was to convince her the threat was gone. Once she had Ransom, she'd do everything in her power to make that happen.

In the meantime, she followed the dot on her phone, ten miles up the highway to an exit near downtown. She didn't know this neighborhood of Dallas very well, but as she drove along the tree-lined streets, she could tell attempts were being made to gentrify it. Well-known restaurants were mixed in with seedy looking convenience stores. This was the perfect place for drug dealers to hide out in plain sight and take advantage of the full range of clientele. It wasn't the kind of place where someone would hide a horse, but maybe Sergio was hiding nearby.

And what will you do if he is? She dismissed the creeping doubt. One step at a time. She didn't know for sure that Razor was the one who'd picked up the duffle bag, but she was fairly certain

Sergio wouldn't trust just anyone with access to the documents it contained. Besides, she wasn't planning to confront anyone. Today was about reconnaissance and nothing more.

Jade continued to follow the path on her phone, noting whoever had the ledger appeared to be circling a particular area. Thinking maybe something was wrong with the app, she pulled over to double-check the settings, but when she looked at the screen again, the light had stopped moving. She enlarged the screen and made a note of the cross streets where the light sat blinking, almost as if daring her to find it. Couldn't hurt to drive by and see if anything struck her as unusual.

On her first loop, she saw the cross street was flanked by a school on one side and a small strip mall that housed a vape shop, a specialty Italian deli, and pawn shop on the other. She ignored the school and focused on the strip mall. There were several vehicles in the lot in front of the deli, but only two were occupied, a VW bug and a Ford pickup. She slowed as she drove past, but couldn't make out anything about the driver of either. She decided to make one more circle around the block before finding a place to wait and see if the light on her phone started moving again.

The same cars were in the parking lot of the strip mall when she drove by again, but this time the Ford pickup was unoccupied. She glanced around, but it only took a second before she locked onto Razor, a few feet from the vehicle. She slid down in her seat, praying he didn't see her or recognize her car. She needn't have worried. He strode across the street completely focused on his destination.

Jade pulled over planning to get an idea of where he was going and then head back out, but it quickly became clear he was walking toward the school. She strained to see him as he walked farther and farther from her, but the buses waiting outside the front doors of the school blocked her view. A second later, the bell rang and students began to pour out the doors of the school. Thinking she had a decent chance of remaining undetected in the swarm of teenagers, Jade grabbed a baseball cap from the backseat and pulled it low over her forehead. Grateful she'd worn jeans and a sweatshirt, she jumped out of the Range Rover and walked briskly toward the school.

Public school was nothing like boarding school. The assortment of fashion was all over the map, and the lack of order was astounding. She waded through the crowd, but she didn't see any sign of Razor.

"Jade!"

Jade spun around, certain she'd heard Emma's voice, but there were too many faces and none of them Emma's. Jade pushed in the direction where she thought the voice had come from while her head swirled with thoughts broken down into simple concrete facts, all related. Emma. Razor. Danger. Razor was here for Emma.

A kid in front of her dropped his backpack, and when he bent over to pick it up, Jade spotted Emma a few yards away to her left. She was standing by herself, off to the side of where the buses were lined up, away from the other kids who were forming into like clusters. When their eyes met, Emma waved, a huge grin on her face.

Jade sucked in a breath and stumbled back a step. She'd let her mind run wild. Razor was probably headed somewhere else entirely, and Emma was not in any danger at all.

Jade raised her hand to wave back when she saw Razor walking toward Emma, slow enough to keep from drawing attention, but fast enough to close the distance in mere seconds. Jade's only thought as she sprang into action was that she had to be faster.

Bianca stared at her phone. Emma hadn't answered her text, and time was running out if she wanted to have any chance of making it back to the office in time to meet with Gellar. She looked out the car window, but from where she was parked, she had no chance of spotting Emma in the sea of kids. Time to go looking.

As she dodged her way past the cars and buses waiting in line, she had a newfound appreciation for her mother and the fact she picked Bianca up most days. With her parents down one car, it was going to be even more of a chore for them to help her out, but she knew she could rely on her mother to make it work. Bianca made a mental note to pick up dinner from one of her parents' favorite restaurants and take it by their house this evening as a small token of thanks.

But right now, she had to focus on finding Emma. She looked at her phone again, but still no text.

"Ms. Cruz?"

Bianca looked up to see Chelsea, one of Emma's friends, was standing beside her. "Hi, Chelsea. Have you seen Emma?"

"Yes." Chelsea pointed toward the east side of the building. "She's over there, waiting for Marisol. Mr. Laramie took Marisol's phone because she was texting in class." Chelsea lowered her voice into a conspiratorial tone. "I think she was texting Emma, but Emma didn't get caught."

For once, Chelsea's gossipy nature came in handy. Emma had probably turned her phone completely off in class and hadn't switched it back on yet. Bianca thanked Chelsea and made her way through the sea of students toward Emma, and finally spotted her on the far side of the teeming crowd. A second later, her phone buzzed in her hand, and she looked down to see Emma had finally responded to her text.

B right there.

Hey, Jade's here :)

Bianca stared at the screen, confused by the message. Jade was here? At Emma's school? Why?

She nearly dropped the phone as a piercing scream ripped through her musings. Icy cold panic gripped her, and Bianca peered back in the direction where she'd seen Emma moments ago, but she wasn't there. Bianca shoved her way through the crowd, moving faster and faster. When she finally spotted Emma again she heard shouts of "watch out" and "he's got a knife." Before she could process what was happening, she saw Jade racing past her, barreling toward Emma while a man approached Emma from the other side. Dread froze her insides. Razor.

Bianca flailed, frantic to get to Emma, but the crowd stampeding in the opposite direction pushed her back. She craned her neck, but as the scene played out in slow motion, she captured only fragments of the action. Jade lunging. Emma falling. A voice shouted, "Stop! Federal agent," followed quickly by the sharp crack of gunfire.

"Emma!" Bianca screamed. She plunged back through the receding crowd, running toward the spot where she'd seen Emma fall.

"Mom!"

Bianca skidded to a stop. Emma, looking completely unscathed, was hunched over Jade who was lying on the pavement, with the palm of her hand pressed against her bloody shoulder. Bianca's heart sank at the sight. She'd been so worried about Emma, she hadn't even considered Jade might be in danger. Her mind flooded with questions about what had happened and what Jade was doing here, but none of that mattered more than finding out if she was okay. She dropped to her knees beside Emma and placed one arm around her and her other hand on Jade's forehead.

"Jade's hurt," Emma said.

"I'm fine." Jade offered a weak smile and tried unsuccessfully to push up from the ground.

Bianca managed to return the smile. "We'll be the judge of that."

"Mom, she saved my life," Emma said. She pointed to a spot a few feet away where a man with a gun was handcuffing Razor. "That guy on the ground was coming after me with a knife. Isn't he the guy you and Agent Cohen showed me a picture of? Anyway, he was this close." Emma placed her hands about a foot apart. "And then Jade like tackles him. You should've seen it!"

Emma finally paused to take a breath, and Bianca placed a finger over her mouth. "Bug, I want to hear all about it, but first I need to make sure you're both okay."

"I was scared for a minute, but I didn't get hurt. I think we better take Jade to the hospital. I can ride in the jump seat."

Jade finally managed to sit up. "No hospital. I have to go."

"No, dear." Bianca pulled Jade into her arms and glanced around, looking for help. She instantly pegged the guy who'd handcuffed Razor as the federal agent assigned to protect Emma, but he was a little too busy to come to her aid. The blare of approaching sirens answered her silent plea. As the paramedics made their way toward them, Jade squeezed her hand and motioned for her to lean down.

"I have to find Ransom. Razor must know where he is. I was following him."

Bianca nodded as the pieces of the puzzle slowly fell into place. Jade had been following Razor, hoping he would lead her to Ransom, but when she'd seen Emma in danger, she'd willingly risked her life and Ransom's too in order to save Emma. Any lingering doubts Bianca had about Jade's loyalties disappeared, and her heart swelled with love for the beautiful woman she held. She kissed Jade on the forehead. "Don't worry, love. We'll get your family back. I promise."

CHAPTER NINETEEN

B ased on your range of motion, it looks like the knife didn't cut any tendons, but I want to take a look at the films just to be sure. I'll be right back."

"I'm fine," Jade yelled to his retreating form, but the young doctor wasn't paying any more attention to her protests than anyone else had. The trip to the hospital in the ambulance with lights and sirens had been bad enough, but when the paramedics rushed her into the ER on a gurney, she felt like she was coming unglued. Jade had been in this room for over an hour, and the lack of information about anything—Ransom, her shoulder, Emma, Bianca—sent her mind racing in a million different directions.

When the door opened again, she was ready to tell whoever walked through to stitch her up or else she was leaving with her wound wide open, but when Emma's grinning face poked through, she bit back her words.

"Jade!"

"Hey, Emma." Jade looked past her for the face she'd been thinking about since Bianca had bullied her into the ambulance.

"I hope you don't mind, but I brought my grandparents. They're waiting in the hall because I told them I wanted to tell you first. Mom sent me in a police car to pick them up and the police took us back to our house, but then I asked if they would bring me here, and we got my papa's truck because Abuela's car got hit by a reckless teenager who wasn't watching where he was going."

Jade blinked as she tried to process Emma's information dump, but she quickly decided none of it really mattered since it hadn't included the one thing she wanted to know. "Where's your mom?"

"She had to go to work. She said to tell you she'd come find you as soon as she's done."

"Thanks for the report, Emma." Jade struggled to hide her disappointment that Bianca wasn't close by, but she'd asked her to find Ransom, so it was her own fault. Now she wished she could take it back. Finding Ransom could be dangerous. What if something happened to Bianca? She couldn't bear the thought she might lose her, and Emma's presence was a reminder of what was at stake. She motioned to the door that was slightly ajar. "I appreciate you coming to check on me, but you can go back home with your grandparents. The doctor's going to put in a few stitches, and I'm going to be as good as new."

The door flew open, and Sophia and Lily strode into the room, followed by Bianca's parents. Jade held back a curse for Emma's sake, but her anger quickly faded into something else. Comfort? Her mother walked over and stroked her forehead.

"Are you okay?"

The refrain she'd been repeating for the last hour came to her lips, but she couldn't bring herself to lie anymore, so she settled on a different refrain. "I will be."

Sophia and Emma made the introductions all around, and Jade lay back on the bed, content to watch as they all settled into companionable conversation that ranged from Razor's takedown at the school—a topic in which Emma excelled at story embellishment—to the weather, ranching, and local news.

When the door burst open again, the doctor looked around at the crowd, seemingly unruffled by the growing population of her room. "Your x-rays showed no areas of concern. We're going to stitch you up, prescribe some antibiotics and pain meds, and you can go home with your family."

Family. That one word had carried so much baggage all her life, but now she craved the security, the peace, the love it could bring. She looked at her mother and her sister. They'd rushed to her side. She hadn't asked—hell, she didn't even know she needed them, but now that they were here, she couldn't imagine getting through this without them. She only needed one more person to make her life complete.

❖

Bianca stood with her colleagues in Razor's hospital room wishing she were in a different room on the other side of the hospital. But she'd given Jade her word she'd find Ransom, so she had to trust the doctors to take care of the woman she loved while she made good on her promise.

Love. Everything had happened so fast, she hadn't had time to digest the revelation, but the bursts of euphoria it sparked signaled this was the real deal, and it took every ounce of willpower she had to focus on the task at hand.

After making sure Emma was taken care of, she'd called Tanner from the school and told her to get the others and head to the hospital. They'd congregated outside of Razor's room and Bianca had filled them in.

"We have to get Ransom back."

"We'll do our best," Mary said, "but we have to look at the big picture instead of just one horse. I think everyone else agrees, right?" Mary looked at the rest of the group, but with the exception of Bianca who was shooting daggers with her eyes, no one would meet her gaze. "What am I missing?" Mary asked.

Peyton reached over and placed a hand on Bianca's shoulder before facing Mary. "There's been a development." She cleared her throat. "That one horse isn't just another animal. He's Jade's family, which means he's now Bianca's family." She looked at Bianca. "Is that about right?"

Peyton's simple but touching explanation left her too emotional to speak, and she merely nodded.

"Well, okay then," Mary said. "Let's do this. Who wants to have the honors?"

Tanner took the lead when they entered the room. The doctors said the gunshot wound had gone straight through his shoulder, which meant no surgery, but he'd be laid up for a while. Once they had him stabilized, he'd be transferred to the nearest federal medical facility until he was well enough to be transferred to Seagoville where Arturo was being held.

Tanner stood next to Razor's hospital bed and didn't mince words. "There are two possible outcomes. In the first one, everyone will think you're dead. You'll cooperate with us in exchange for a new life, but no one will ever know you helped us, and you will be assigned protection for the rest of your life.

"Your second option is to wait for trial at Seagoville with Arturo Vargas. We will tell him you cooperated with us whether you do or not, but there will be no deals, no reduced sentence. With your past history, we have enough to send you away for life, no parole, and you'll do your time at the supermax in Colorado. But here's the deal," Tanner dropped her voice to a low growl. "No matter which option you choose, you better fucking tell me where that horse is or you'll wish you were dead."

Razor's answer was a cold, flat stare.

Bianca flinched but didn't look away as Tanner pinched the tube sending medicine into Razor's veins, and then barked at them to leave the room. Bianca stood in the hall with the others, but no one was talking. She glanced occasionally at her phone, second-guessing her decision to leave Jade, but knowing at least she was getting the medical attention she needed.

Finally, Tanner emerged from Razor's room. She walked over to Peyton, and everyone else gathered around. "We're going to need to get the marshal's service involved right away. Make it look like he died here in the hospital. Should be fairly easy since a crowd of people watched him get shot. He told me where to find Ransom. If that checks out, we can move forward with full protection, and he'll give us Sergio."

Bianca would hardly believe it. "But what about Gellar? Doesn't he have to sign off on this? We'll have to tell him everything."

"Let me handle that," Peyton said. "I think with what Neil told you and Tanner about Gellar, we have enough to get someone at Main Justice to dig a little deeper into what he's up to and I can talk to them about signing off on witness protection for Razor while we're at it."

"Okay, then," Tanner said. "Let's start putting together a team."

Bianca watched while they stepped away to make the necessary calls. Tanner pulled out her phone, but before she could dial, Bianca tugged on her arm. "I'm coming with you."

"No, you're not."

"I promised her we would get Ransom back."

"And you'll keep that promise, but you're going to have to trust us to do the legwork." Tanner dropped her stern voice to a gentler tone. "It might get dangerous. She may love that horse, but I bet she loves you more. Go, be with her. I promise the minute we have Ransom, I'll let you know."

❖

"It's time for your pain pill," Bianca said.

Jade waved away the bottle. "What time are they going in?"

"They didn't tell me a specific time. Pretty sure they don't like to spread around that kind of information on cell phone lines." She leaned down and kissed Jade on the forehead. "They'll call when it's done."

Jade looked at the pill bottle in Bianca's hand. The pain was making her edgy, but so was the not knowing. Bianca had shown up at the hospital to take her home just as the doctor finished stitching her up, and the entire Cruz family, along with Sophia and Lily, had converged on Bianca's house. Lourdes and Sophia had prepared a feast for dinner while the rest of them engaged in lively conversation in the living room. Jade didn't say much, content to watch from her vantage point on Bianca's sofa as their two families fit together so seamlessly. But now it was getting late and she was tired, which made it harder to contain her worry. Emma had gone to bed, and Mr. and Mrs. Cruz had gone home an hour ago. Now Sophia and Lily were getting ready to leave to head back to the Circle Six.

Sophia donned her coat, walked over to Bianca, and held out her hand for the medicine bottle, shook out a pill, and handed it to Jade. "Take your medicine."

Jade started to protest, but Sophia shook her finger. Jade picked up a glass of water and swallowed the pill and then made a show of opening her mouth wide to show she hadn't cheeked it. "Satisfied?"

"I'll be satisfied when you're healed and back to work," Sophia said, letting a small grin sneak across her lips. "In the meantime, I trust this wonderful woman to take good care of you." She bent down and kissed Bianca on the cheek.

Jade watched the exchange, blinking back tears. She'd never been a crier, but today had tested every preconceived notion she had, so she wasn't surprised by much.

"See you, Sis," Lily said.

Jade laughed, thankful for the dose of levity. "We'll get there," she said, close to believing it was so.

Once they were gone, Bianca went to the kitchen to finish cleaning up. She'd only been gone a few minutes when Jade heard a loud squeal, and Bianca rushed toward her.

"What is it?"

Bianca shoved her phone into Jade's sightline. "See for yourself. It's from Peyton."

She read the text five times before she let herself believe it was true.

R is safe. All good. Call you later.

Jade pushed up from the couch. "I need to go see Ransom, make sure he's safe. Should we call Lily and Sophia and let them know?"

Bianca shook her head. "Peyton will call Lily and Sophia's with her. And I know you want to go, but trust me, if Peyton says it's all good, it is. She'll call when you can see him."

Jade considered her options. She could leave Bianca's side or she could trust and wait. The choice was clear. She settled back into the couch cushions and pulled Bianca close. "We're finally alone."

Bianca sighed. "I want this to last."

"This?"

"Us. You and me. This really super romantic thing. Mysterious ranch owner, crime fighting attorney." Jade laughed and Bianca put a finger against her lips. "You laugh now, but wait until a tired, hungry eleven-year-old comes bounding down the stairs in the morning. It has a way of sucking all the romance out of the room."

"Are you trying to chase me away?"

"Not in a million years, but am I?"

Jade used her good arm to pull Bianca closer, and she buried her face in her hair, breathing in the sweet scent of this woman who'd captivated her world and changed her life. She dipped her head lower and brushed her lips against Bianca's neck. "I'm so in love with you," she murmured.

"I'm in love with you too. I think I might have fallen madly in love with you the minute you rode up on Ransom, that first day I was at the ranch." Bianca pressed closer. "Whatever comes next, let's just enjoy this moment."

"I hope it's more than a moment."

"Oh, Jade," Bianca said, stirring against her. "You can have all the moments. I want to be with you forever."

THE END

About the Author

Carsen Taite's goal as an author is to spin tales with plot lines as interesting as the cases she encountered in her career as a criminal defense lawyer. She is the award-winning author of over a dozen novels of romantic intrigue, including the Luca Bennett Bounty Hunter series and the Lone Star Law series. Learn more at www.carsentaite.com.

Books Available from Bold Strokes Books

Forsaken Trust by Meredith Doench. When four women are murdered, Agent Luce Hansen must regain trust in her most valuable investigative tool—herself—to catch the killer. (978-1-62639-737-8)

Her Best Friend's Sister by Meghan O'Brien. For fifteen years, Claire Barker has nursed a massive crush on her best friend's older sister. What happens when all her wildest fantasies come true? (978-1-62639-861-0)

Letter of the Law by Carsen Taite. Will federal prosecutor Bianca Cruz take a chance at love with horse breeder Jade Vargas, whose dark family ties threaten everything Bianca has worked to protect—including her child? (978-1-62639-750-7)

New Life by Jan Gayle. Trigena and Karrie are having a baby, but the stress of becoming a mother and the impact on their relationship might be too much for Trigena. (978-1-62639-878-8)

Royal Rebel by Jenny Frame. Charity director Lennox King sees through the party girl image Princess Rosa has cultivated, but will Lennox's past indiscretions and Rosa's responsibilities make their love impossible? (978-1-62639-893-1)

Unbroken by Donna K. Ford. When Kayla and Jackie, two women with every reason to reject Happy Ever After, fall in love, will they have the courage to overcome their pasts and rewrite their stories? (978-1-62639-921-1)

Where the Light Glows by Dena Blake. Mel Thomas doesn't realize just how unhappy she is in her marriage until she meets Izzy Calabrese. Will she have the courage to overcome her insecurities and follow her heart? (978-1-62639-958-7)

Escape in Time by Robyn Nyx. Working in the past is hell on your future. (978-1-62639-855-9)

Forget-Me-Not by Kris Bryant. Is love worth walking away from the only life you've ever dreamed of? (978-1-62639-865-8)

Highland Fling by Anna Larner. On vacation in the Scottish Highlands, Eve Eddison falls for the enigmatic forestry officer Moira Burns, despite Eve's best friend's campaign to convince her that Moira will break her heart. (978-1-62639-853-5)

Phoenix Rising by Rebecca Harwell. As Storm's Quarry faces invasion from a powerful neighbor, a mysterious newcomer with powers equal to Nadya's challenges everything she believes about herself and her future (978-1-62639-913-6)

Soul Survivor by I. Beacham. Sam and Joey have given up on hope, but when fate brings them together it gives them a chance to change each other's life and make dreams come true. (978-1-62639-882-5)

Strawberry Summer by Melissa Brayden. When Margaret Beringer's first love Courtney Carrington returns to their small town, she must grapple with their troubled past and fight the temptation for a very delicious future. (978-1-62639-867-2)

The Girl on the Edge of Summer by J.M. Redmann. Micky Knight accepts two cases, but neither is the easy investigation it appears. The past is never past—and young girls lead complicated, even dangerous lives. (978-1-62639-687-6)

Unknown Horizons by CJ Birch. The moment Lieutenant Alison Ash steps aboard the Persephone, she knows her life will never be the same. (978-1-62639-938-9)

Divided Nation, United Hearts by Yolanda Wallace. In a nation torn in two by a most uncivil war, can love conquer the divide? (978-1-62639-847-4)

Fury's Bridge by Brey Willows. What if your life depended on someone who didn't believe in your existence? (978-1-62639-841-2)

Lightning Strikes by Cass Sellars. When Parker Duncan and Sydney Hyatt's one-night stand turns to more, both women must fight demons past and present to cling to the relationship neither of them thought she wanted. (978-1-62639-956-3)

Love in Disaster by Charlotte Greene. A professor and a celebrity chef are drawn together by chance, but can their attraction survive a natural disaster? (978-1-62639-885-6)

Secret Hearts by Radclyffe. Can two women from different worlds find common ground while fighting their secret desires? (978-1-62639-932-7)

Sins of Our Fathers by A. Rose Mathieu. Solving gruesome murder cases is only one of Elizabeth Campbell's challenges; another is her growing attraction to the female detective who is hell-bent on keeping her client in prison. (978-1-62639-873-3)

The Sniper's Kiss by Justine Saracen. The power of a kiss: it can swell your heart with splendor, declare abject submission, and sometimes blow your brains out. (978-1-62639-839-9)

Troop 18 by Jessica L. Webb. Charged with uncovering the destructive secret that a troop of RCMP cadets has been hiding, Andy must put aside her worries about Kate and uncover the conspiracy before it's too late. (978-1-62639-934-1)

Worthy of Trust and Confidence by Kara A. McLeod. FBI Special Agent Ryan O'Connor is about to discover the hard way that when you can only handle one type of answer to a question, it really is better not to ask. (978-1-62639-889-4)

Amounting to Nothing by Karis Walsh. When mounted police officer Billie Mitchell steps in to save beautiful murder witness Merissa Karr, worlds collide on the rough city streets of Tacoma, Washington. (978-1-62639-728-6)

Becoming You by Michelle Grubb. Airlie Porter has a secret. A deep, dark, destructive secret that threatens to engulf her if she can't find the courage to face who she really is and who she really wants to be with. (978-1-62639-811-5)

Birthright by Missouri Vaun. When spies bring news that a swordswoman imprisoned in a neighboring kingdom bears the Royal mark, Princess Kathryn sets out to rescue Aiden, true heir to the Belstaff throne. (978-1-62639-485-8)

Crescent City Confidential by Aurora Rey. When romance and danger are in the air, writer Sam Torres learns the Big Easy is anything but. (978-1-62639-764-4)

Love Down Under by MJ Williamz. Wylie loves Amarina, but if Amarina isn't out, can their relationship last? (978-1-62639-726-2)

Privacy Glass by Missouri Vaun. Things heat up when Nash Wiley commandeers a limo and her best friend for a late drive out to the beach: Champagne on ice, seat belts optional, and privacy glass a must. (978-1-62639-705-7)

The Impasse by Franci McMahon. A horse packing excursion into the Montana Wilderness becomes an adventure of terrifying proportions for Miles and ten women on an outfitter led trip. (978-1-62639-781-1)

The Right Kind of Wrong by PJ Trebelhorn. Bartender Quinn Burke is happy with her life as a playgirl until she realizes she can't fight her feelings any longer for her best friend, bookstore owner Grace Everett. (978-1-62639-771-2)

Wishing on a Dream by Julie Cannon. Can two women change everything for the chance at love? (978-1-62639-762-0)